LOUISE'S WAR

BOOK TWO OF THE TRENWITH TRILOGY

ROSIE CLARKE

First published in 2008 as Love and War. This edition first published in Great Britain in 2024 by Boldwood Books Ltd.

Cover Design by Colin Thomas

Cover Photography: Colin Thomas

A CIP catalogue record for this book is available from the British Library.

Paperback ISBN 978-1-83518-180-5

Large Print ISBN 978-1-83518-181-2

Hardback ISBN 978-1-83518-179-9

Ebook ISBN 978-1-83518-182-9

Kindle ISBN 978-1-83518-183-6

Audio CD ISBN 978-1-83518-174-4

MP3 CD ISBN 978-1-83518-175-1

Digital audio download ISBN 978-1-83518-178-2

Boldwood Books Ltd
23 Bowerdean Street
London SW6 3TN
www.boldwoodbooks.com

1

'Take care of yourself, Jack,' Rose Barlow said and hugged her brother. 'Don't be a hero. Keep your head down and come back to us in one piece.'

'I'm not daft, love,' her brother said. He grinned confidently as the train came chugging into the station, sending clouds of steam into the air. 'When I come home it is all going to be different. I've had enough of being a servant. I'm going to study hard and learn all I can in the army. When the war is over I shall be a mechanic and own a small garage.'

'You wish.' Rose made a face at him and then nodded. 'Why not? You deserve it. You've always been good with your hands. Just don't get yourself shot!'

'I applied to join the mechanics,' Jack told her. 'I shan't be on the front line, Rose. Blokes like me are too valuable, because there aren't many of us around. They will need me to keep their vehicles on the road.'

'Like I believe that one,' Rose scoffed. The train was stationary now and people were about to get on, jostling and bumping as they pushed by to the carriages. She hugged her brother again. 'Go on then, you daft lump! Why you had to volunteer I don't know. You're as bad as Troy Pelham! And didn't that upset Miss Sarah! Write to me when you can. Mum is going to want to know if you're getting enough to eat, and if you have a clean shirt.'

Jack chuckled, kissed his sister on the cheek and swung his bag on to the train. He leaned out of the window and waved to her as the engine let off steam once more and then set off down the line. Rose stood waving to him until the train had left the station and they could no longer see one another.

Jack moved away from the door, stowed his bag safely on the rack above his head and sighed with relief, because the parting was over. He took the only empty seat left in the carriage and glanced round at the other occupants. A pretty young matron wearing a blue coat was sitting opposite him, a small child dressed in red on her lap. An older woman sat next to her; young men occupied the other seats.

'Off to join your unit?' the man in the next seat asked in a friendly tone. 'I'm Joe Briggs...'

'Jack Barlow.' Jack offered his hand. 'I've joined the army – how about you? I've asked for mechanics.'

'Good with engines, are you?' Joe said. 'I'm a black-smith so I'm handy at most things. They might put us in the same division with a bit of luck.'

'If you can make parts or mend them, you could be a big help,' Jack replied with a grimace. 'If I know any-thing of the army, they will always be short of spares. I had an uncle who was an army man. Ted always said they never had enough of what they needed. He died a couple of years back, but he told me what it was like for him. I don't suppose it will be any different now.'

'I've always had to use me head when it came to fixing things,' Joe told him. 'I daresay it won't be far different. Horses are difficult sods to deal with at the best of times, and farmers aren't much better.'

Jack nodded his agreement. They started talking about horses and one of the other men joined in until the older lady sitting opposite frowned at them. She clearly did not approve of so much talking in a public place.

The child hopped off her mother's lap and offered Jack a bullseye peppermint from a paper twist. He thanked her but refused. She put her finger in her mouth and climbed back on her mother's lap. Jack felt Joe nudge him in the ribs and saw him wink at the girl's mother, then lean back, closing his eyes. Jack took out a newspaper. Reading wasn't his strong point, though he could manage everything but the more difficult words. He had made up his mind that he would use his spare time to good advantage. He was going to improve his education all round, because when the war was over he wanted to be his own man. No more working for a master – even though Luke Trenwith had been a good master, as they went. His mother and father belonged to the old school, expecting servants to pull their cap and look down respectfully when spoken to. Mr Luke was different, but while his father lived, things would not change very much at Trenwith.

Luke had been disappointed he was leaving so soon. 'You will be missed, Jack,' he'd said and smiled in a way that looked as if he meant it. 'I shall be joining up myself before long I expect. Things will be very different here when all the young men go. I think we shall have to make changes after the war. I would like you to come back one day, Jack. Perhaps not as a groom, but a chauffeur. I know you like driving and fixing engines.'

Jack had murmured something vague about hoping they both came back in one piece. He was making no promises, because he had his own ideas.

Even if Luke were the master at Trenwith, Jack still wouldn't want to go back to work there. He would serve his time in the army, keep his head down like Rose said, and then, when it was all over, he might be able to set up his own business. In the meantime, he would read something every day to improve his mind...

* * *

'So your brother got off all right then?' Mrs Barlow asked as Rose came into the kitchen and took off her coat. 'I hope he didn't mind that neither your father nor I were at the station. Your father isn't one for good-byes, and I didn't want to weep all over him.'

'He understood, Ma,' Rose said. She unpinned her felt hat and put it on a chair.

Mrs Barlow had been cooking and the large, spot-lessly clean kitchen smelled of baking and herbs. Her eyes travelled round the room, appreciating the oak dresser packed with her collection of blue and white china. There were expensive pieces of Spode china bought for birthdays and anniversaries, as well as the cheaper stuff used every day, and the collection was Mrs Barlow's pride and joy. She took great pleasure in keeping her cottage neat and clean, as she was herself. She had been an upper parlour maid at the house until she married John Barlow, and was loyal to the family.

'Jack wouldn't want a fuss. You know how he is over sentimental things,' Rose went on.

'He's the same as his father,' Mrs Barlow said, looking pleased with life. She had done well for herself when she married Barlow. He was well respected and had recently been made up to under butler. 'Mr Luke came to see me, Rose. He said he would miss your brother up at the stables. He understands he had to go, because he is thinking of joining up himself soon.'

'Yes, he told Jack the same thing,' Rose said. 'Lady Trenwith won't like it when Mr Luke goes, Ma. He's her favourite, always has been.'

'Yes, well, he is her only son. She has two daughters but only one son – and now her eldest daughter is married. What a shock that was, after the way she jilted Mr Pelham. Lady Trenwith must have been mortified. Miss Marianne was lucky she wasn't ruined.'

'I think Miss Marianne got a fine scolding from her mother at the time,' Rose agreed. 'We all knew about it downstairs. I think she deserved it, all the trouble she caused – and she's a spiteful cat to poor Miss Sarah. I don't like her much.'

'Now, Rose, you shouldn't talk that way.' Mrs Barlow gave her a look of disapproval. 'It isn't your place to take sides.'

'I told you how they made Miss Sarah stay in her bedroom for days, Ma – and they sent Mr Troy away without letting him ask for her. That's all down to Miss Marianne if you ask me.'

'She is the Honourable Mrs Bernard Hale now,' Mrs Barlow said. 'And you don't know she had anything to do with her father's decision to send Mr Pelham away.'

'I didn't hear her say anything,' Rose admitted honestly. 'But I know it was her. She is jealous because she still wants Mr Troy if you ask me.'

'Now that is enough of that,' Mrs Barlow said and looked at her severely. 'I don't hold with gossip, Rose. You will show your employers respect if you please.'

'Well, I shan't be working for the Trenwith family much longer,' Rose said and picked up a rock cake that was still warm from the oven. 'I stayed for Miss Sarah's sake, but she's going to stay with a cousin of Lady Trenwith's soon, and I'm off to join the VADs.'

'Well, I suppose it is your duty,' Mrs Barlow said, her expression softening as she looked at her pretty daughter. Rose was out of the ordinary with that dark red hair of hers. She got it from her father's side of the family. 'I dare say Lady Trenwith will give you your place back when the war is over. They say it won't last more than a few months.'

'Jack thinks that is just paper talk,' Rose said. She sighed, because she would miss her brother. 'I suppose I'd better get changed. I'm working this afternoon. They let me have the morning to see Jack off, but I'm not free until this weekend.'

'Free!' Mrs Barlow snorted. 'You wait until you start work at the hospital, Rose. You've had it easy up at the house, mark my words.'

Rose didn't answer as she went upstairs to change out of her best frock into her uniform. Her mother still felt intensely loyal to the family, because she had worked for Sir James's family as a young woman. She had never actually worked for Lady Trenwith, and she might feel differently if she had. Rose respected her employers, and she liked Mr Luke and Miss Sarah, but Lady Trenwith had a sharp tongue like Miss Mari-anne. Rose had no intention of returning to service after the war. She was hoping the voluntary services would let her join the nursing section, and in time she might even apply to be a nurse. Her mother didn't know about that yet. Mrs Barlow wouldn't approve, but Rose had been planning her escape for a while. She had only stayed on this long for Miss Sarah's sake. She hummed a little tune as she began to change her clothes. She would be glad to leave service, but she wished her brother hadn't joined the army. She didn't like to think of him in danger.

* * *

'I am proud of you for wanting to do your duty,' Sir James told his son Luke as they drank a glass of wine in his study. 'I cannot pretend that I like the idea of your entering the army, but in times like these we must all make the best of things. When will you join?'

'I promised I would take Sarah to Mama's cousin Amelia in Sussex,' Luke said. 'I have an engagement to visit some friends after that – and then I shall join the flying corps, Father. I had thought of the army, but I prefer the Royal Flying Officers Corps. I don't see the need to rush, though I must say that I expect things to hot up pretty soon now.'

'Yes, I am sure you are right.' Sir James frowned.

'You heard that Troy Pelham has joined the army, I suppose?'

'He went for officer training,' Luke agreed. 'I imagine he always meant to join; as soon as the trouble started he made it his excuse. His brother Andrew is a career officer and I think that is what Troy truly wanted. Naturally, Lord Pelham was against it, but I suppose he feels he cannot forbid it in the circumstances.'

'Pelham wanted his heir at home, as I do, Luke. However, I shall not prevent you doing your duty – as long as you remember that your true duty lies here once all this fuss is over. There's no need to be a hero. Just do what is required and come home in one piece.'

'Yes, of course, Father.' Luke's expression remained unchanged. All his life he had been reminded of his duty to the estate, his own desire to be an artist dismissed as mere fancy or a waste of time. There were times when Luke was tempted to rebel, to stick out for what he really wanted. However, he respected his father and felt affection for his mother, though she was not an easy woman to love. 'I have always known where my duty lies.'

'You have never been a trouble to me, Luke. I could wish that your sisters would remember their duty to the family, as you do.'

'Sarah is young and passionate.' Luke thought of his sister with affection. 'I am sure she is sorry that she was discourteous to you. She ought not to have been, but she was in some distress.'

'Perhaps,' his father agreed. 'All that is at an end since she has apologised. I leave for London tomorrow. I hope that you will come home again before you join up, Luke.'

'Yes, Father, of course – if I can.'

The expression on Sir James's face told Luke that their time was at an end. He left his father's study. He ought to take a stroll down to the stables. Now that Jack Barlow had gone, they would find it difficult to keep the carriages and horses to the standard his mother expected. One elderly groom and two stable lads would find it difficult to cope. Jack hadn't been the first to leave, and two others had handed in their notice as soon as they knew he was leaving.

Lady Trenwith had resisted the change to an automobile, preferring her carriages and horses, but Luke was sure his father would agree to reduce the stables once the war actually started. Luke frowned as he thought of the inevitability of war. He did not relish the idea and had not participated in the rush to join up. Troy Pelham and Jack Barlow wanted to get in before the outbreak of war, but Luke could wait a bit longer. He wouldn't shirk his duty, because he knew that he would have no choice once war was declared. He wasn't a coward, though he hated the idea of having to kill people. He wasn't sure he would be able to do it, but he would have to try. It was his reason for applying to join the RFOC. Killing from the air might not be so personal as hand-to-hand fighting, though the end result was the same of course.

Thrusting the unwelcome thoughts to the back of his mind, Luke decided that he would pay a last visit to the horses before changing for dinner. He was relieved that his sister Sarah had come to her senses at last. She had quarrelled with Sir James because he refused to listen to an offer from Troy Pelham. She ought to have known it was too soon. Troy had been engaged to Marianne and Sir James had disliked the scandal, which resulted from his eldest daughter's decision to jilt her fiancé. It wasn't Sarah's fault, and it was hardly fair that she should be denied her happiness. Luke was certain his father would relent in time, but Sarah was impatient. He sympathised with her, but believed his father was entitled to expect courtesy from his daughter. Sarah must learn to curb her tongue and her temper.

Luke smiled wryly. His favourite sister would probably get what she wanted in time, if she remembered to behave and be patient. It was unlikely that Luke would ever be free to follow the life he preferred. His father expected him to knuckle down and help him run the estate. After the war, Luke would do exactly that, because he had no choice.

* * *

He completed his tour of the stables, making sure that the horses were comfortable for the night. It was peaceful standing there in the warm silence of the stables, talking to the horses as they snuffled and shifted in their stalls. He would have liked to stay longer but knew he must change for dinner.

As he walked back to the house, Luke saw Rose Barlow leaving. She had taken off her cap, her rich red tresses falling freely about her face. She looked beautiful. The sight of her made him catch his breath, because he knew he was unlikely to see her again for a long time – if ever. Rose had told him she was leaving. They had spoken briefly earlier that afternoon. He had wished her luck, but what he had really wanted to do was to take her in his arms and kiss her until she melted into him.

For a moment Luke allowed himself to indulge in picturing her in his bed, lying naked beneath him, her eyes soft with passion as she gazed up at him, mouth moist and parted for his kiss. His stomach tightened with desire and he groaned.

'Damned fool!' Luke made a wry face at his weakness. Rose wasn't for him. The divide was too great; the prejudices on both sides too entrenched to overcome. He laughed softly as she walked from his sight without even noticing him. Rose hardly knew he existed. He was just Mr Luke, someone she worked for – and that was the way it had to be. Luke knew his duty to the estate. He would be given a few years to sow his wild oats and then he must settle down with a suitable young lady to raise the next heir.

Rose was both above him and beneath him. He liked and respected her too much to suggest making her his mistress, and his family would never accept her as his wife. He was a moonstruck idiot if he hoped for love. Men like him looked for a suitable girl and love didn't enter the equation.

He headed back to the house. Once alone in his dressing room, Luke glanced at himself as he tied a neat bow at his neck. He looked the perfect English gentleman with his dark blond hair, his neat moustache, which gave him that little bit of distinction, and eyes that were more grey than blue. He didn't consider himself handsome, but he supposed he was attractive enough to the ladies. So why hadn't Rose given him so much as a second glance? A wry smile curved the mouth that could look sensuous at times, and he chuckled deep in his throat.

It was just as well that he could laugh at himself, Luke thought. He had best hurry and go down. Lady Trenwith was not pleased when people came late to her table.

2

'Maman is dying,' Louise said as she looked up from her letter. 'This is from her neighbour, Isabelle Renard; she has been caring for Mama for some weeks and she begs me to visit her.'

Jacques Saint-Claire scowled at his wife across the large kitchen of the French farmhouse. 'I need you here. I can't manage all the chores alone. You hated your mother. Throw the letter on the fire and get down to the cowsheds.'

'I want to go, Jacques,' Louise said. She felt sick inside as she saw his angry expression. Jacques was handy with his fists, especially when he had been drinking. He was sober now, but he wouldn't be by bedtime. 'I never hated Maman. I did not approve of the way she lived. It was her men I hated – especially as I grew up.'

'She will expect you to stay and look after her.' Jacques poked at the kitchen fire with a vengeance and then stood with the steel fire iron in his hand. His eyes narrowed, as if threatening her. 'I've told you, I need you here.'

'The letter says there may be something for me,' Louise said. Her greenish-blue eyes held defiance as she looked at him, her sensuous mouth set hard. She could be stubborn when she set her mind to it. 'Maman's lawyer has asked that I come to settle things.'

Jacques cursed and spat into the fire. He was thoughtful for a moment, then turned to look at her. 'A week,' he growled. 'If you must go I can spare you for a week, but no longer. If you aren't back by then you can stay away for all I care.'

'Thank you, Jacques. A week should be long enough to settle things.' Louise dug her nails into the palms of her hands to stop herself screaming in frustration. He was such a bully these days and she was sick of being told what to do.

'When are you leaving?'

'I thought today, after I milk the cows and feed the chickens.'

'I don't know how you think I shall manage

without you,' Jacques said. 'But you were always a selfish bitch...'

Louise held back the retort that rose to her lips. She had been a fool to marry him. It had seemed like the answer to her prayers when Jacques Saint-Claire asked her to be his wife, but she had gone from one miserable existence to another. Though if she were truthful, it had not been so very bad at the start. Jacques's temper had steadily worsened since the accident to his leg, which he had broken falling from the hayrick the previous summer. Until then he had been generous in his way, though he had always expected her to do what he wanted.

'I am sorry if you think me selfish,' she said, and for a moment her eyes glittered with anger. 'I do my best to help you, but I can't stop the pain, Jacques.'

'Damn you!' he muttered and stomped off towards the back door. 'I don't need you or your pity.'

Louise felt the sting of tears but refused to cry. Sometimes she felt that her husband hated her and she did not understand why. She had not caused his accident, and she'd nursed him faithfully until he was on his feet again. There was no doubting the accident had changed him, but it wasn't her fault that he was in constant pain with his leg.

Her frown eased as she left the house and walked

down to the cowsheds. She would have a week away from the farm and the backbreaking work that kept her busy from dawn to dusk. Louise had no illusions. If her mother were still alive when she reached Boulogne she would expect Louise to nurse her. Her time away from the farm would not be a holiday, but at least she wouldn't have to listen and tremble at the sound of Jacques's heavy footsteps as he came up the stairs at night.

These days she never knew what to expect. If drunk he might fumble at her breasts and attempt intercourse before falling asleep and snoring all night. The worst times were when he hadn't drunk quite enough. That was when he took pleasure in hurting her. Sometimes, she thought about leaving him for good.

* * *

'Bloody boots,' Joe muttered. He sat down on a bale of straw and unlaced his boots, pulling the sock down to look at the blister on his heel. 'I had a perfectly good pair of my own. Brown, they were. I don't know why the sodding sergeant said I had to wear these, because they are black.'

'They're army issue,' Jack said and looked at the

blister. 'You want to put a bit of lint over that or it will get worse.' He took his rucksack from his back and opened it, offering a roll of clean linen. 'Try this, mate. It will keep the flesh clean and stop your sock rubbing the skin raw.'

'Thanks,' Joe said. 'You got any chocolate in that bag of yours?'

'Sorry,' Jack said. 'Ma sent me a parcel of stuff she thought I was sure to need, but no chocolate.'

'I'm sick of army rations,' Joe said. 'The food they give us ain't fit for pigs.'

'It will get worse once they ship us over there,' Jack said and grinned. He shrugged off the hardships of training as part of army life, accepting that he must manage as best he could, but most of the men never stopped complaining. 'It's a pity we weren't in Captain Pelham's unit. I heard they got fish and chips the other night. He sent out for them and paid out of his own pocket.'

'Some buggers have all the luck,' Joe muttered gloomily. 'I thought we signed up to fight, but all we do is dig bloody trenches.'

'You'll get plenty of fighting once we get out there,' Jack said. He watched as Joe replaced his boot. 'Do you think you can make it back to camp?'

They were on a ten-mile hike through the English

countryside, carrying their rations and rifles plus all the other equipment they'd been given. The sergeant had told them they needed toughening up in preparation for the marches they would have to do once they got to France.

'Got no choice, have I?' Joe muttered. 'I'll hobble as best I can, mate. You go on without me.'

'I saw a place that hires bikes when I came this way a couple of days ago,' Jack said. 'Are you up for it?'

'Cycle instead of walk?' Joe grinned at him. 'Lead me to them! The sergeant will have our guts for garters if he finds out, but I'm past caring.'

'Come on then,' Jack said. 'We'll worry about Sergeant Morris when we come to it...'

Jack knew their sergeant was one of the worst, seeming to delight in punishing the men whenever he got the chance, but he could see that Joe could hardly hobble and there was no way he was going to leave him behind. Besides, it was a bit of initiative. Surely they were going to need that when they got over there?

He saw the small shop hiring out cycles just ahead of them as they crested the rise. For half a crown they could ride the rest of the way back to camp and he could return the cycles the next day. If they got caught he would take the blame. Sergeant Morris might put him on a charge, but he was prepared to take the risk.

Besides, they were being given a two-day pass and after that they would be shipped off to the front line.

Sergeant Morris would be staying here, putting a new intake of young men through their paces. The poor devils had no idea what was coming to them. Some of them were so young they were still wet behind the ears. Jack had seen a few of the lads reduced to tears by the bullying sergeant. He had been tempted to belt the brute a couple of times, but he knew that kind of behaviour would land him in the cooler.

Jack had held his temper, because he'd joined up to fight Germans. He might hate the sergeant's guts, but he could live with the aggravation.

He paid for their cycles, and watched Joe wobble off ahead of him. Grinning, he got on himself. He was used to a bike and he soon overtook Joe, waving to him as he sailed past and freewheeled down the hill. The feeling was terrific, and he was congratulating himself on his brilliant idea when the officer's car went past him.

He didn't see much of the man in the back seat, but knew he was being watched and cursed the ill luck that had sent an officer down this lonely country road. If he happened to mention it and Sergeant Morris heard the story he was going to lose his rag...

* * *

Luke caught sight of the soldier enjoying himself on the bicycle as he passed him. He was so amused by the sight that he turned round to look through the back window and grinned as he realised it was Jack Barlow. He hadn't expected to bump into Barlow, because he was based with the RFOC and they didn't often mix with the army chaps. However, he had been asked to attend a meeting at this training camp. He wasn't quite sure what it was about, except that it had come up after he'd mentioned that he was an artist to his CO.

It was good that he had happened to catch sight of Jack Barlow. He would try to get a few words with him before he returned to Cheshire. Jack would like news of his family, which Luke could tell him, because he had visited Trenwith recently – and Barlow might in his turn just have some news about Rose...

* * *

'Barlow!' Sergeant Morris bellowed as Jack was on his way to the mess hall for supper that evening. 'I want a word with you!'

Jack stopped in his tracks. He didn't like the sound of the sergeant's voice. There was a gloating, menacing sound that told him he was in trouble. He turned to face the sergeant, waiting for the axe to fall as he saluted.

'Yes, sir,' he said. 'What can I do for you, sir?'

'You can take that smirk off your face for starters,' the sergeant snarled. 'You were on the hike today. Clever bugger, aren't you? Thought you could put one over on me, didn't you – but I've got eyes in the back of me head. You came back on two wheels instead of two legs. I want an explanation and it had better be good.'

'It was initiative, Sarge,' Jack said. 'That's what they told us when they briefed us. Show initiative and bravery in the face of the enemy.'

'Smart arse!' the sergeant growled. He shot a look of hatred at Jack. 'You weren't in the bloody face of the enemy. You should have been following orders.'

'Yes, sir. Sorry, sir.'

'You will be bloody sorry,' Sergeant Morris said, a glint of malice in his eyes. 'You're on a charge and your leave is cancelled.'

'You can't do that,' Jack objected. 'We're off straight after our leave.'

'We're off straight off after our leave, *sir*.'

'Yes, *sir*,' Jack saluted. 'You can't do it, *sir*.'

'I'll decide what I can do,' Morris said. 'In the

meantime you can run round the parade ground with your rifle over your head until I tell you to stop.'

Jack bit back the retort that he hadn't eaten properly for hours. He knew that he'd made his punishment worse than it need have been by his sarcastic manner, but he had no intention of landing Joe in it. Obviously, he'd been seen by an officer and reported. If Joe hadn't been noticed that was all to the good.

Jack longed to smash his fist into the sergeant's face, but he knew that would be playing into Morris's hands, and he wouldn't give him the satisfaction. Morris was trying to break him, but he had picked the wrong man.

He looked up at the sky as he felt the first tiny spot of rain touch his face. That was all he needed. The punishment would be hard enough without having to do it in the rain.

* * *

Luke came out of the officer's mess hall feeling slightly bemused. He hadn't seen this coming and he was both shocked and pleased to discover that someone thought his talents had a use. Accustomed to everyone speaking of his painting as a nice little hobby, he hadn't known what to say when General George

Thompson had told him that he could do them all a huge service if he would agree to become an official war artist.

'You know how it is, Trenwith,' General Thompson told him. 'We need to keep up the morale – here at home as well as at the front. We don't want the people to realise what it is really like out there, do we? I suggested that we needed an artist's impression of what was going on. I dare say you can produce some stirring stuff for us – the heroic soldier going off to do his duty, ready to die for King and country. You understand what I'm after?'

'Yes, of course, sir,' Luke told him. 'You know that I joined the RFOC and I'm training to be a pilot?'

'Yes, of course. I am sure you will do well, Trenwith. Your special duties need not interfere with your training, but we would rather you flew on special missions for us than just waste you in combat. There are plenty of others for that... We need someone who can sum up a landscape for instance and make a quick drawing...'

'You're asking me to do reconnaissance missions, aren't you?'

'Well, that might be a part of your special missions, but we do want the propaganda pictures.'

Luke nodded. He understood that he was being

painted a rosy picture, the kind of thing they were asking him to do for the people at home, to keep up the idea that the war was a piece of cake. He didn't mind that some of the things he was asked to draw might mean landing in a dangerous location. At least he wouldn't be asked to go out and kill people every day. He shuddered as he thought of having to shoot a man the way the British Tommy did, face to face.

'When do you want me to start on the propaganda stuff?'

'Immediately,' General Thompson said and nodded his appreciation. 'Good man. You've got three days before you need return to your unit. Could you do a few sketches, let me approve your ideas and then work on them back at base in your own time?'

'Yes, of course,' Luke agreed. 'So you want me to show the new recruits coming in, and then what they look like after a few weeks training. Call it the *Pride of Britain* or some such thing?'

The General beamed. 'You've got the idea, Trenwith. Wander around the camp and see what you can find of interest. You have my permission to go where you like – and if you want one of the men to pose for you, you can pull him out of whatever training he is doing.'

'I was going to ask about that, because I'll need a

face for my pictures. Some of it will be just my view of army life, but we'll need an impressive face for the hero. Someone who looks brave and full of enthusiasm for the task ahead.'

'See what you mean,' Thompson agreed. He arched his brow. 'We've fixed you up in officers' quarters. If you would like to change before dinner?'

'Yes, thank you,' Luke said. 'My driver will have taken my kit to quarters. I'll see you shortly.'

'We shall be glad to have you as a guest, Trenwith.'

Luke was crossing the parade ground when he noticed a soldier running round the square with his rifle above his head. The man was soaked to the skin for it had been raining this past hour, though it was easing off now. He saw that a sergeant appeared to be watching while sheltering under a porch. The soldier must be on a charge, but this was surely taking the punishment too far? As the soldier came closer, Luke saw it was Jack Barlow. He walked up to the sergeant, who saluted him.

'At ease, Sergeant,' Luke said. 'Why is this soldier being punished?'

'He disobeyed orders, sir.'

'Indeed?' Luke raised his brows. 'Not to be encouraged, of course, but he has clearly been out here for a while. Do you think he has been punished enough?'

'Begging your pardon, sir, but this is an army affair.'

'Yes, I know – but actually I have been given permission from General Thompson to recruit anyone I need for my work. I need Jack Barlow. So if you wouldn't mind taking him off charge now, Sergeant.'

'Begging your pardon, sir. Do you have that in writing?'

'Not yet,' Luke said. His manner was polite but he had the breeding of centuries behind him, the pride of his ancestors in every line of his body. The sergeant's arrogance vanished: he knew when he was beaten. 'But I could always go to General Thompson and explain the situation. I imagine he is changing for dinner at this moment, but if you insist, I can...'

'No, sir!' Sergeant Morris stepped forward. 'Barlow! Get your arse over here sharp! Officer needs you!'

Luke's face remained impassive. He knew the sergeant was fuming inside, but he was also aware that he would not dare to draw the attention of a high-ranking officer to what had been going on. He was probably a bully and enjoyed lording it over the new recruits. Whether he took his bullying too far was another matter. Luke had no authority to inquire, though had it been at his own base he would have got to the bottom

of what the man had done to incur such a punishment.

Jack Barlow came up to him. He saluted, his expression giving no indication that he had recognised
the RFOC officer. Sergeant Morris scowled and walked
off, clearly smarting from the encounter.

'Sir! Private Barlow reporting, sir!'

'Barlow, I need you for special duties. Would you
get changed out of those wet clothes, put on a dry uniform and meet me at the pub in the village at nine this
evening please?'

Jack's eyes gleamed, but his expression remained
unchanged. 'Is that an order, sir?'

'Yes, Barlow, it is. General Thompson wants me to
paint some pictures of a hero for use by the War Ministry. You are my chosen model – if you are prepared to
sit for me?'

'I was due to go on leave for forty-eight hours before being shipped over there, sir,' Jack told him. 'Sergeant Morris cancelled my leave, but if you want me to
sit for you I'll be happy to do it.'

'If you wanted to go home, Barlow – I am sure I
could swing it. I'll have a word with your CO...'

'No, sir. I hadn't planned to go home. Ma would
only get upset, because she'd know where I was going.
Rose has a couple of days off too. She was coming here

and we were going to have a nice meal out, walk a bit and go to the theatre in the evening.'

'Rose is coming here?' Luke was pleased when Barlow confirmed it. 'Well, I don't think your sitting for me need interfere too much with your plans, Barlow. If you would allow me to take you both out for a meal somewhere decent, I think I could make as many sketches as I need. Then you can have the rest of the time to yourselves.'

'Yes, sir.' Jack grinned suddenly. 'Thank you, sir. Rose will be proper made up with that, Captain Trenwith. I'll see you in the King and Crown later.'

Luke nodded as Barlow went off at a run. He took a cigarette from his silver case, tapped the end against the metal and transferred it to his lips before lighting up. Sergeant Morris was watching him from a distance, a scowl on his face. If Barlow was due to ship out any time now, he would probably be safe from his brutality until then. However, he must warn Barlow to be careful of the man if the two of them should ever meet again...

* * *

'She asked for you many times, Louise,' Isabelle Renard said. 'I am so sorry. Even last night she spoke fondly of you, but this morning she took a turn for the worse and she slipped away just an hour ago.'

'I came as soon as I had your letter,' Louise said. She glanced round the parlour of the boarding house her mother had run for many years. It still smelled of Maman's perfume. In the background lingered another smell – that of tobacco and sweat. Her throat felt tight and she blinked hard. It was so foolish to feel like weeping. She had been glad to marry and leave her mother's house after the last argument over one of her mother's lovers. 'Did she suffer much, Isabelle?'

'I can't lie to you,' Isabelle said. 'She was sick for a long time before she would let me send for you. She wrote you a letter but she decided not to send it. She asked me to give it to you if you came when I sent for you.' Isabelle hesitated. 'I am not sure what is left to you, but the lawyer says there is something...'

Louise shook her head. 'I don't want to talk about that yet, Isabelle. Is she upstairs?'

'Yes. She looks peaceful. I wasn't sure what you would want to do for the funeral...'

'Did Maman speak to you of her wishes?'

'It may be in your letter.' Isabelle took an envelope from her pocket and handed it to her. 'Now that you're here I should go – but if you need me I am only next door.'

'Thank you,' Louise said. 'You were so good to Maman. I do not know how she would have managed without you.'

'She was my friend.' Isabelle hesitated, then leaned forward to kiss Louise's cheek. 'She would have done the same for me – and she loved you, Louise. Whatever happened between you that last day before you left... it haunted her. She always loved you and she was glad that you were happy.'

Louise turned away as the hot tears stung her eyes. She'd sent her mother only birthday or Christmas cards and not once had she complained of her miserable life. She had not forgiven Maman for not believing her – for pretending to think that Louise had been willing. A shudder ran through her and she thrust away the memory of hateful hands touching her, invading her body.

'I shall go up now,' she said. 'I shall see you later...'

She was remembering the good times as she went up to her mother's bedroom. Her English 'uncle' had been kind to both Maman and Louise. It was after Freddie left them that the other uncles came; they did not stay for long and they were not so kind. As Louise left her childhood behind she had begun to feel their eyes on her. Sometimes they tried to touch her and they looked at her in a way that made her feel dirty.

She grew to hate them, and when she was eighteen she had known that she must leave. If only her mother had believed her when that pig had forced himself on her...

Louise blocked out the hurtful memories. Maman had been kind when she was a child. Her rages began when Louise grew up and the men started to look at her instead of Maman.

Brushing away the tears, Louise went into the bedroom. It was too late for weeping now. She was here to say goodbye.

* * *

'So how do you find it in the VADs?' Luke asked as Rose Barlow got into the back seat of his staff car. He was driving it himself, having decided it would be best to leave his official driver behind that morning. Rose's brother was sitting up front beside him. 'Is it terribly hard work?'

'Yes, sir,' Rose said and looked slightly awkward, as if she felt she ought not to be getting into his car. 'But it is worthwhile and they gave me work on the nursing side, which was what I wanted. I'm not a nurse, but I do get to help the patients sometimes, though it is mostly scrubbing bed pans and floors.'

'That is hard work for you!'

'Yes, but I'm used to it and I may be allowed to train for nursing in a year or so. They say I have potential.'

'You must be pleased,' Luke said. 'I hope you don't mind that I've arranged to take you and Jack out to a meal? I'm sketching him and it seemed a good way of combining your visit and a couple of sittings. I shan't keep you all day. After tea you can just go off together and enjoy yourselves.'

'I was on a charge from Sergeant Morris,' Jack put in as Luke got into the driving seat. He turned his head to look at Rose. 'If it were not for Captain Trenwith I shouldn't have been able to meet you at all today. Sergeant Morris cancelled my leave, but Mr Luke told him he needed me for his war work. He is going to paint propaganda pictures for the War Office – and he decided to use me as the model.'

'That was good of you, sir,' Rose said from the back seat. 'I don't mind watching you work at all. It will be something to tell the girls when I get back to the hospital.'

'I thought we would go to a rather nice pub I've been told about,' Luke said. 'It is such a lovely day and they have tables in the gardens. We can use it as a sort of studio. I'd like to make half a dozen sketches of Jack, walking or sitting... Maybe having a drink at the bar. I can use them in different ways when I come to do the actual paintings. I believe they serve reasonable food there too.'

'Anything would be better than what we get!' Jack said and grinned.

'Fancy Jack being in one of the government's posters,' Rose said and gave her brother a teasing look. 'You'll be famous, Jack.'

'His face will certainly be well known if they use my pictures,' Luke agreed. 'It's a pity you weren't wearing your uniform, Rose. It might be nice to have a picture of our womenfolk doing their bit too.'

'Oh, you wouldn't want to paint me in that.' Rose pulled a wry face. 'It's awful. You could always sketch my face and then paint me in a nurse's uniform. Some of them are nice, nicer than ours anyway.'

Luke glanced at her in his driving mirror. 'Yes, maybe I will make a quick sketch of you – if you don't mind?' He had always wanted to paint her, but it had been impossible to ask. She would have felt uncomfortable, suspicious. She was all right with the idea now, because of Jack's involvement.

'Of course I don't mind, Mr Luke. If you put me in a poster, Ma would love to have one.'

Luke wanted to tell her she could drop the formality. His family no longer employed her, but as her brother was forced to address him as sir or Captain Trenwith it wouldn't seem right if he encouraged the familiarity. Besides, Rose might find it even more awkward if he tried to break down the barriers. He would have liked to invite her to be his friend, but he couldn't do the same for Jack, because of the difference in their ranks, so it was best to keep to the old ways.

He glanced at Rose in the mirror. She was wearing a dress he hadn't seen before and a pretty straw hat. She had probably bought the clothes in London. The dress had a certain style, though the material was cheap. She looked beautiful, her hair seeming to catch fire in the sunlight. He imagined her wearing the kind of clothes society ladies wore, a string of pearls about her throat, and then dismissed the idea as ludicrous. Rose would feel stupid. He was a fool even to let himself imagine that it could ever happen.

He should keep his mind on the job. He had been scrupulous about keeping the proper distance between them when Rose worked for his family. Nothing had changed. The divide was still there, as wide and insurmountable as ever. He could enjoy her company for a few hours and then he must put her out of his mind.

If he survived the war, he would come home and

marry a suitable young lady, someone who would provide the sons his father required to carry on the family traditions.

* * *

'Well, that was a surprise,' Rose said as they queued for the theatre that evening. She offered her brother a toffee wrapped in paper, but he refused. 'You could have knocked me down with a feather when Mr Luke opened the car door for me and told me to get in!'

'It was a bit of luck for me that he came along last night when he did,' Jack said. 'That bastard would have near killed me if Captain Trenwith hadn't pulled rank on him.'

'He must be a right pig,' Rose said. 'I mean Sergeant Morris – not Mr Luke.'

'You shouldn't call him that now,' Jack told her with a frown. 'You're not part of the family now – not that you ever were really.'

'Mr Luke and Miss Sarah always made me feel I was,' Rose told him. 'I know we had to be respectful, but Mr Luke has a lovely smile. Not that he smiles often... though he did today. He seemed different, happier.'

'I doubt he had much to smile about at home,' Jack

said with a grimace. 'He was always being told to do his duty. It isn't much different now, but he was pleased about being offered the chance to be a war artist. He caught you to the life in that sketch, Rose.'

'And you,' Rose agreed. 'I've seen some of his landscapes before. He didn't know, but I used to look at his work when I cleaned his rooms. He has real talent, Jack. It is a pity Sir James can't see how clever Mr Luke is at painting.'

'Well, maybe he will if the War Ministry uses his posters,' Jack said. He hesitated as they approached the box office. 'Do you want to be at the back or in the circle?'

'Can you afford the circle?' Rose teased.

'Considering that Captain Trenwith paid for our lunch I think I can stretch to it – and some chocolate if there's any going.'

'It was a nice lunch. I'm glad we ate in the garden, Jack. I didn't feel a bit awkward, and I really enjoyed myself.'

'Yes. The food was good for once,' Jack agreed. 'Better than we get in the army. Not as good as at home though. I shan't taste anything like Ma's cooking until this blasted war is over.'

Rose looked at him anxiously. 'Are you all right

with things, Jack? I know you're going over there soon...'

'We don't need to talk about that,' Jack said. 'It's what I joined up for, Rose. I want to get out there and do what I'm paid for...'

'Well, as long as you keep your head down and don't take risks.' Rose hugged his arm and gazed up at him. 'You're my big brother and I want you to come home in one piece.'

'Don't you worry about me.' Jack grinned at her. 'I thought it might be all over before I got out there, but by the looks of things it is going to take longer than everyone thought...'

They were inside the theatre now, lapsing into silence as they searched for and found their seats. Rose settled down as the lights were dimmed. She knew she would worry in the next weeks and months, just as every other sister, mother and sweetheart would worry while their men were away fighting. However, she wouldn't mention it to Jack again. She would make the most of the few hours they had left. They had worked at Trenwith together for years and she'd missed him since they'd left to go their own ways. She had been looking forward to this leave for weeks.

Rose hadn't really minded that they had spent most of the day with Mr Luke. She had always liked him, even though sometimes when he looked at her she had a strange feeling inside. It was ridiculous to think that he might like her more than he should. Mr Luke was a gentleman, and even though she was no longer a servant for his family, there could never be anything between them. Now what had made her think that? It was ridiculous! Mr Luke wouldn't fancy her, of course he wouldn't. Not with all those society ladies to choose from when he was ready.

Rose had never had a steady boyfriend. Lady Trenwith hadn't encouraged followers. Rose hadn't met anyone at home that she fancied enough to wed. She liked to go dancing with a group of friends now that she was in the VADs, and she enjoyed a bit of flirting once in a while, but she still hadn't found anyone she wanted to settle down with, though she'd had offers.

Maybe she was too fussy, but most of them didn't match up to her ideal. She wasn't really certain what kind of a man would make her want to settle down. It hadn't occurred to her before, but she would want someone with nice manners – someone who smelled clean. A lot of the men she met didn't bother with that kind of thing, but Rose wouldn't go out with someone who didn't keep himself right. She thought he would probably have to be a cross between her brother and Mr Luke.

* * *

Luke made certain that he bumped into Barlow on the morning the unit was due to leave for the coast and the ship taking them to France. He had some chocolate wrapped in brown paper, also some decent cigarettes instead of the cheap muck a lot of the soldiers smoked.

'I wanted to give you these, Barlow,' he said, thrusting the parcel at him. 'It was good of you to give up a day of your leave for me. I hope Rose got off all right?'

'Yes. I saw her on the train to London. She said to thank you for a lovely day, sir.'

'It was nothing.' Luke would have liked to be giving Rose presents, but that would be stepping over that invisible line. 'It's just some chocolate and cigarettes – no packets, because we don't want to tell the enemy where you came from, but you may find the case useful. Good luck, Barlow. I hope we shall all meet again after the war.'

'Thank you, sir. It's no picnic your side of things either. Make sure you come through it safe, Mr Luke.'

Luke nodded, smiling as Barlow lapsed into the familiarity. For a moment they were master and head groom once more, bonded by a mutual respect. Then

Jack saluted and moved off to join the queue for the truck taking his mates to the coast.

Luke turned away. The chocolate and cigarettes might come in useful if Barlow chose to barter them for food rather than consuming them himself, and the silver cigarette case could help him out of a sticky situation if the need arose. It had been an impulse to make the gift and he did not regret it, because Barlow had been almost family. That was the thing about servants you grew up with, Luke decided. Some of them had been closer to him than his blood relatives. Barlow's father had taught him to ride and Nanny had sat with him during the thunderstorms he'd found so terrifying as a lad. His mother had visited him for twenty minutes in the mornings.

This war was going to change things. He doubted that men and women who had known the freedom to work where they pleased would wish to return to domestic service, and that would leave people like his parents short of help. The huge house they lived in was a liability. If they wanted to survive in the future they would need to make changes. Luke wondered how his mother would feel if they had to give up the house and move into something smaller.

He took out his own silver cigarette case, extracted a Passing Cloud, his favourite brand, and lit up. He had a few more sketches to do here today and then he would be making his way back to his base in Cheshire. It shouldn't be too long before he was sent out to join an RFO base in France. After that, life was bound to change. He wondered how he would feel when it all started for real.

The men in the army were already having a hard time of it, and the defeat at Mons had been a terrific shock to everyone. Most people had thought it would be a short sharp war and over in a few months; they hadn't expected the Germans to break through as they had. It wasn't surprising that Rose was working hard as a VAD. The injured were coming home in droves. And far too many were dying out there.

Luke frowned as he remembered a letter he'd received from his sister, Sarah. She was helping set up a home for injured soldiers in Sussex. She might have been married by now or at least engaged if their father had been more reasonable. Luke had hoped to have a word with Troy Pelham, tell him that it would probably all come right if he were patient for a few months, but Troy had been shipped out a week or two before Luke had got round to trying to locate him.

Sarah was probably feeling miserable, but like a lot of other women whose men had gone to war, she would just have to put up with it. Luke would write to her soon, tell her to be patient and wait. If she did nothing to upset the apple cart their father would come round.

Luke found himself thinking about Rose again. She had been wearing some kind of perfume. A lot of the maids at Trenwith had worn cheap stuff when they had their days off. Rose's perfume smelled like flowers...

* * *

Back at the hospital, Rose soon forgot about her brief spell of leave. There had been another new intake of patients. She was kept busy every minute. Sister would have had her guts for garters if she'd caught her day-dreaming.

She wrote a letter to her mother that evening. Mrs Barlow would want to know all about her leave and what Jack had looked like. She hesitated over saying anything about Mr Luke, but if she didn't mention it to her mother, she would think it odd if she heard it from someone else. She wrote:

Jack is going to be in some war posters. Mr Luke is the artist and he took us both out to lunch at a pub so that he could make the sketches.

She didn't mention the sketch of her, because it probably wouldn't be used and her mother might get the wrong idea.

Rose finished her letter and then started one for Jack. She knew she would be lucky to get a postcard from France, but she had promised to write often and she wouldn't let him down. Letters and parcels from home meant everything to the boys over there.

She decided to tell him about a fundraising event she had been to and what one of the girls had been telling her about her young brother who'd had the measles. By the time she had finished she'd covered six pages. She smiled as she sealed the envelope. Jack might think it was all nonsense, but it was a slice of normal life and he wouldn't get much of that once he got to the front.

3

'When are you going home?' Isabelle asked. They had returned from the funeral two hours earlier and the few guests that had come for wine and a pastry had departed. 'Will your husband be expecting you?'

'He said I could stay for a week,' Louise said and sighed. She had felt sad burying her mother, but now it was over and she had a sense of freedom. Jacques hovered at the back of her mind like a menacing black cloud, but she tried not to think of him. 'I shan't go back before that...'

'Why go at all if you are unhappy?' Isabelle asked. She was an attractive woman some years older than Louise, unmarried with a child of her own. 'You could stay here. This house is yours. You could find work, perhaps in one of the cafés.'

Louise looked wistful, because the idea appealed. It was exactly what she wanted, except that she would prefer to work in Paris. 'Jacques would come looking for me. As soon as he learns there is some money he will make me go back.'

'Why tell him?' Isabelle shrugged her shoulders. 'The Germans are driving towards Paris. If they break through the British lines we are in trouble. Soon they will have control of the whole country. Jacques might not find it easy to come after you. We are inundated with British soldiers here. Your maman always liked the English.'

'My English uncle was the best of them,' Louise said. 'Maman's letter says that he gave her this house when he left us. He was married and he went back to his wife, but he sometimes wrote and sent money. She saved the money for me.'

'She loved you,' Isabelle said and looked thoughtful. 'Why don't you come out with us this evening? Yvonne and I are going to a dance in the town. It will be fun. It is for the British Tommies – to make them feel at home in France.'

'Do you think I should? We have just buried Maman.' Louise hesitated, but she was tempted. It was so long since she'd had any fun. Once she went back to Jacques the grinding work would start again, and if he knew about Maman's house, he would demand that she sell it and give the money to him. Louise would have to tell him about the five thousand francs her mother had left her, but she might keep the house secret. The lawyer could let it to tenants and put the money in the bank for her... just in case.

'Your maman would not want you to go on grieving,' Isabelle said. 'She would tell you to enjoy your life, Louise. If I were you I would not return to that brute at all, but it is your choice.'

'I have no choice. He is my husband...' Louise smiled suddenly, her face lighting up. 'I'll come this evening, but I shall need something to wear.'

'I have a pretty blue dress that will suit you well,' Isabelle said. She laughed as she caught Louise's excitement. 'I had it before my daughter was born and wore it only twice. It is too tight for me now but it will fit you...'

* * *

'This is a bit of all right,' Joe said. He glanced around the taproom, lifting his tankard to the group of Frenchmen who had sent it over to their table. 'My father said the Froggies were rubbish, but this lot seem pleased to see us.'

'They are afraid the whole country will be overrun by the Germans,' Jack said. 'They think we're here to protect them. I suppose we are in a way.'

'Cannon fodder more bloody likely,' Joe muttered and scowled into his tankard. He put the pewter pot down in disgust. 'I don't know what they call this stuff but it tastes like dish water.'

Jack chuckled. 'Let's have a walk round the town. We might find somewhere better. We need to make the most of tonight, because they'll have us on the move soon. You never know where we'll be by this time tomorrow.'

'Yeah, all right,' Joe agreed. 'I heard there was a dance on somewhere. It's free for British servicemen. They might have some decent beer there.'

Jack nodded his agreement. 'I think I saw the posters as we came into town. It has to be better than this place.'

'Anything would be better than this,' Joe said. He took another swig of his tankard and shuddered. 'Come on, let's get out of here before they send us another one.'

Joe got up and Jack followed him. He nodded to the group of men who had sent over the drinks, thanking them with the few words of French he'd picked up in the couple of days they had been stuck here. They should have moved on almost at once, but there had been some trouble further up the line and they had been given some surprise leave.

'Get to know the locals, learn a bit of the lingo – but be polite and no fighting,' the officer had instructed them. 'Make the most of this chance, lads. You'll find it different when you get up to the line.'

Jack had found most people willing, even eager to be friendly with the British Tommy, and he had decided to use his time to good purpose. You never knew when you might need to make yourself understood. He saw the poster advertising the free dance and pointed it out to Joe. They could hear the music playing, songs that had been popular at home, and grinned at each other. Evidently, the locals were doing their best to welcome them. It looked as if they were in for a good night.

* * *

Louise laughed, shaking her head as the British soldier offered her another glass of wine. She had already drunk three that evening. If she had any more she would be too drunk to dance. She wanted to dance, because it was fun, and she hadn't had this much fun in years.

'Will you dance, Mademoiselle – *sil vous plait?*' She turned at the sound of a pleasant voice. She hadn't seen this man before and the look in his eyes held her. He was in uniform, clearly English and his accent was awful, but at least he'd made an attempt to learn her language. She took to him immediately.

Most of the men she'd danced with that evening hadn't even made the attempt to speak one word of French. Louise smiled and took his hand. He was polite and very good looking, and, as she caught the fresh smell of soap on him, she thought him attractive. His hair was dark with red undertones, his eyes a greenish brown that some people called hazel.

'Thank you,' she said in English. 'How long have you been here?'

'Two days,' Jack said. He grinned at her. 'Your English is much better than my French, Mademoiselle.'

'Yes,' Louise agreed, her eyes filled with laughter. 'Much better, but at least you tried and that is good.'

'I want to learn all I can while I'm here,' Jack told her, his face alight with eagerness. 'I've got plans for when the war is over.'

Louise nodded. There was something about this Englishman that reminded her of her husband before he injured his leg – but Jacques wasn't as bright as this man. He would never have tried to learn anything new.

'Learning a new language is always good. I learned to speak English as a child, but I had a good teacher.'

'I didn't have as much schooling as a child as I should have liked. I am reading something every day, because one day I want my own business.' Jack had won a French phrase book in a game of poker with one of the lads, and he had found it stimulating reading when there was nothing else to do.

'You dance well,' Louise told him. She smiled up at him, feeling excited. He was different from any of the men she had known before she married and she was pleased that she had taken off her wedding ring, as Isabelle had advised. He might not have asked her to dance if he had known she was married. 'Tell me about yourself. What are you called – and what did you do before you joined up?'

'I'm Jack and I worked as a groom at a big house in the country,' he said. 'But after the war I am going to have my own garage. Automobiles are the thing of the future.' His eyes went over her appreciatively. 'So what do you do with yourself?'

'Oh, this and that,' Louise said. 'One day I should like to have my own café. I like to bake and I think I should enjoy doing this for customers. I am called Louise.'

'I'll bet you're a good cook,' Jack said. He kept hold of her hand as the music came to an end. 'Do you fancy going for a walk with me, Louise? I shan't try it on – it would be good to be quiet for a while and just talk...'

Louise hesitated. She ought to say no, but he was nice and she felt reckless for some reason. 'Yes,' she said and smiled up at him. 'Let's go for a walk, Jack. I too think it would be good...'

She linked her arm through his as they went out into the night air. It was late, but there was a moon and it still felt warm. Somewhere in a garden, night blooms were giving off a strong perfume. Louise glanced up at her companion, feeling a thrill of pleasure, the first stirrings of desire. Jack had promised not to try it on, but she knew that if he tried to kiss her she would let him. She might go further if he persisted, because she was feeling adventurous. Freedom was a heady thing. She wanted this night to go on and on, and she wished that she need never go back to the farm. She would be happy if this night never ended...

* * *

Louise brushed the sleep from her eyes as the doorbell rang the next morning. She reached for the small clock beside the bed and looked at the time. It was past eleven! She was usually up long before this and she groaned as she remembered that it had been nearly six before she finally crawled into bed.

Pulling on a robe that had belonged to her mother, Louise looked out of the window and saw the post boy. He appeared to have a letter for her. She opened the window and looked out.

'Put it in the box please.'

'You have to sign for it, madame.'

'I will be down in a moment.'

Louise ran down the stairs and opened the door. She signed for the letter and then saw it was for her mother. Opening it, she discovered it was from a man who signed himself Freddie... Her English uncle!

Reading it as she made coffee and ate a croissant, Louise smiled. Her 'uncle' had not forgotten them. He had written to say that he was now a widower and to offer both Louise and her mother a home in England – *a place you can stay in safety until the war is over...* He had sent some money for them to use as their fare to come to England. It wasn't much, but it was thoughtful of him and it touched her.

Louise's mouth curved in a smile. The English

were gentlemen. Her soldier had told her she could stay with his mother if she wanted to get away from France.

'There are plenty of jobs going, up at the house or on the farm,' Jack had said the previous night after he'd kissed her. 'Ma would welcome you if you told her I'd sent you.'

Louise smiled as she recalled the kiss. It had been soft and gentle, though she had sensed the hunger and passion Jack had kept in check. He had been so determined to treat her like a lady that she hadn't dared to tell him she was ready to sleep with him: she hadn't wanted him to think she was a whore, because he so obviously respected her.

Instead of bringing him back to her mother's house and taking him to her bed, Louise had allowed him to take the lead. They had walked and walked for hours. Some of the time Jack had talked about his home and his family, though he'd never mentioned his family name. Louise had talked about her mother's death, but she hadn't told him she was married or that she lived on a farm. She hadn't told him why she'd left home to marry a man she now disliked, because her secret was buried somewhere at the back of her mind.

She must write to her uncle, to the address he had

given. Louise looked at her letter once more. She would thank him for the money. She must also tell him of her mother's death. She thought it would make him sad, because clearly he had never forgotten the woman he loved.

One day, after the war, perhaps Louise would visit Freddie. She had thought about him often, wondering where he lived and who he really was. She took the letter upstairs to pack in the trunk containing Maman's things. She wanted some of her mother's clothes and the linen from the house, and there were one or two items of sentimental value, nothing worth much. If she took anything that could be sold, Jacques would sell it when he was short of money for drinking. The best furniture could go into store somewhere. She would call and see the lawyer later this morning, tell him to let the house to tenants and bank the money he got in rent in her name.

She would catch a bus that afternoon. Returning to the farm might be more difficult than leaving it had been. According to the papers, the Germans had made advances since she came to Boulogne. It might not be possible to get through at all – but that was wishful thinking. Louise smiled wryly. She was French, her papers were in order and she had paperwork to prove that she had been to her mother's funeral. She might be stopped and asked for her papers, but she would be allowed to go on.

She had no real excuse not to return to her husband. It was tempting to take up the offer she had received and leave France – or even stay here with Isabelle and find work at a café. However, she had married Jacques and she knew he needed her. He couldn't manage everything on his own. His leg was so painful. Louise knew that he relied on her and her conscience would not let her desert him.

She thought wistfully of the previous night. It had been special somehow, but she wasn't likely to see the English soldier again. They would not have met at all if his unit had not been delayed by some problem further up the line. He was expecting to leave to join the fighting at any moment. He might even be killed. Louise read the newspapers and she knew that a lot of the British troops were being killed all the time. It would be foolish to weave dreams about a future that could never happen.

Louise was a Catholic. Divorce was not an option for her. She couldn't leave Jacques, because her conscience wouldn't let her and he would never consent to a separation. The interlude with her English soldier was just something to keep tucked away at the back of her mind. When she was feeling low she would remember and smile, but it was just a dream, like the one she had of living in Paris one day and owning a little café.

* * *

'You disappeared last night,' Joe said in an accusing tone. 'I saw you leaving with that girl in the blue dress. She was a bit of all right! You lucky bugger! Did you get your leg over?'

Jack frowned. He didn't mind Joe's coarseness in the normal way, but applied to Louise it annoyed him. Louise wasn't the kind of woman you had a quickie with up against the wall. He had liked her, respected her, and wished he could know her better. He had meant it when he'd suggested she go to England, because it would be safer for her than staying so near the fighting.

Louise had smiled and shaken her head. Jack remembered the feel of her mouth as he'd kissed her: warm, soft and responsive. He had wanted so much more, but he'd kept his desire under control. Maybe he would come back and find her when he got some leave. They could really get to know each other and...

The order to move on broke into Jack's thoughts. The troops' train had arrived early that morning and they were being taken to base camp. After that the next stop was the front line and everything that went with it. He wouldn't have much time to think about Louise once he was in the thick of things.

'Nothing happened,' he said to Joe. 'She wasn't a whore. I liked her too much to try it on.'

'More fool you,' Joe said. 'I took her friend outside. She didn't say no. I made the most of it. You never know when you'll get another chance.'

'Did she have a friend?' Jack asked. 'I didn't see Louise with another girl. I don't blame you if the girl was willing, but it wasn't what I wanted.'

Jack wasn't sure what he did want. A permanent relationship had never entered his head when he was working in the stables at Trenwith. He had ambitions and a wife and family would have made his dream impossible. The feelings he'd had for Louise were new and strange; he didn't understand them and no doubt he would forget her after they got up to the line. He would have more than enough to occupy his thoughts once he was faced with the enemy.

No, he wouldn't forget her. If he got through this thing he might come back one day and look for her.

* * *

Louise had arranged for her trunk to be sent ahead by carrier. She took the bus for a start, then changed to a train for the last part of her journey. She had wondered if she would be challenged by German patrols. When the train passed into German-controlled territory, some soldiers came on board. They walked through, looking at the occupants and demanding to see papers, but the one who approached Louise was young and hesitant. He had a quick look at her papers, but didn't ask any questions. One or two of the men were questioned but the Germans seemed satisfied and departed without taking anyone off, leaving the passengers to continue in peace.

Louise walked from the station. When she entered the farmhouse it looked deserted. Almost every plate and mug they owned had been used and left on the wooden draining board. Louise grimaced. She wondered whether Jacques would have got round to washing the dishes if she hadn't come back. He clearly believed that it was her job and that she could do it on her return.

The fire had gone out in the range. Louise knew she must light it if she wanted hot water to wash the dishes. It would take a while to get going enough to boil a kettle. She wondered if there was any food in the house, but a brief look in the pantry told her it was almost empty. Jacques had just used what she'd left and not bothered to replace anything.

Once she had the fire started and the kettle filled, Louise took a basket and went out to investigate whether the eggs had been collected. At least there was flour in the pantry. She could make a pudding and she had brought some bacon with her, as well as butter and bread. She could make a supper of some sort, though she would need to buy supplies from the market the next day.

She found enough eggs to fill her basket in the hen house, which meant they probably hadn't been collected since she left. She would have to test them in water before using them; if any floated she would discard them as being bad. If most of them were fresh she might be able to barter a few in the village in return for foodstuffs they needed.

She could actually afford to spend a little more if she chose, but once Jacques knew about the five thousand francs her mother had left her he would demand she give it to him. If she refused he would hit her. He would probably find some excuse to hit her anyway when he got back, because he would be angry that she had stayed away longer than she needed.

Louise sighed as she started on the piles of dirty

dishes. Isabelle had told her she was a fool to return, and she was right.

* * *

'So you came back then?' Jacques grunted as he walked in late that evening. She could smell the odour of strong drink on his breath, and the scowl on his face told her he was angry. 'So what did the old bitch leave you then? Was it worth the trip?'

'Don't talk about Maman that way,' Louise said, resentment stirring. He hadn't shaved in days and by the look of the clothes he was wearing he had slept in them while she was away. 'She never did you any harm.'

'Only because I never went near her,' Jacques muttered. 'What is for supper?'

'I bought bread and I made a quiche with bacon, onions and eggs...' Louise caught her breath as she saw his eyes narrow. 'There was nothing left in the cupboard... I baked a pudding...'

'Damn your puddings,' Jacques grunted. 'I'm sick of eggs and bacon.' He advanced towards her, a menacing look on his face. Then he lifted his hand and struck her across the face. 'I asked you a question – what did the bitch leave you?'

'Five thousand francs and her personal things; they are in my trunk upstairs but there's nothing much of value.' Jacques's eyes gleamed for a moment, and then he turned away and spat into the fire.

'The stupid old bitch should have had more than that for a lifetime of spreading her legs for any man who would pay her.'

'Jacques! Don't you dare say that,' Louise said. She was really angry now. She could taste blood in her mouth and her lip felt sore, but she faced him bravely. The thought of her mother's house was comforting. He wasn't going to get a penny from that if she could help it. 'Five thousand francs is something.'

'Where is it?'

'The solicitor said he would put it into an account for me.'

'Then you had better tell him to get on with it.' Jacques lifted his fist to her again. 'Unless you want some more of this, you get that money here fast. It's time I had something for taking on a whore's daughter! Now get upstairs. I'm going to teach you a lesson.'

'No...' Louise was shaking inside but determined not to give in to his brutality. 'I don't want you touching me. You can sleep in the spare room...'

She gasped as he hit her with such force that she went staggering and fell to the floor. He stood over her as she lay there trying to recover her breath, and then he kicked her in the stomach. Louise screamed with pain, curling into a ball to protect herself.

'You'll do as you're told, bitch,' Jacques warned. 'Otherwise I'll beat you until you can't stand up...'

Louise closed her eyes as the tears trickled down her cheeks. She hadn't hated him before this; she had been sorry for his pain and she'd tried to be a good wife despite his temper and his neglect, but now she hated him.

She got to her feet and stumbled up the stairs, holding back the tears. She wouldn't show weakness. Let him do his worst! She wouldn't give him the satisfaction of seeing her weep, even though she was weeping inside.

* * *

Louise vomited into the toilet. As she wiped her mouth afterwards she saw blood in the vomit. She had been bringing up small amounts each day since the beating Jacques had given her. She was feeling sore and her stomach hurt. She was in two minds as to whether she should go to the doctor, but her face was still badly bruised and she had hesitated because people would stare if they saw her.

She went downstairs as she heard Jacques moving in the kitchen. She knew she had provoked him to the beating, and she sensed that he was ashamed, even though he hadn't apologised. He was making up the fire in the range as she went in and a kettle was boiling.

'Why were you being sick?' he asked.

'I don't know.' Louise gave him a hard look. 'I've been passing blood since you kicked me in the stomach.'

'I shouldn't have done that,' he said, and for a moment there was fear in his eyes. 'I was angry and I'd been drinking. It won't happen again.'

'If it does I shall leave you,' Louise said. His eyes narrowed and she thought he might fly into a temper again, but he didn't.

'I suppose I deserve that, but you know how I am...' He hesitated, then, 'Did you hear them passing in the night?'

'I heard rumbling – as if there were several vehicles.'

'Germans,' Jacques said. 'I got up and went to look. I thought they might come here.'

'Why should they? There's nothing here to interest them.'

'Nothing, except for a few hens and pigs,' he

agreed. 'I am going to the village to see what is going on. I should think they were just passing through, but one of these days they will stop here.'

'I don't see why they should,' Louise said. 'If they do they will take what they want and move on.'

'Hide yourself if they come while I'm gone. The Germans are brutes. They might rape you.'

Louise threw him a challenging look and he turned away. She didn't tell him that it would be no worse than what he'd done to her a couple of nights previously, but he knew it. She thought he was remorseful, but that didn't change what had happened. Nothing could wipe away the pain and humiliation he had inflicted.

'You can do nothing,' she told him, and Jacques glared at her. 'It isn't your fault they wouldn't take you with the others for the army. No one thinks you a coward. Besides, we are doing important work. The government needs us to grow food for the troops.'

'Be quiet, woman,' Jacques muttered. His face was still unshaven and he had not bathed in days. 'You have no idea what it feels like to be rejected as useless. Get on with your chores and leave me to do what I think fit.'

'You should be careful,' she warned. 'Otherwise,

the Germans might cart you off somewhere to work for them.'

'With my leg?' Jacques asked with a sour twist of his lips. 'I would be no use to them. What would you care if they did?'

'They won't know you can't work from looking at you. Be careful, Jacques.'

'As if you care,' he said and stumped out of the room without another word.

Louise let him go. She would care if the Germans took him, if only because she couldn't do all his chores as well as her own. She couldn't bring herself to tell him that she did still care in her way. Before the beating, she would have gone after him, told him again to make sure the Germans didn't see him. She was still too raw inside; too angry over the way he had behaved towards her.

Louise stood at the door of the old farmhouse shading her eyes against the sun. She had heard the rumble of cartwheels and heavy machinery passing again at some time during that morning and since then there had been gunfire in the village. Jacques had been gone for hours.

Louise had done all the work that Jacques should have shared with her. She was accustomed to milking their three cows: feeding and watering the pigs, chickens and ducks were just one of her usual chores, but her husband should have seen to mucking out the stables and the cow byres. She did as much as she could, but she knew that she would not manage to lift the root crops alone. If the field was not ploughed they would be short of food next year, but Jacques never listened to her. He had become so bitter since the men of the village joined the French army and marched away.

The light was beginning to fade from the sky. Louise went into the kitchen and lit the oil lamp. She was hungry and the smell of the soup she had been preparing was tantalising. She had baked bread early that morning, and there was some good cheese and pickles she had made herself. There was also a small piece of ham left from the gammon she had boiled the previous day. Jacques would eat that for his supper when he eventually came home. If she ate it herself he would probably be angry, and she would rather manage with some soup and cheese.

She always waited for him until eight o'clock. If he did not come back by then she would eat her supper alone and go to bed. She was almost falling asleep, and her back ached. The pain in her stomach was beginning to ease, but her hands were sore where she had raked out the pigsties. She rubbed a little cream into them and sat down. There was always a pile of mending and it would help to pass the time until Jacques returned.

She pushed away the tiny nagging fear at the back of her mind that Jacques would not come. The shooting she'd heard earlier meant that the Germans had fired on someone. She prayed it wasn't Jacques. He wasn't much of a husband. She didn't love him, but life was hard enough on the farm as it was. Without him she would find it impossible to do some of the chores that needed urgent attention.

* * *

'How are you, Ma?' Rose asked as she walked into the comfortable kitchen and saw her mother busy at work. As usual, the room smelled of baking and herbs. 'Guess who I saw as I came from the station?'

'Not your brother?' Mrs Barlow asked, looking expectant. 'He hasn't been sent back wounded?'

'Not that I've heard,' Rose said. 'Has he written to you?'

'I had a postcard a few weeks back, before he went overseas. So who did you see then, Rose?'

'Miss Sarah. She was on her way up to the house.'

'She's back then,' Mrs Barlow said and wiped her floury hands on a small towel. 'I suppose Lady Trenwith wanted her home. What with Marianne married and expecting her first – and Mr Luke gone off to the wars...'

'I saw him the day I went to meet Jack for my two days of leave, but I told you in my letter.'

Mrs Barlow looked at her oddly. 'I hope you're not getting ideas because he took you to lunch and drew your brother's picture? We've got propaganda pictures all over the village, telling the young men they are needed, but I haven't seen one of Jack yet.'

'No, of course I haven't got ideas, Ma,' Rose said and laughed. 'Whatever made you think that, Ma? Mr Luke is one of *them*. He wouldn't be interested in the likes of me.'

'He might be interested in one thing,' her mother replied with a little sniff. 'It wouldn't be fitting, Rose. Your father still works for the family, and you may want to go back there after the war. Don't do anything foolish. You wouldn't be the first girl to be taken advantage of by someone who should know better.'

'Ma! Of course I shan't,' Rose scoffed. She picked

up a jam tart that had just come from the oven. 'Besides, Mr Luke isn't like that, honestly.'

Her mother made a disbelieving face at her. 'Given the chance, who knows? That tart is hot. Watch you don't burn your mouth!'

'Yes, Ma,' Rose said. She went out of the kitchen and upstairs to her bedroom, blowing on the hot jam. She liked coming home, but her mother seemed to think she was still a child. Rose knew that a relationship between her and Luke Trenwith would be doomed from the start. It hadn't stopped her thinking about him a few times, but she was sensible enough not to start dreaming. Besides, her work was hard for the Voluntary Aid Division and she had met lots of new friends, some of them men.

Rose did not lack for opportunity if she wanted a follower. Thus far she'd stuck to going out with a group of girls or mixed company. She hadn't met a man who made her melt inside... The way she might feel about Mr Luke if she let herself.

That was nonsense! Rose shut the thought out of her mind. Her mother was right. It was quite out of the question. She couldn't help wondering whether Mr Luke had been shipped over there yet, and how he was getting on with his work as a war artist. She smiled as she remembered the sketch he had done of her. It would be strange if she suddenly saw her face looking out at her from a War Office poster!

* * *

Luke waited as the three men examined the paintings he had brought in. He knew that they would like three of them, which were exactly the kind of thing that had been suggested to him; a heroic portrayal of men becoming soldiers, eager to fight for King and country. He had also painted a picture of a nurse helping a wounded soldier. The girl wasn't Rose. He had painted a picture of Rose, but it wasn't for anyone else. He wanted it for himself. He kept the sketch of her with him in his breast pocket. He wasn't sure why... Unless it was a reminder of home and a time before war.

'These three are very good,' General Thompson said. 'I like the face you picked for this poster, Trenwith. It is a good strong face, not too young and quite bold – the kind of image we want to portray of our heroes.'

'Yes, Barlow was a good choice,' Luke agreed. 'What about the other two?'

'I'm not sure we can use those,' the general said. 'Severely wounded men are a bit depressing for the public. They like to think of their boys marching off with flags flying... They don't want to see them come back blinded and with lost limbs...'

'No, I dare say not,' Luke agreed. 'But it is what happens in many cases. I visited a hospital and saw these men myself.'

'I dare say. It isn't what we need, however. I thought I had made myself clear?'

'Yes, you did,' Luke said. 'I thought you might like to show what sterling work the nurses are doing?'

'Not like this, Trenwith – these scenes are too raw for general consumption. But the other pictures are good. Have you thought about those special missions we mentioned?'

'Yes, sir. Of course I'm up for it – if you think I'll be any good? I'm not clear exactly what you want...'

'We can't get good enough images from the air,' General Thompson said. 'The idea is that you take your kite in, land somewhere you're not likely to be noticed and then do a spot of scouting for us.'

'Spying?' Luke said and frowned. 'Wouldn't photographs be better than sketches?'

'The images aren't always clear. You might sketch details that wouldn't show up on film – but you can take pictures too.'

'Yes, I get the idea,' Luke said. 'I am ready when you give the order, sir.'

'You will be going over sometime next week. When we need you for a special mission, your CO will brief you – at other times you will fly with your squadron.'

'I understand. Thank you for putting your trust in me, sir.'

'You're a good man.' The general extended his hand. 'And thank you for the pictures. I'll hang on to them all if you don't mind.'

Luke wanted to protest. Thompson was making sure that the pictures he hadn't approved were kept away from the light of day. However, it didn't matter. Luke had others and he had no doubt that he would be storing up memories in the weeks and months to come. One day he would put his memories on canvas. When the war was over he would have a show – if he managed to produce anything worth showing. In the meantime he had a job to do and it was best to keep his opinions to himself.

'Thank you, sir.' He saluted and went out.

The door closed behind him. Thompson turned to his companions.

'What do you think? About using him over there, I mean?'

'It's a bit risky. If he isn't shot down before he gets into enemy territory he will find it hard to hide the kite. Even if he gets the stuff we're after, there is no guarantee that he will make it back.'

Thompson shrugged. 'If he doesn't we'll have to go back to aerial shots, but it would be good to have some idea of what their side of the line is like. If Trenwith makes it back he will have the right material. It is a pity we can't use these pictures – they are damned good. He has captured the pathos, the bravery of these poor devils...' He held up the pictures of wounded men for them to see.

'But inflammatory,' the government official said. 'We have to keep up public morale and we don't want the new recruits scared off before we even get them.'

'What do you suggest I do with these pictures?'

'Lose them for the duration of the war. If he returns to claim the damned things you can take your time finding them. It's more than likely that he won't...'

* * *

'Bloody boot,' Joe muttered and unlaced the offending article. 'I'm damned if I'm going to wear these again. I shall go back to my brown ones and they can say what they like.'

'I shouldn't worry,' Jack said and grinned. 'With the

state of things out here they won't know if they're black or brown.'

'I don't give a bugger if they do,' Joe grumbled. 'I've had nothing but blisters for weeks.'

Jack nodded but made no answer. There was no point in grumbling about a little thing like blisters. The conditions in the trenches were hellish, and it wasn't much better back here at base camp. The men were filthy when they came back for a rest, riddled with lice and other pests. Most had some kind of sores or skin irritation, and it wasn't easy to get a bath. They were using old wine vats and they had to stand in line for their turn. They were lucky if they got clean water, because they were expected to use it again and again until it was disgusting.

A lot of men had worse things to worry about than blisters or skin rashes. There were casualties every day and the stretcher-bearers were busy ferrying the injured back through the lines ready to send to the field hospitals. If the injured were lucky enough to get a Blighty wound they could expect to be shipped back to England, but if you got away with a flesh wound you would be sent back to the front as soon as you could walk. Perhaps the luckiest ones were those who died swiftly.

'You ain't got any more bandages?' Joe asked in a plaintive tone.

'Sorry, mate,' Jack said. 'Tell you what, there's a nurse I met the other day. She might have something you could use. I've got a couple of hours to myself. I'll walk down to the field hospital and ask.'

'They won't give you anything. I've tried.'

'Jane might. She's a decent lass.' He tossed Joe a pack with a couple of cigarettes. 'Stay here and rest. I'll see you later.'

'Are you coming to the village this evening? I told you I met a girl last night. She says she has a sister – Andrea is an obliging girl, if you know what I mean. Her sister would do the same for you. They like the English.'

'Thanks. I'll think about it,' Jack said. 'I'll see what I can scrounge for you, mate. Leave your foot open to the air. It will give the skin a chance to harden up.'

'Cheers, mate,' Joe said and lit up the first of the cigarettes. 'I'll do the same for you one day.'

Jack walked out of the tent they shared with two other privates. He hadn't expected he would be sent to the trenches, thinking he might be more use working on the vehicle detachment. However, thus far his skills seemed to have been overlooked. It was because they had been forced to withstand a barrage of fierce attacks from the Germans. He'd hardly had a breather since he got here. The order to stand down and return to base camp had been a welcome relief.

He whistled a tune as he walked towards the line of tents that were known as the field hospital. Conditions were far from good this close to the line, but as a rule they just did their best to patch up the worst of the men's wounds and then sent them on their way.

He watched a makeshift ambulance being unloaded, the stretchers carried from the van that had once belonged to a high-class department store in London. Talk about the government being unprepared! They had drafted in all kinds of vehicles, because they didn't have anywhere near enough of the right kind. Men and arms could quite easily be transported in a wagon with horses, which were slow and vulnerable if one of the German planes came over and shot at them. It was time the damned fools in high places got their act together and realised this was the twentieth century. Not that the government gave a damn. Men were expendable, because there were always more young fools ready to answer the recruitment drives.

Rose had told him that the papers were full of articles about the need for another five hundred thousand men at the front. Her frequent letters were always filled with news of what was going on at home. Apparently, the Queen had called on the women of England to knit socks for the troops. At least Jack never went short of parcels from home. His mother and sister were always sending him something. Post from home was something all the men looked forward to receiving. The lucky ones often shared with their mates, because they were bonded together by mutual suffering.

Jack paused to watch the stretcher-cases. As one of them was carried past him he did a double take. That couldn't have been who he thought it was! Bandages covered half of the man's face, but Jack was almost sure he knew him.

He went after the stretcher-bearers as they entered the tent, his stomach heaving as he caught the awful smell. It was the sickening stench of gangrene. He recognised it, because one of the farm labourers had died of it slowly after neglecting a flesh wound at Trenwith. He could hear men sobbing, crying out in pain, and his stomach tightened. He felt sick, but he didn't turn and run. He needed to know if he really had seen Troy Pelham being carried in on that stretcher.

He saw the stretcher being placed on the ground and went over to investigate. The two men were preparing to leave again immediately: there were more men needing attention, because the guns had been pounding their lines since early morning.

'Who is he?' Jack asked, catching the arm of the nearest bearer. 'I thought it was Captain Pelham?'

'Yeah... Know him, do you?'

'Yes, a little,' Jack said. 'He looks bad. What chance does he have?'

'He was burned,' one of them said. 'And he has a thigh wound but nothing internal. He will probably make it, poor devil. He might have been better off dead.'

Jack's stomach heaved as he looked down at the face of the man he remembered as being very handsome. The bandage had slipped, revealing the raw red flesh where his face had been burned by the blast. Jack felt a wave of pity for the poor devil lying there. He remembered his sister saying that Sarah Trenwith had wanted to marry Troy Pelham. She would have to be brave to want him now.

As he hesitated, Troy moaned and then opened one eye. Jack saw the agony he was enduring. There wasn't a damned thing he could do, because the doctors and nurses were already rushed off their feet. Captain Pelham would receive attention when they got round to him.

Jack did the only thing he could think of to ease

Troy's suffering. He lit a cigarette and then put it to the injured man's lips. Troy took a drag at it and then whispered something. Jack couldn't hear the words but he guessed he was being thanked.

'The doc will be here soon, old chap,' he said. 'Can I get you some water?' Troy moved his head slightly. Jack offered the cigarette again. Troy turned his head away and closed his eyes. 'I'll hurry the doc up – and I'll come and see you again.'

Jack felt his stomach heaving as he left the tent. It took more guts to work in here than it did to go over the top. He would rather make the run between the British lines through No Man's Land to face German fire than stay there and listen to the wounded screaming and crying. He spoke to one of the nurses about Troy, forgetting all about Joe's blisters.

As he walked swiftly away after delivering his message – a message that had been received with a curt nod – he felt the vomit rising in his throat. He relieved himself at the side of one of the dirt tracks that passed for roads in these fields. Wiping his hand on the back of his mouth, he glanced at a car that had just arrived. The driver turned his head to stare at him and he recognised Sergeant Morris. He knew from the sudden gleam in his eyes that the sergeant had recognised him too.

With the whole of the British front to choose from, why did that evil bastard have to turn up here? Jack had expected he would stay in England for the duration, using his special talents on the poor devils he treated like dogs while he taught them what army life was all about.

A cold shiver went down Jack's spine. Sergeant Morris hated him because of what had happened the day Luke Trenwith had pulled him off a charge. He would do Jack harm if he could.

* * *

Louise came out of church that Sunday morning. She waited to speak to the few old men and women who attended the service. None of the younger women or children had bothered to come. She knew that many of them were frightened that the Germans might notice and start rounding up anyone they found wandering around. It had frightened them because Jacques had been taken. No one knew where he was or even if he was still alive, but most felt that he would not have survived long.

Louise had been told that Jacques had been foolish. The villagers had told her what he'd done. It seemed that he had taken his shotgun and started waving it at the German officers who had been the first to arrive in their staff cars. It was such a stupid thing to do, because he must have known they would shoot anyone who resisted them. The truth was that he hadn't cared; he had been so bitter and angry that he threw his freedom and maybe his life away for nothing.

Louise couldn't cry for her husband. The tears had all gone. She felt empty, drained from months of living with a man who had been dead inside. Her tears had been shed long ago. She would miss another pair of hands about the farm, but she would not miss Jacques's rages or his drinking; she would not miss the times he had beaten her when he came home late from the inn and found his supper cold or dried up in the oven.

'May I walk home with you?' Louise said to the only woman present for whom she felt any empathy. Madeline Bonnier was in her early forties, still more than fifteen years older than Louise, but the youngest of the women who had attended the service. 'Would you like to come to the house for a bowl of coffee?'

'I shall come another day to see how you are,' Madame Bonnier said as they fell into step. 'You must be careful, for you are alone and these are difficult

times. If the Germans come looking for food... give it
to them.'

'I thought the Germans would come to the farm
before this, but they pass straight by,' Louise admitted.
'They go on to the Chateau Lorraine. People say it is
where they have their headquarters...'

'We are too close to the line,' Madame Bonnier
said grimly. 'The sound of the guns would disturb
their beauty sleep.' She spat on the ground. 'Bosch
pigs!'

Louise laughed, the first time for days, perhaps
much longer. At that moment traces of the girl she had
once been were in her face and she looked almost
beautiful again. Once she had been known as the most
beautiful girl in the district. She still had soft fair hair
and green eyes, but her hair was lank and her clothes
were washed so often they looked faded and drab. She
hadn't bothered much with her appearance since
Jacques was taken. She felt as if she were in shock, and
it had taken her several weeks to get over the beating
Jacques had given her.

'You must take care,' Madame Bonnier warned
again. 'I shall ask my son Pierre to come and help you
get your potatoes up, but I need him too, and he works
from morning to night. With the men gone there are

not enough hands to help with the root harvest this year.'

'Thank you,' Louise said. 'Pierre is a good boy. You must be careful the Germans do not notice him. He is tall for his age and they might think he is older than thirteen.'

'Yes, they might,' Madame Bonnier agreed. 'As long as they keep passing through the village we should be safe enough. They would not have taken Jacques if he had not waved his shotgun at them. They shot him, Louise, and threw his body into a truck.'

Louise shuddered. 'Was he dead? Why did they take him?'

Madame Bonnier shook her head. 'I do not know. They are brutes – animals! I hope the British will break through soon. If we were on their side of the line it would be better.'

'How do you know?' Louise asked. 'Men are men, Madeline. Even a Frenchman can be a pig...'

'You should not speak ill of the dead,' Madeline crossed herself. 'I know Jacques was harsh sometimes, but...' She shook her head as Louise turned away. 'He was not so bad before the accident I think?'

'No...' Louise sighed. 'I thought he loved me once. I married him because he had his own farm and I thought he would give me a better life than the one I had, but I was wrong. I should have gone away to Paris. Perhaps there I should have found something different.' She frowned. 'Besides, we do not know he is dead. He might have been taken to work somewhere.'

'With his leg? He would be no use to them. If he could not work fast enough they would shoot him anyway. They shot him in the shoulder, Louise. I doubt that he lived long, though he moaned as they picked him up. He was alive then.'

'Perhaps it would be best if he died quickly.'

'Perhaps.' Madeline looked anxious. 'It would be better if you knew for certain one way or the other. It is difficult for you alone. If you need help you can always come to me. I will do what I can...'

Louise nodded and turned away. She took off the black scarf she had worn for church, shaking her hair. It felt dirty, greasy. She would wash it this evening. It was time she shook off the apathy that had fallen over her after Jacques was taken. Madame Bonnier was right. It would be better if she knew one way or the other. Jacques had gone, but she was not sure if he still lived. She was in limbo, neither a wife nor a widow. She was not alone. So many women had lost their men to this war, and some of them would never come back.

Louise could hear the boom of guns in the distance. She wished the British would advance a few miles, force the Germans back. They were close to the line here and she would not have minded seeing a few English soldiers in the village.

Louise thought about the English soldier that she had met briefly when she was staying at her mother's house. He had been kind... Gallant. He had kissed her so sweetly, almost tenderly. She had sensed that he wanted more from her, but he hadn't asked. She had wished that he had spoken, but perhaps it was best that it hadn't happened. She had nothing to reproach herself for; she had not betrayed her marriage vows, even though she had wanted to. Unless you counted that kiss as a betrayal?

Louise dismissed it. The kiss had been innocent. Jacques had had no reason to beat her as he had. She hated him for it. She knew Madame Bonnier thought she should grieve for her husband's loss, but Louise couldn't weep for Jacques.

She missed his help about the farm. The chores were too much for her. She wasn't sure how long she could carry on alone – or even if she wanted to. Jacques had no relatives. She supposed that she owned the farm now. At least, she would if Jacques did not come back.

Did she want to spend the rest of her life like this? She could go back to Boulogne if she wanted, live in her own house or another, find work in a café... She could even go to England. Her English uncle had given her an address.

Louise smiled inwardly as she remembered Jack telling her that she would be safer in England with his mother. He had seemed to truly care about her and she had liked the feeling. She wondered where he was and whether he was safe.

They didn't get much news of the way the war was going. It was hard to get newspapers from behind the lines. The official story was that the Germans were winning the war. Louise hoped it wasn't true. She hadn't seen much of them as yet, but she had heard stories that made her flesh creep.

She didn't know whether they really bayoneted babies and raped all the women they found. Everyone talked about things they didn't know for sure. Madame Bonnier had shown her one paper that reported the situation from the British point of view. Someone had brought it through the lines, because there were still ways of getting past the Bosch if you were clever. It had been passed from house to house, but the news wasn't encouraging. The allies seemed to be getting a battering and the Germans seemed stronger, more prepared for this war.

Back at the farm, Louise was aware of the silence.

The guns must have stopped for a while. It happened every now and then, as if both sides got tired of the fighting and decided to take a breather. Why couldn't they all see how stupid it was and go home? Would Jacques come back when the war was finally over?

The weather was much cooler now because autumn had set in hard. In a few more weeks it would be winter. Louise would have long dark nights alone in the house.

She thought about Isabelle and the night they had gone dancing. Louise suspected that her mother's friend had found herself a lover that night. It was her privilege, but it wasn't what Louise wanted – though she had liked Jack. She would have slept with him if he had asked. He wouldn't be in Boulogne now anyway. He would be up at the front, fighting.

4

'Barlow! I want you. At the double!'

Jack's blood chilled as he heard Sergeant Morris's voice. He had done his best to stay out of the sergeant's way, believing that he would be back at the front line in a few hours and out of the man's way.

He turned and walked back to where the sergeant waited. 'Yes, sir!' he saluted smartly. 'What can I do for you, sir?'

'You can take that smart-arse look off your face for a start,' Morris said. 'I've got a job for you.'

'Yes, sir.' Jack's heart sank. It was no use protesting that he was supposed to be resting or that he was officially on leave.

'You can drive, can't you?'

'Yes, sir.'

'We have a convoy stuck in thick mud halfway up to the front. Captain Martin wants a volunteer to take him up there and find out what is going on. Apparently a truck has broken down and it is holding everything up because no one can get by it.'

'I might be able to help there. I am a mechanic.'

'Yeah, I've heard that one before. If you're looking for a transfer, hard luck, Barlow. This is just a favour for an officer – right?'

'Yes, sir!' Jack saluted. 'Where do I pick up the car and the officer, sir?'

'Outside the officers' barracks,' Morris said. 'Don't look so pleased with yourself, Barlow. There have been reports of Gerry planes buzzing the men stuck up there. It isn't going to be a picnic.'

'I didn't think it was, sir.' Jack saluted and walked off.

'Don't think I've finished with you, Barlow. I've got a score to settle and this isn't the end of the little jobs I've got lined up for you.'

Jack resisted the temptation to look back. He balled his fists at his sides, itching to punch the bugger's lights out. One of these days he was going to show that devil just how thin the ice was where he stood.

* * *

Rose came off duty that night feeling tired to the bone. She left the hospital and walked through the gloomy streets. It would soon be winter and that was never her favourite time of the year, and her hands felt sore after so much scrubbing. There were times when she almost wished herself back at the house. Everyone was feeling down because of the news from the front. The British were struggling to hold the line, though recently things had seemed a little brighter for the allies. There were stories that the Germans might have been held, that their relentless progress towards Paris had been halted. Rose prayed it was true. She had been invited out that evening, but she didn't feel much like going anywhere.

She would go home and write another letter to her brother. She had some news about Miss Sarah that he might find interesting. Lady Trenwith would be in a stew when she found out that Sarah hadn't gone to her cousin as arranged. Rose wondered if Mr Luke knew that his sister had instead run off and what he would think about it when he did...

* * *

Luke took off his goggles and helmet as he walked into the mess room early that evening. He had been flying with his squadron up near some woods that were pretty close to German lines. In fact, if you wandered into the middle of them you would probably cross the line without knowing it. He and the men flying with him had gone up to help protect the convoy that had bogged down on its way to the front. The Germans had been having fun shooting at the poor devils until the RFOC boys had turned up and given them a run for their money. Luke was pretty pleased with himself, because he knew he had shot two of the enemy down. He had seen both pilots parachute out and felt glad that they hadn't crashed in flames.

'There you are, Trenwith,' Squadron Leader Henshaw said as a round of spontaneous applause broke out in the room. 'I understand you bagged two Gerry kites today. Well done!'

'Thank you, Henshaw,' Luke said. 'But we worked as a team. I just got lucky.'

'We all did a good job today,' Mike Henshaw agreed. 'We lost Smallwood – did you know that?'

'No...' Luke felt the glow of triumph disappear. 'I am sorry – did he get out?'

'No.' Henshaw looked bleak for a moment. 'His kite went up in flames. He never had a chance.'

'Damned bad luck,' someone said behind Luke. 'But we got five of them so we came out on top.'

Luke nodded, but he couldn't join in the mood of celebration. Crashing in flames was a terrible way to die. He thought that if he were ever hit he would try to land and get out if he could – but of course it didn't often happen that way.

'I was told that you were to report for a special mission in the morning,' Mike Henshaw said. 'We're going for a drink in the village this evening – want to come?'

'A drink in the village?' Luke hesitated and then nodded. He knew that his special mission was likely to be dangerous. Tomorrow night they might be talking about him not making it. 'Yes, why not? We need a bit of light relief now and then.'

'There's a rather pretty girl I met,' Henshaw said. 'In fact, there are one or two... and they are friendly if you know what I mean.' He winked at Luke suggestively.

Luke nodded. He didn't often indulge in sex lightly, but he wasn't a virgin by any means. Perhaps this evening he might take what was offered – if he liked the look of the girl...

* * *

Mrs Barlow looked at her husband as he told her the news. She was shocked; stunned might be a better word.

'Are you telling me that she has disowned Miss Sarah?' she asked. She frowned as her husband confirmed it. 'I'm not condoning what Miss Sarah has done, mind. If it is true what they are saying, she has been a very foolish girl – but her mother should have stood by her. Besides, it wouldn't have happened if she'd been allowed to marry the man she loves.'

'They were overheard arguing,' Barlow told his wife. 'It seems that Lady Trenwith was furious and banished her to stay with some old harpy in the north of the country. She was taken to the station and put on a train, but she never turned up the other end. She has run away and Lady Trenwith has forbidden anyone to mention her name in her presence.'

'Well, that is unkind,' Mrs Barlow said. 'I feel upset, Barlow, and that's the truth. Miss Sarah has always been a favourite with me. She used to come and sit in my kitchen and have a glass of my lemon barley and a cake. If her father hadn't refused to let her marry Mr Troy it need not have turned out this way.'

'I'm not sure if it's right,' Barlow said. 'But Jack wrote something about Mr Troy having been injured – badly as well.'

'It's all of a piece,' his wife replied and set her mouth. 'Poor Miss Sarah! If he doesn't come home and marry her she will be ruined – if she isn't already.'

'Her ladyship said she would like to see you. I think she wants to ask if you'll go in and give Cook a hand in the kitchen.'

'Does she now?' Mrs Barlow looked cross. 'Well, I'm not sure about that, Barlow. There was a time I would have done anything for the family, but I don't know if I care to now...'

'Ah, well, Jack may be right,' Barlow said. 'He told me he wasn't coming back here after the war. He's got big plans, our Jack.'

'All I care about is that he comes back safely,' Mrs Barlow said. 'I'll speak to her ladyship, Barlow – but I am not promising anything. Did you get me them cigarettes I asked for? I'm making up a parcel for our Jack and he always appreciates his smokes...'

* * *

Jack had no doubt that Sergeant Morris had picked him for the driving job that day because he thought it was dangerous and he might get killed. Morris could have no idea that he was doing him a big favour. Jack chuckled to himself as he gave his boots a final polish.

He wanted to look smart as he presented himself for his new job.

Captain Martin had been impressed with the way he had sorted out the mechanical fault in the ammunition lorry. Within half an hour, Jack had got the line moving again, much to the relief of the men who had feared it might be blown to smithereens and them with it.

'That was a little bit of wizardry, Barlow. Well done,' Captain Martin said once the line was moving off once more. 'Why aren't you with the division looking after the mechanics? A man with your skills is invaluable.'

'I applied, sir,' Jack replied. 'I think perhaps my request didn't go through.'

'Someone shelved it I suppose,' Captain Martin said, looking thoughtful. He couldn't have been much older than twenty or so. Struggling with the command he'd been given, he was trying to make the best of it. A lot of the young officers didn't make it beyond the first few weeks. The word was that they were considered expendable, but Captain Martin had been out here from the start so he had to have something going for him. Some said he had the devil's own luck. 'I can't arrange a transfer without a lot of paperwork – but I can ask for you to be my driver. It isn't an easy option, Barlow. You won't be in the trenches, but I'm what I call a fixer for want of a better word. Any trouble along the line and they send me to sort out the problem. We may be called to go anywhere – and I do mean any- where. I've been through the German lines a couple of times. More by accident than design I will admit...' He gave Jack his boyish grin. 'Want to throw in your luck with me?'

'Yes, sir!' Jack couldn't keep the eagerness out of his voice or the grin from his face. It sounded just up his street and a hell of a lot better than sitting in a muddy trench with wet feet. 'You can count on it, sir!'

'Good man. I can do with someone who can show some initiative and you certainly did that today. I'll square it with your CO – present yourself tomorrow morning, early.'

'You jammy bugger,' Joe said, coming into the tent they had been sharing as Jack was lacing his boots. 'Trust you to come up smelling of roses! The last driver, Mad Martin, took a fancy to getting his face blown off! But you'll breeze through it I reckon.'

'I didn't ask for the transfer,' Jack said. 'I hope you won't bear a grudge? We can still be friends?' He offered his hand tentatively. They had formed a strong friendship and he would be sorry to leave him behind.

'Yeah, of course,' Joe said and pulled a wry face. 'I shall miss you, mate. We've been together from the start. It won't be the same without you, but you would be mad to turn the chance down. I'd swap places with you in a minute. It's better than wallowing in the mud.'

'I know.' Jack clasped his hand. 'I'll miss you, Joe. We'll get together next time they send you back for a rest – yes?'

'Yeah, why not?'

'Good luck, Joe.'

'Good luck to you, mate. I've heard about that Captain Martin. They say he takes risks; should have bought it months ago, but he has the luck of the devil. Keep your head down! If there's a bullet coming it will get you, not Mad Martin, so watch out!'

'I'll try,' Jack said and laughed. 'You know my motto – run away to fight another day.'

'Likely tale,' Joe scoffed. 'Get off then. You don't want to keep Captain Martin waiting.'

'No, I don't,' Jack said.

He was whistling to himself, smiling as he set off across the camp towards the officers' quarters. Joe was right; he had landed on his feet. Instead of sending him to certain death, Sergeant Morris had done him a favour. He wouldn't be pleased when he found out, and Jack had better watch himself because he wouldn't put it past the sergeant to make trouble if he could.

Jack would need to watch his temper. He would be bumping into Sergeant Morris from time to time, and the last thing he wanted was to land himself in trouble by knocking the rotter off his feet.

* * *

'I had another postcard from Jack this morning,' Mrs Barlow said as Rose walked into the kitchen one morning in December. 'He says he has a wonderful new job, but they blue pencilled the rest of it so I couldn't read what else he had to say.'

'That's the censors,' Rose said and rested her basket on the kitchen table. 'I brought some Christmas presents, because I'm not sure I shall be able to come down then. I expect to be working.'

'That is a shame for you, love,' her mother said. 'I was hoping you might get here for Christmas dinner, and I haven't got anything for you yet.'

'It doesn't matter,' Rose said and kissed her mother on the cheek. 'I'll come again when I can. There are a couple of things for Jack in the basket. You will be sending him a parcel for Christmas? Or am I too late?'

'I shall send that tomorrow. I thought you might bring something for him when you came so I waited. He did send a postcard last time he got a parcel. He seems to appreciate the things I put in for him – and the bandages and ointment you sent last time went down well.'

'I've brought some more of that and some chocolate and lemon sherbets,' Rose told her with a smile. 'Jack sent me a letter when he got his new job. I think he is driving an officer, though some of my letter had been blue pencilled as well. I know he wanted some more socks and a scarf. He lost the one he had and he says it is cold at nights.'

'Not as cold as it has been here,' her mother said and shivered, though it was actually very warm in the kitchen. However, the outside scene was frosty and icicles had formed above the window where the guttering dripped. 'So what news have you got to tell me? You said that you'd seen Miss Sarah in your last letter...'

'You knew she had run away from home?' Mrs Barlow nodded. 'She came to find me in London and she got herself a job. I never thought she would stick it but she did. She was a real trouper, Ma!'

'Well, fancy that...' Mrs Barlow frowned. 'Should you tell Lady Trenwith? She was very angry when Miss Sarah ran off and she told the maids they were never to mention her name again.'

'No, I wouldn't tell her if she were the last person on earth,' Rose said, looking angry. 'Miss Sarah isn't with us now anyway. She heard that Troy Pelham had been badly wounded and she went down to see him at the hospital. She wrote to tell me they are getting married as soon as Mr Troy is well enough – and she invited me to go down and stay with her at his home as her guest. She says I can go whenever I like.'

'She never did!' Mrs Barlow was astonished. She stared at her daughter doubtfully. 'You won't go, Rose? You wouldn't feel right staying in a house like that as a guest.'

'I can't go for the moment,' Rose told her. 'I wanted to see you before Christmas – but if she asks me to the wedding I shall try to get there.'

'I'm not sure you should,' Mrs Barlow said, and sighed as she saw Rose's stubborn expression. 'Mixing with your betters never works, love, believe me. I've seen it before.'

'Things are changing fast, Ma,' Rose told her. 'This war is making people see things in a different way. We're not living in Victorian times any more. Lady

Trenwith and her sort have had their day. She'll find it hard to get servants after the war.'

'She already does,' Mrs Barlow agreed and picked up the kettle to make their tea. 'She asked me if I would go back to the house for a few hours a week. I told her I would think about it, but I don't really feel like going into service again – and your father is against it. He says that he may leave Trenwith after the war and find us a little guesthouse by the sea. We shall still have a few good years left to us. Your father says my cooking would bring the guests in droves.'

'Your cooking is the best – but would he go?'

'He says he's had enough of service – wants to make a change.'

'No!' Rose stared at her in surprise. 'Did he really say that? I never would have thought it.'

'He's been putting money by for years, and he had a few bob left to him by his Uncle George. I'm not sure what to think of the idea, but it might do if he really wants to make the move.' Mrs Barlow made a face. 'He might change his mind yet, of course.'

Rose was thoughtful. 'Why do you have to wait until after the war? Why not make the move now?'

'You know your father. He makes his mind up in his own good time. I think it was partly the pair of you going that made him think of it, though he liked the sea when we went on our honeymoon. He will decide in time, but you can't rush him.'

'I know.' Rose smiled. Her father never did anything in a hurry, but when he made up his mind there would be no changing him.

* * *

Louise's back was aching as she finished scraping out the cowshed and then cleaned her spade. She was accustomed to hard work these days, because the weeks since the Germans had taken Jacques had been hard. Madame Bonnier's son Pierre had come to help her a few times, and she'd managed to hire a couple of elderly men to help with the root crop. The field had been left late and some of the crop had been lost, but she had enough feed for the cows and there was hay to feed the horse for a while. One of the neighbouring farmers had offered to buy two of the horses a month earlier and she had let them go, because she only needed one to pull the small cart, which was all she could manage these days.

Louise decided to take a rest from her chores. She had done most of the important ones, and the others could wait until she'd had something to eat and drink. One benefit of living alone was that she could please herself when she took a break and when she ate. She knew that she had lost weight recently, because the work was hard. However, she made herself eat properly, because if she didn't she would be ill.

As she approached the house she saw the post boy. He waited for her to come up to him rather than pushing the letter through the box.

'It's from Boulogne,' he told her cheerfully. 'From that lover of yours I expect.'

Louise made no comment. She knew that people wondered about the letters that came regularly these days. They probably did think she had a lover. The letter would be from her bank or her lawyer. He had found it difficult to let the house while the threat of being overrun seemed imminent, but thankfully the Allies had stopped the German army's advance.

Louise read the news avidly these days. She knew that the troops of both sides were bogged down in the trenches. Since the German advance had been successfully halted no one seemed to move much either way. It was almost a stalemate, though the boom of the guns was constant in the distance. The opposing armies continued to bombard each other all the time, but no one seemed to get anywhere. She could only guess at the casualties, but from what she'd seen in the few papers that got through she guessed there must be a lot of men dying.

Louise had seen German patrols moving through the village several times recently, but they never seemed to stop. She hoped they never would.

She took her letter into the kitchen and read it. The house was successfully let to a good tenant and the first few weeks of rent had been paid into an account for her in Boulogne. She could draw from it at other accounts if she needed to by using her pass book, and if she went to Paris she could transfer her account.

Louise tucked the letter into her pocket and then pulled on an apron over her dress. She had been thinking a lot about going to Paris recently. Her life on the farm was so hard and now that she had a little money coming in she could surely find some sort of work to support herself. Her dream was still to have her own café one day, though she didn't think she could afford that just yet.

Perhaps if she sold the farm... But she couldn't do that, because she didn't know if Jacques was alive or dead. If he came back and found she had sold some of the stock he would be furious. If she went to Paris he might not be able to find her.

She sighed as she made herself a bowl of steaming

hot coffee and spooned sugar and cream into it. She wished she knew for sure if her husband was still alive or not. It would be so much easier if she could sell the farm and move away...

* * *

Luke opened the letter and frowned as he saw it was from his mother. His father's letters were always informative, telling him about the estate and the mood of the country, but Lady Trenwith seemed to do nothing other than complain these days.

Your father has given Sarah permission to marry, Lady Trenwith had written. *I think it is absolutely disgusting that she should behave so badly and be rewarded. She has disgraced us, Luke, and I have told Trenwith that I shall not receive her here. He told me that she asked for an address so that she can write to you. I dare say she will, though whether you will think it right to reply to her is a matter for your conscience.*

Luke scanned the remainder of the letter. His mother had written of his elder sister's bad temper and of the shortage of decent servants. Only at the very end did she say that she had sent a parcel for him for Christmas. He folded the letter and put it in his breast pocket.

Luke did not often write home. However, he would write to Sarah now that he knew where she was staying. He felt sorry that his father's refusal to allow her to marry the man she loved had led to her being in disgrace, but he would not condemn her. Since he'd been out here he had come to realise that she was the only one of his family he really cared for. Marianne had never cared for anyone but herself, but Sarah had always been warm and loving.

Somehow Luke's luck had held these past weeks. He had been sent on a couple of missions behind the enemy lines, and his photographs and sketches had proved useful. At least his CO had told him so. However, for the past couple of weeks he had been flying routine missions with his squadron. Most of them had been uneventful; there had been a couple of skirmishes in the skies over the troop lines. He and others had helped to protect the convoys making their way up the lines from attack by enemy planes.

If things continued this way he might actually get to enjoy whatever his mother had sent him for Christmas, Luke thought – though she didn't seem to have much idea of what was useful. A tin of Gentleman's relish and salted biscuits wasn't really what was needed out here. At least he wasn't forced to lie in muddy trenches in the freezing cold, Luke thought. His mother never seemed to think he might need some warm socks or a scarf.

'Ah, there you are old chap,' Mike Henshaw said cheerfully as he came into the room the officers shared when waiting for the order to scramble. 'Are you coming to the party this evening?'

'What party?' Luke looked up. He wasn't too keen on the kind of parties some of the others seemed to enjoy. Getting wildly drunk and pawing the local girls didn't feel like having fun to Luke. He would prefer to be somewhere quiet, working at his paintings or reading a book.

'It's just some drinks and fun down at the local in the village. The landlord is putting on a bit of a do for us.'

'I don't think I'll bother. I've got some letters to write.'

'Lillian was asking for you,' Mike said. 'She likes you, Trenwith. I know she isn't the kind of girl you would want to take home to your mother – but she is warm-hearted and attractive. You should take advantage while you can.'

Luke shook his head. He had been back to the girl's

home once, but he hadn't stayed the night after he'd seen the small child in the cot upstairs. Lillian told him she relied on the money she earned from sleeping with the British flying officers.

'You look kind,' she'd said as she'd began to undress. 'You will give me money for the baby – yes?'

'Yes, of course,' Luke said. He'd taken some French bank notes from his wallet and given them to her. 'Here, take this for the child – but don't bother to get undressed. I've changed my mind.'

'You don't like me?' Lillian looked disappointed. 'I can make you happy...'

'I am sure you could,' Luke said. 'But I don't take advantage of girls like you. You shouldn't have to do this, Lillian. It isn't right.'

She had tried to stop him leaving, but Luke had walked out into the night, stopping to light a cigarette only when he was clear of her home. He wasn't sure why he had refused her. She was clean and she smelled nice, and she was a pretty girl. But something about her had reminded him of Rose and after that he just couldn't do it.

He would have felt as if he were abusing her, treating her as something less than she was; a decent, pretty girl who had a child to support. Luke hated to think of Rose being in a similar situation.

Luke hated the idea of her going with any man, though he knew it was a stupid attitude. The idea of Rose being abused by someone who didn't care for her made him frown. It could never happen! She would find a decent man to marry one day, and it would not be him.

'Sorry,' he said as the squadron leader looked at him expectantly. 'I have some letters to write...' If he got a chance he would go into town and buy a present for Sarah and send it to her. He would have liked to buy Rose a present but that would be foolish. He supposed that he would have to try and find a gift for his mother too...

* * *

'Give us a kiss,' the soldier said and lunged at Rose. She could smell the beer on his breath and recoiled. He had been drinking far too much and she thought he might be drunk. 'I'm on me way back out there to-morrow – give me something to remember.'

'No. I'm sorry but I do not want to kiss you.'

Rose pushed him aside and walked away. She had come to this party because some of the other girls had asked her. Most of them were getting in the mood for Christmas, and she had noticed one or two of them going outside with the soldiers they had been dancing with all evening. She might have done the same if she had found someone she really wanted, but so far she hadn't been lucky. Perhaps she was too fussy. One of the girls she worked with had told her that she would never get herself a lad if she persisted in being stuck up.

Rose didn't think she was stuck up, but she was choosy about the men she went out with occasionally. She wasn't in a hurry to find herself a boyfriend, because she wanted to become a nurse and most men didn't like their girls to work once they were married. She wouldn't have been allowed to work as a nurse if she married anyway.

In the cloakroom Rose splashed her face with cold water. She wasn't wearing make up; she hardly ever wore much and she'd come here straight after work, so she hadn't bothered. She thought she might as well go home. She'd had enough of this party and she had to be up early in the morning.

As she went outside, she hesitated for a moment, pulling her coat collar up around her face to keep out the cold. She was just deciding whether or not she wanted to walk or catch a bus when someone put an arm round her. She turned and saw the soldier who had tried to kiss her earlier.

'Leave me alone please.'

'Come on, darlin',' he persisted. 'Just a little kiss. It won't hurt a bit...'

'Please leave me alone,' Rose said and gave a scream as he grabbed her and pulled her close. She struggled, trying to push him away. Suddenly, he was pulled off her and sent flying. She looked at the man who had rescued her with relief. 'Oh, thank you! I told him earlier I wasn't interested, but he didn't seem to listen.'

'He's drunk,' the man replied and smiled at her in a way Rose liked. He offered his hand to her, the way a gentleman would. 'My name is Flight Lieutenant Rod Carne. I'm a Canadian and I came over to join the fly-boys. I wondered if you needed a lift home?'

Rose hesitated. She didn't know this man and she would generally have turned his offer down instantly, but there was something she liked about his manner. In a way he reminded her of Luke Trenwith.

'I only live a few streets away,' she said. 'If you wouldn't mind walking me home?'

'Sure thing, Miss...?'

'It's Rose – Rose Barlow,' she told him with a smile. 'I'm with the VADs. My brother is in the army, but I do know someone in the Royal Flying Officers Corps.'

'Is he your fiancé?'

'No. I don't have a fiancé.' Rose smiled as he offered her his arm. 'I don't have a boyfriend either...'

* * *

Jack opened the parcel his mother had sent him and grinned as he saw the contents. He knew exactly what had come from his mother, and what Rose had sent. The lint and ointment would be useful. He didn't have much use for them himself since he'd been transferred to driving for his officer, but he would give them to Joe next time he saw him.

There were only a few hours left until Christmas now. At base camp they had tried to celebrate as best they could. Jack had joined the choir for the hymn-singing service. There had been a good gathering for that, officers and men from the ranks. He had seen some RFOC officers among the crowd that gathered in the open air. Jack had looked for Luke Trenwith but couldn't see him. He hoped he was all right. Just because he hadn't come to the carol service it didn't mean he'd bought it, though so many of the young flying officers were being shot down that they were having trouble replacing them. But Luke could be stationed miles away for all Jack knew. It was unlikely that they would meet out here.

Jack broke a piece of chocolate and put it in his mouth, letting it melt on his tongue as he went outside. Captain Martin was on a three-day leave, so that left Jack at a loose end. He hadn't been given a pass himself, but as his officer was away he probably wouldn't have much to do.

'Barlow! Get yourself over here double sharp!'

Jack groaned inwardly as he heard the sergeant's voice. He did his best to stay out of Morris's way, but the man was always turning up out of the blue and trying to make things as difficult as possible.

'Yes, sir! What can I do for you, sir?'

'I've got a job for you,' Sergeant Morris said, an evil grin on his face. 'Christmas cheer for the boys at the front line. I told Major Harkness I knew just the man for the job. I'm sure you volunteered for it, Barlow.'

'Yes, sir.' Jack grinned at him, knowing it would infuriate him more. He wanted to needle Jack, get under his skin. It wasn't going to happen. 'I'm your man, what do I take and where?'

Sergeant Morris looked as if he had swallowed a pint of vinegar. If he'd imagined he was going to spoil Jack's Christmas he was wrong. Jack had been pleased to get his own parcel from home and he had nothing else to do – nothing that compared with the grins and thanks he would get for delivering Christmas parcels to the lads in the trenches.

He returned to his own quarters and picked up the lint and ointment for Joe. He was whistling as he strolled off in the direction of the decrepit old van in which the parcels had already been loaded. Maybe the Germans would give it a break since it was almost Christmas, and if they didn't it would be no more dangerous than driving Captain Martin.

Anyway, it was nearly Christmas and if he was lucky he would see his mate Joe.

* * *

Louise looked at the baking she had been busy with all morning. The smell of pies, tarts and cakes was tantalising. She had invited a few neighbours to a small party on Christmas Eve. It was something she hadn't done since she married Jacques, because he had never wanted anyone at the house. She had heard nothing of him. People said he must be dead. Louise wasn't sure. Sometimes she hoped he was dead; it would surely be better than being a prisoner of war, especially since he was always in pain. Yet such thoughts made her feel guilty. She had confessed them in church and the priest told her that she should say fifty Hail Marys.

Perhaps he'd heard a similar story from other lonely wives.

Louise had done her penance, but she still felt guilty because she was much happier with Jacques gone. She didn't really wish him dead, but it would be much better for her if he never returned. If she could be sure he was dead she would sell the farm. She had been asked to sell more of her stock, namely her milking cows, but so far she had refused. It was one of the chores she liked best, putting her head against their warm bodies and feeling the milk squirt into her pails as she gently stroked their teats. A couple of them had kicked Jacques in the past, but they never kicked her, perhaps because she treated them with respect.

Leaving the kitchen, Louise went upstairs. She had risen early so as to finish her chores and the baking. She wanted to wash her hair and wear a pretty dress for the party that evening.

She sighed as she looked at herself in the dressing mirror. It was one of the things she had brought from her mother's home and much better than anything Jacques had provided. It was a long time since she had bothered to wear something pretty...

The last time was at that dance. Her mouth curved in a smile as she thought about the man she had danced with... and kissed. The memory was fading now, lost in the continual round of work from dusk until dawn. He had urged her to go to England to his home. She allowed herself to wonder what kind of a reception his mother would have given her if she had gone. Of course she couldn't go, because she was married to Jacques.

It was hard to remember that she was still married sometimes. Louise had noticed one or two of the men in the village looking at her, speculation in their eyes. She knew what they were thinking. She was alone and might need a friend. It was probably only a matter of time before one of them came knocking at her door. They would be disappointed.

Louise kept a barrier in place. She didn't need that kind of a friend – and especially the men who had been Jacques's friends. She was alone but most of the time she was too busy to worry. Sometimes at night when she had lit the lamps and locked all the doors she felt isolated, but she was usually too busy to worry about whether or not she was lonely.

If she thought she could get to Paris easily she might go after Christmas. But she would need to sell all the livestock. She couldn't expect Pierre Bonnier to do all the work while she was away. She was torn between wanting to sell and leave for good and staying to take care of things. After all, the house and land must be worth a good bit if she could sell it.

Louise pushed the thoughts from her mind. There was no point in going over and over the same things. She was going to celebrate Christmas Eve with her neighbours and then she would take a couple of weeks to decide...

5

Jack was pleased that he had accepted Sergeant Morris's orders to bring the Christmas parcels up to the front. It had felt good handing them out to the men, and he'd been able to find Joe and give him the ointment and rolls of lint for his feet.

'Thanks, mate,' Joe said. 'I didn't expect to see you here?'

'Captain Martin had a three-day pass. I was at a loose end so I volunteered,' Jack said, bending the truth a bit. 'How are things up here?'

'Quiet at the moment,' Joe said. 'The Gerrys seem to be in the Christmas mood. They've been singing carols over there...' Joe nodded towards the German trenches. 'Don't know if they're tryin' to lull us into a false sense of peace or what.'

'Probably feeling fed up like us,' Jack said. 'We're all blokes. We didn't make this damned war – it's governments that do that...'

'Yeah, too right,' Joe said and offered him a Woodbine. 'I got these in my parcel. Have one if you like.'

'Thanks, I will,' Jack said and took the cigarette. 'I'll smoke it later if you don't mind.' He didn't care for the brand and would pass it on to someone else later, but he wouldn't offend Joe by refusing. 'What's that...?' He cocked his head to one side, listening. Joe listened too, staring at him in surprise.

They could hear voices, laughter and shouting coming from the open stretch between the British and German lines. Jack scrambled up the muddy bank, Joe right behind him.

'Well, bugger me!' Joe exclaimed as they looked over the top of the trench. 'I don't believe it.'

Jack stared and then grinned at him. 'Looks like there's a truce for Christmas. Come on, let's join them!'

Soldiers from both armies were standing out in the open. Muffled with hand-knitted scarves and hats, thick gloves to protect their hands from the cold, they gathered in small groups. No one was shooting at anyone. They were exchanging gifts, cigarettes for British jam, chocolate for fruit cake, anything someone had they wanted to exchange. Jack saw a couple of them shaking hands. Officers were talking in French, interpreting what the Germans were saying for others. And then someone produced a football and a huge cheer went up as several men rushed to join in the impromptu football game.

'Never thought I'd see anything like this,' Joe said as he headed the ball back to a German soldier. 'Bloody good show, that's what I say…'

Jack agreed. He wandered over to one of the German soldiers and took the cigarette from his pocket, offering it to him. The German took a wrapped sweet from his pocket and Jack accepted it. They grinned at one another and then the football came their way and they both went for it, laughing as they tackled one another, all the world as if it were Sunday afternoon on a village green.

Jack chuckled to himself as he imagined what Sergeant Morris would think if he could see him now. He would probably have him court marshalled and shot.

* * *

'Did you manage to have a good Christmas?' Captain Martin asked as Jack reported for duty two days later. 'I should have arranged leave for you, Barlow. I did try but somehow it didn't come through before I left. You should have been told you were on a pass – did anyone give you the message?'

'No, sir,' Jack said. 'It didn't matter. I exchanged a few gifts and had a bit of a kick about with a football. I was quite happy.'

'Good man,' Captain Martin told him with a nod of approval. 'That is what I like about you, Barlow. You don't hold grudges and you're always ready for anything. I am giving you the rest of the day off to write letters home, do anything you really need to do – write your will if you haven't done it already.'

'Yes, sir – any reason for that?'

'Tomorrow we're going on a trip. I can't tell you much more at this moment, Barlow. It's secret and it's important.'

Jack nodded. Clearly it was also dangerous. He hadn't made a will, but he thought perhaps he should, because he had a few bob put by. If anything happened to him he would want Rose to have that money. It hadn't occurred to him before, but now that Captain Martin had reminded him he would do it. He would write it out, get someone to sign it and enclose it with a letter to his sister.

As he was walking back to his quarters he saw Sergeant Morris coming towards him. The scowl on the sergeant's face told him he was in trouble.

'What's this I hear about you playing football in No Man's Land?'

'It was Christmas Day,' Jack said. 'The Germans started it. I think – one of them stood up and offered to exchange goods. Then someone produced a football and we had a bit of fun.'

'Treason! It's bloody treason if you ask me. You will all be lucky if you don't get shot – fraternising with the enemy!'

'It wasn't like that,' Jack said. 'There were officers out there... Everyone just wanted a breather on Christ's birthday. I can't see much wrong with that myself.'

'You might not, but heads will roll for this; you hear me, Barlow! If I have anything to do with it the lot of you will face the firing squad – and I'll dance on your grave!'

'I am sure you will, sir.' Jack grinned at him insolently. 'Excuse me, I'm on a special mission for Captain Martin. Oh, and it's a bit late – but Happy Christmas, sir.'

Jack whistled as he walked away. He was sure that the sergeant wasn't the only one who would find the behaviour of both British and German soldiers odd.

There might be some discipline on both sides of the lines, but he didn't think it was a treasonable offence. No one had deserted and no doubt they would all go back to killing each other now that Christmas was over.

* * *

Rose stopped to speak to the soldier in the end bed by the wall. He had been in a bad way when they brought him in a couple of weeks earlier. He had lost both legs and one hand and Sister had told them that he probably wouldn't make it. However, Terry Mannering was a fighter and somehow he had defied the odds. Rose had formed a habit of stopping to have a few words with him every night before she went off duty.

'I came to say goodnight,' she said as she looked down at him. A feeling of distress went through her as she saw the fine sweat on his brow. He wasn't looking as well tonight. She thought he might have taken a fever. 'I'm sorry. I'll get the doctor...'

'Please stay with me.' Terry's eyes opened. He looked at her and for a moment she saw his old spirit in his eyes. 'I shan't be here when you come tomorrow...'

'Of course you will...' Rose hesitated as she saw his expression. 'What is it?'

'They told me my wound has gangrene. It has gone too far for them to do anything. Besides, I can't stand much more. I'm ready to go now.'

'You mustn't talk like that,' Rose said and moved forward to take his hand. It felt warm and clammy. 'I am sure you are getting better.'

'It looked that way, but it's best if I go. I'll only be a burden to my family. If I can't work they will be better off without me.'

'No!' Rose hesitated and then sat on his bed. Sister didn't encourage this sort of thing, but she sensed his need. 'They love you. You've had visitors every day. Your mother was here and your sister.'

'Not my wife. She has the kids to look after. She doesn't have time to nurse me.'

'She will when you are well enough to go home. Besides, they will do something for you. You can have new legs... they will help you.'

'You've got more faith than I have,' he said and held on to her hand. 'I suppose you need it working here.' His eyes met and held hers. 'Do you have a boyfriend – someone special?'

'I'm not sure,' Rose replied honestly. 'I've just met

someone I like. He wants to see me again, but it isn't a real relationship yet.'

'Supposing it was and he got hurt – the way I am. Would you want to give up everything and devote yourself to him?'

Rose hesitated, then, 'Yes, if I loved him. I would never desert someone I love. My friend Sarah married her boyfriend after his face was burned. Some of us love whatever happens. You mustn't give up hope, Terry. I know it means another operation...'

'No, they said it is too late. It's gone inward. Even if they operate there isn't much chance I'll live.'

Tears stung Rose's eyes. He had been so brave, never complaining whatever the nurses did for him, and now he was dying. She knew there was no point in lying to him or herself. Sometimes if the poison had spread too far before the patient got to them there really was nothing they could do except nurse them until the end.

'I'm sorry,' she said. 'Is there anything I can get you – a drink of whisky or something to help you sleep?'

'I don't want anything, but I'd like you to sit with me until I go to sleep. They gave me something for the pain. It shouldn't be long.'

'Yes, of course I'll sit with you,' Rose said. She

leaned forward and then kissed his cheek on impulse. 'You are a brave man, Terry Mannering.'

'And you're a great girl, Rose Barlow...'

Rose sat back, holding his hand, watching as he drifted into a drug-induced state. The tears were trickling gently down her face.

It was nearly two hours before she left him. As she reached the end of the ward where Sister Harris sat at her desk, the senior nurse got up and came to her.

'Is he sleeping now?'

'Yes, Sister. He said the doctors told him there is no hope.'

'He was left too long before his right leg was amputated,' Sister Harris replied. 'The poison has taken a hold. It is only a matter of treating him for the pain now, Barlow.'

Rose rubbed the back of her hand over her eyes. 'I thought he was getting better.'

'It looked that way for a start, but the damage was inside. I'm sorry. I know you've been saying goodnight to him before you leave. I doubt if he will last many days.'

Rose blinked. 'This war has a lot to answer for, Sister.'

'Yes, it does,' Sister Harris said. 'I've been hearing

good things of you, Barlow. I think you should seriously consider putting in for nursing training next year.'

'Yes, I shall.'

'And they tell me you have a good singing voice?'

'I joined the others singing carols at the party but I wouldn't say I had a good voice.'

'Well, that isn't the opinion I've heard.' Sister Harris frowned. 'You look tired to death. Go home and get some rest or we shall have you as a patient.'

Rose shook her head. It was good to hear praise on Sister Harris's lips, because she wasn't known for it. She would have to think hard about putting her name down for training.

Rose was thoughtful as she walked home. Rod Carne had asked to see her again when he got his next leave. He hadn't told her much, but she thought he was probably about to go on a tour of duty in France. She liked him but she didn't know him. He might forget all about her...

* * *

Louise hung her pretty dress in the big old-fashioned armoire with regret. She had enjoyed taking a break over the Christmas period, something she couldn't have done if her neighbour's son hadn't helped her out. She was walking down the stairs when she heard a loud knocking at the back door. Her heart caught with fright. Was it the Germans? Had they come at last? What would they want of her?

She ran down the stairs and went to the door, taking a deep breath as she opened it. She saw Madame Bonnier and knew at once that something was terribly wrong.

'Come in,' she said and took her arm. She could feel the other woman shaking. 'I am sorry the door was locked but I was upstairs. What is the matter?'

'The Germans have taken Pierre,' Madame Bonnier said. 'A convoy came to the village this morning. They rounded up anyone who looked as if they could work. Pierre was on his way to school. They took him and three other lads who look old for their age...'

'Oh no!' Louise looked at her in consternation. 'That is terrible! What can we do? The children are too young to be forced to work for the enemy.'

'I wish I thought that was all it was about,' Madame Bonnier said and gave a little sob of despair. 'There was an ambush on a convoy going from Chateau Lorraine up to the line. Several Germans were killed. They say someone used explosives to blow a truck up and then a group of Frenchmen fired on the others before they could get past.'

'But what has that to do with the children?'

'The Germans have been demanding to know who ambushed them,' Madame Bonnier told her tearfully. 'This morning a dozen of them were knocking on doors and smashing windows; they said they were taking hostages. If no one confesses they will kill them all...'

'They can't do that,' Louise said. She was horrified. 'Pierre – the other children. They can't kill innocent people because some other people have been trying to fight them...'

'They can and they will,' Madame Bonnier told her. 'You are isolated here at the farm, Louise. If you came to the village more you would hear the stories.'

'I have heard stories of the Germans bayoneting babies but I thought it was just a scare story...'

'It probably is propaganda from the British or the Allies,' Madame Bonnier agreed. 'But the Germans who came to the village meant business. They took a couple of women as well. They threatened to kill one person a day if no one owns up to what is happening.'

'Does anyone know who is behind these attacks?'

Madame Bonnier shook her head. 'They say there

are men and women hiding in secret – living in the woods and caves all over the country. They smuggle out British airmen who crash their planes, taking them through the lines to safety...'

'Is it possible to get through to Paris?' Louise looked thoughtful. 'But you don't know – this is all speculation...'

'Pierre knew,' Madame Bonnier said, and the fear was in her eyes. 'I know a little but I think he was meeting them. They call themselves Freedom Fighters: old men and children! I don't know what else Pierre did, but if they hurt him... he might betray the others. He won't be able to stand the pain. He is only a child! Those fools should never have let him help them...'

'Oh, Madeline...' Louise looked at her with sympathy. 'The Germans wouldn't... they wouldn't torture a boy? Surely they couldn't be cruel enough to do such a thing!'

'Pierre looks like a man. He thought like a man. All he wanted to do was kill the Bosch pigs who had invaded his country.'

'I am so sorry,' Louise said. 'If there is anything I can do...'

'No one can do anything. Pierre has gone the way Jacques did. I wanted to tell you not to expect Pierre to help you. If I were you I would sell as much as you can and leave. Go away... Go to Paris if you can or to friends. I would if I could, but I have my father and my younger boys...'

'I'm not sure,' Louise replied. 'I have thought of going – but supposing Jacques comes back and finds the stock gone and the land neglected?'

'You can't keep running this place alone,' Madame Bonnier said. 'I am not sure how long I can manage now that Pierre has gone...' She choked back a sob. 'Damn them to Hell! I swear that if I get a chance I'll kill every German who comes near me...'

Louise nodded silently. At the moment she was feeling very much the same way.

* * *

It was a morning much like any other, Jack thought as he reported for duty. Captain Martin looked pleased with himself, an air of expectancy about him as he approached Jack, who was standing by the car they had been allocated.

'Is this thing going to get us there and back today, Barlow?'

'Depends where we're going, sir, but it should do. I've got my tool kit if anything should go wrong.'

'We're going on quite a trip,' Captain Martin said. 'Some of our men are having a terrible time of it further down the line. There seems to be extra-heavy fire coming from the German lines in this particular area and we need to find out why. That means we're going to cross over at a certain point and try to come round on their position from the back. See if we can pinpoint where they are entrenched and what our people can do about it.'

'Sounds interesting,' Jack said and grinned. 'Just where do we cross over? You'd better brief me so that I don't make any mistakes.'

Captain Martin took out his map and spread it on the bonnet. 'There is a small village here, hardly shows up on most maps but one of our flyboys took a spin over that way and found the weak spot. He says the Germans don't seem aware of how easy it is to get through at this point. He took pictures and made some sketches on the ground. The German headquarters is here somewhere, at a place called Chateau Lorraine, at least that is my information. These woods are thick and pretty big. One side of them is British controlled, more or less – and the other side is this village. The main road is here beyond the village, and there are frequent troop movements along it. We think they must be concentrated just about here.' He tapped his finger on the map. 'If we can get confirmation we might be able to work out a strategy. We could send someone to attack them from the air. We are finding that kind of manoeuvre more and more helpful these days. Once we can break through there we can make significant gains.'

'It is certainly worth a try, sir,' Jack said, studying the map. 'Do you have any particular orders for me?'

'If we come under enemy fire it is every man for himself, especially if either of us has the information headquarters needs. Even if we haven't managed to discover what strength the Germans have at their position, I want you to remember that. No heroics, Barlow – and don't expect them from me. We are there to do a job and that comes first, right? If you don't make it back on time I shan't wait.'

'Yes, sir.' Jack was thoughtful as he climbed into the car and released the brake. Their missions had become increasingly more dangerous, and this one sounded the worst of the lot so far. At this moment he could almost wish himself back in the trenches.

* * *

Louise could hear the rumble of heavy wagons and machinery passing. The Germans had been reinforcing their position for the past few weeks. She wondered how long it would be before one of them got curious about the bumpy track leading to her farm and came to investigate. She wouldn't stand much chance here alone and she was beginning to think she should try to get through to Paris. It seemed at the moment as if the Allies were holding the German advance. If she could manage to get through to the British side she would feel safer. Besides, there was too much work on the farm for one person. She had just about been holding her own, but with Pierre gone it would get harder and she certainly couldn't plant root crops for next year. She didn't think Jacques was coming back, at least not until the war was over and goodness knows when that would be. He might already be dead. Madeline Bonnier was sure he must be by now.

Thinking of her friend made Louise feel guilty. How could she leave before there was news about Pierre and the rest of the children? Louise couldn't let her friend down. Madeline was in much the same boat as Louise now, though she had her younger children and she had more family in the district than Louise. She had been a good friend.

Louise looked at the basket of eggs she had collected that morning. Most were chicken but some were duck eggs. She had far more than she needed living here alone. She would take the hens' eggs to the village shop and exchange for some flour, and she could call at Madeline Bonnier's house on the way there and see if she would like a few of the duck eggs. It would be an excuse to ask if there were any news about Pierre and the others.

Madame Bonnier had advised her to leave, but for the moment she was undecided. Something was holding her back, but she wasn't sure what it was.

* * *

It was early afternoon when they stopped to check the map references again. They knew they must be getting near their destination, because they had heard heavy firing for the past hour or so and they had seen planes overhead a couple of times, but fortunately they had been friendly. One British pilot had dipped his wings and done a loop to them, showing off his dare-devil skills.

'Silly young devils,' Captain Martin said with a wry look. 'It is no wonder that some of the raw recruits don't last a week. They've had a few hours' flying lessons and they can do tricks. They seem to think this is all a great lark.'

'I suppose it seems that way,' Jack agreed and frowned. 'Some of them can't be more than eighteen. They have no idea what war is really like.'

'Bloody mayhem half the time,' Captain Martin agreed. 'Some officers just send their men over the top to no purpose. Half of them get killed or wounded, and those who make it back will carry the memories until they die. That's why our mission is important, Barlow. If we can pinpoint the reason for this increase in activity at least the men sent on that mission will be dying for a good reason. We have to make a break-through somehow. Otherwise, the troops could be bogged down in the trenches forever.'

Jack said nothing. Captain Martin was enthusiastic. He believed in what he was doing and Jack was willing to go along with him, because he knew the man was genuine. Whether the information they were risking their lives for would be put to good use was another question. He hoped it would, because he just wanted to do whatever was needed to get this war over and done with. He had volunteered to fight, but he was damned if he wanted to sit in muddy trenches ducking enemy fire. He had always been relieved when they were sent over the top; it beat sitting with your feet in freezing water by a mile.

'I think this track leads to the village,' Captain

Martin said. 'It is way off the main road, a bit isolated. The woods are there, the village here – and there seems to be nothing much in-between. I think we'll go that way. We shouldn't meet many German patrols along a road like that...'

Jack wasn't sure the track led anywhere, but Martin was the officer. He was here to drive and do as he was ordered.

'Right you are, sir,' he said. 'If we have to abandon the car because the track is too rough we can leave it and do some scouting on foot.'

'Agreed,' Martin said with a nod of his head. 'The German position we're interested in is over here some-where. If we can't take the car there we'll split up and make our way there as best we can.' He grinned at Jack. 'Here's where your initiative comes in, Barlow. We get there and then meet back here. If you are back by midnight and there's no sign of me, leave me to make my own way back.'

'Is that an order, sir?'

'Yes, Barlow, that is an order.'

Jack nodded. He frowned as he concentrated on the way ahead. He felt uncomfortable with the order, and vowed to himself that he was going to get them both home in one piece if he could. If he happened to get back first he would wait for a while despite his orders.

* * *

The farm looked deserted as they passed along the dirt track. Jack heard the sound of cows bellowing. They needed milking if he knew anything. Whoever was in charge round here needed their heads banging together. The place looked a mess.

'There's the main road – just through those trees,' Captain Martin said. 'Leave the car here behind the haystack, Barlow. The enemy position must be just over there. We have to cross the road, and then the trees will shelter us again. You go to the right and work your way back in a circle. I'll go left and do the same.'

'Yes, sir. Good luck, sir.'

'Good luck, Barlow.'

Captain Martin hesitated and then offered his hand. Jack took it firmly and grinned. 'Don't worry, sir. I've got the luck of the devil.'

The main road looked deserted as Jack made a dash across into the trees at the other side. He lingered, watching as Martin did the same thing and then set out to his right. The enemy position could be anywhere along a certain line. They needed to know what kind of strength the Germans had and what the defences were like. The chances that one or both of them would be caught were probably high, but that was the risk they took. If he was ordered to halt he would surrender rather than waste his life, but he didn't intend to get caught if he could help it.

Hearing harsh voices speaking a language he knew instinctively was French and not German, Jack froze in his tracks. He hid behind a tree, waiting for them to pass. His brow creased in a frown as he saw they had guns and caps pulled down over their eyes; some had scarves across their faces. They didn't look like farm labourers. What were they up to?

Jack decided to tag along behind to see what was going on. He had a suspicion that he knew, but it would be interesting to observe the men. If his guess was right, they would lead him exactly where he wanted to go.

* * *

Louise returned later than she had intended. She could hear the cows calling out and felt guilty, because she knew that they needed to be milked. She had stopped longer in the village than she normally did. Everyone was talking about the latest German troop movements. It seemed that the Germans had been building up their forces in the area for weeks. Something had to be going on.

'They may be planning another advance,' one of the old men of the village told her. 'If they break through again Paris may fall this time. The British are stretched to the limit. We should be doing something to help them this side.'

'What do you mean?' Louise asked, feeling a chill down her spine. 'How can any of us fight the Germans?'

'There are ways,' the old man told her. He tapped the side of his nose. 'You'll see, Madame. The Germans think they have broken us but a few of us are still willing to fight on...'

Louise shook her head. 'Isn't it enough that they took Pierre and some of the others? If there is any more resistance they will return and kill women and children.'

'War is like that,' the old man told her. 'Give me a gun and I'll fight them until they kill me.'

Louise thought about his words as she walked home. Some of the villagers were angry enough to do anything, but she could not see that they could make a difference. They could blow up a few trucks, kill some

Germans, but they would only bring trouble to the village.

She fetched hay from the stack to feed the cows and then froze as she saw the car. Someone had tried to cover it with sacks taken from outside her barn, but it was still obvious what it was. She looked but could see no number plates; they had clearly been removed. A tingle ran down her spine. She spun round, looking for any sign of who the vehicle might belong to, but could see no one.

She took a closer look, moving a couple of sacks and then replacing them. Something told her the car wasn't German. Besides, Germans wouldn't try to hide a car; they knew they were in control here. It must belong to a stranger, because she hadn't seen it in the village. She backed away, half inclined to bolt herself into the house and stay there, but then she knew she couldn't hide forever. The cows needed milking and she had to feed all the stock. But as soon as she could, she would go inside and lock the door. Whatever was going on, she did not want to know about it.

* * *

Jack saw the men ahead of him halt as they approached what was clearly the road leading into a

German supply dump. Jack stood back, watching as the trucks and wagons were driven into the depot. If his guess was right this was the ammunition store. It was from here that the Germans were supplying the troops up at the line, and by the size of it they were planning on more than just making the lives of the British Tommies miserable.

With all this stuff building up here the Germans must be planning on making another advance. Jack felt excited, because he could have walked for hours and not found this place. It was well hidden in the woods. Clearly the Germans needed to be stopped. A raid on this depot could set their plans back for months, and by the looks of it, these Frenchmen were set on making as much trouble as possible. Could they be planning on trying to blow up the depot? It was a hopeless task. The place was too heavily guarded and also cleverly positioned. Here in the woods it was protected from attack from the air. What was needed here was a well-armed and briefed attack force. These vigilantes would be totally ineffective. Surely they knew that they would be slaughtered?

The best thing Jack could do was to get back to the car and wait for Captain Martin to return. Headquarters needed to be told about this place. Hearing a rumbling sound, Jack followed his instincts and ducked down. It was then that he saw what the men he'd been following were after. A small convoy was approaching the depot, and there were some heavily laden trucks among the slow-moving vehicles.

The damned fools were going to attack. In broad daylight and armed with shotguns that looked as if they had come out of the ark! Jack watched in horror as he saw the small party of men break cover and charge towards the convoy. What the hell did they imagine they were doing? Some of them were old, some mere boys. They were like gnats against an elephant. It was brave but stupid. Jack wanted to walk away and leave them, but his feet wouldn't move. He was fixed to the spot as he watched the brief battle.

The Germans turned their superior firepower on the raiders, mowing them down one after the other. Jack saw one of the young lads falter and fall face down on the earth. Suddenly, he found himself charging down the small incline towards the lad. He got to him despite the bullets flying over his head from either side and started to drag him away from the chaos. He could see that one of the trucks had been hit. It was on fire and even as he lifted the lad over his shoulder to carry him there was an almighty explosion that blew Jack off his feet into a ditch at the side of the road. Knocked unconscious, he lay still, unaware of the battle that continued for a few minutes longer.

The two Frenchmen that remained alive fled back into the woods. The bodies of the others lay where they fell, most of them already dead before the Germans started shooting them through the head to make sure of it.

Somehow, Jack had rolled under the reeds growing from the ditch. No one saw him as they collected the bodies of their comrades and the dead Frenchmen. Another two trucks were on fire and the Germans were frantically trying to move them out of the way of a second ammunition lorry. In the confusion, no one thought to look in the ditch.

Jack lay still, blood trickling from cuts to his face, hands and his right thigh. He was still unconscious by the time all the commotion had settled and the rest of the convoy had made it into the depot.

It was dark when Jack's left leg began to twitch. A few minutes later, his eyes opened and he stared into the pitch black, too dazed to wonder where he was or what had happened to him. He could feel pain and cold and nothing else.

Some deep instinct for survival made him crawl out of the ditch. He must have lain in an inch or so of water and his clothes were soaked. It took him several tries before he could stand, and it was agony to move. He could only limp slowly up the incline towards the woods. The pain in his thigh was excruciating, but he kept going. He didn't know where he was going but his instinct seemed to drive him in a certain direction.

Jack didn't know it consciously, but he was heading for the farm where he had left the car earlier that day.

* * *

The hour was past midnight when Louise heard the car engine start. She saw the lights flash as it reversed and went back down the narrow track it must have come along to reach the farm. She breathed a sigh of relief when it had gone. She had heard the explosion earlier and knew it had come from one of the German supply dumps. Like everyone else in the village, she had known it was there somewhere in the woods. She thought there might be more than one, but she had never tried to take a look. It would be dangerous and stupid, because the Germans would shoot on sight. She was glad that whoever had parked the car there had taken it away again or she might have been accused of being involved.

She wondered what had happened to cause the explosion. Had there been some kind of an accident –

or was it the French freedom fighters? She hoped they hadn't been foolish enough to do something like that, because it might mean more reprisals in the village.

Louise was nervous when she went to bed that night. She lay restless for hours, because the strange car parked in her yard and the explosion had unsettled her. At last, unable to rest, she got up and fetched a storm lamp from the scullery. It was nearly dawn but still dark for the moment as she went down to the yard. She was heading towards the stack, though she wasn't sure why. She knew the car had gone much earlier, just after midnight, but something had made her come this way.

She felt a cold shiver as she saw the figure limping towards her through the dim light. Could it be Jacques? The figure was of a similar build and height as her husband, and the limp brought a lump to her throat. She could still feel pity for him despite what he had done to her.

'Jacques...' she cried as she began to walk faster. 'Jacques, is that you?'

She halted as the man stumbled towards her. She could see even in the poor light of her lantern that he had been badly injured.

'Help me...' he croaked in English. 'Help me, Madame...'

It wasn't Jacques. Louise could see that now, even though the man's face was filthy and streaked with blood. His clothes were hanging off his body in tatters and he was wet, soaked to the skin. She could see blood on his hands and more of it seeping through what remained of his trousers. Louise knew instinctively that he was English. He must be looking for the car – but what was he doing this side of the line?

Had he been involved in whatever had caused that terrible explosion earlier? Smoke had drifted this way and she could still smell it on the air. If the Germans came looking here and found him, he wouldn't stand a chance.

'Please help me...' the man said and stumbled, almost falling. 'Please...'

Something stirred in Louise. She didn't know if it was pity or anger against the Germans for taking the children, but it banished her doubts. To hell with the Germans! If they came to the farm looking for him she would make up some excuse, pretend this man was her husband or something... anything!

'Yes, I shall help you,' she said and went to him, putting an arm about him, taking his weight on her shoulders. Louise was strong because of all the work she had done on the farm, and she was used to handling Jacques when he was drunk and needed putting to bed. 'Trust me, I shall look after you. You need to rest...'

She had spoken in English. He did not answer but seemed to trust her. Perhaps he had no choice. He would never make it back to the British lines in his present condition. He was leaning heavily on her but managing to limp.

They began to walk towards the house. At the kitchen door, Louise paused and put down the storm lantern. She would fetch it in later. This man needed all her attention for the moment. His wounds looked nasty but she did not feel that they were life-threatening. He had been cut on the face and hands and was clearly in pain, but when she had him cleaned up and put bandages on to stop the bleeding he would probably live. She was going to do all she could to help him. It was one small act of defiance against the brutes that had invaded her country.

Louise knew that the wounded man was almost exhausted. It was a huge effort to get him up the stairs. He stumbled and fell against her once, knocking her backwards so that she had to let go of him and grab for the banister. As she lifted him again, he mumbled something she knew was meant to be an apology, but she didn't waste her breath answering. She needed every bit of the strength she had to haul him up there and into her bedroom. By the time she got him on the bed she was too weary to bother undressing him. That would have to wait for another time. For the moment she must concentrate on cleaning his wounds and patching him up as best she could.

If her patient needed a doctor she would have to fetch one later, once she'd done all she could for him. It would mean going to the village, and that could be dangerous if the Germans were looking for the men who had attacked their ammunition depot. She imagined that the loud explosion had had something to do with the freedom fighters operating in the area. There might be more reprisals, so it would be best to stay away from the village for a while if she could.

After examining her patient, Louise discovered that most of the bleeding came from superficial cuts. There was one deep gash on his thigh. She decided to bind it tightly for a start and then wash the cuts and apply ointments and bandages. She didn't know much about nursing, though the doctor had told her she'd done everything possible for Jacques when he broke his leg in two places. She remembered the doctor had put moss on the open wound and she knew where the same moss grew in the wood near a swampy pool. She would fetch some if the wound looked infected. However, the doctor had set the broken bones and put a splint on to hold Jacques leg. All Louise had needed to do was run after Jacques and give him something for the pain.

She remembered she still had some of the pills the doctor had given her for Jacques when he was in such terrible pain. If the British soldier cried out the way her husband had, she would give him a pill to help him through it.

Having patched him up as best she could, Louise went to fetch some cordial and the pills. When she returned she saw that her patient had fallen asleep. She stood looking at him for a moment. Something about him looked familiar. Where had she seen him before? He threw out his arm and murmured something, and suddenly it hit her.

'Jack...' she said aloud. 'You're Jack... from Boulogne.'

Surely she must be mistaken! She hadn't recognised him at first, but the light had been bad and then she'd been too busy trying to stop the bleeding to look at his face. She reached down and stroked the damp hair from his forehead. It *was* the man she had met at a dance. Louise's throat tightened. Her eyes stung. She had thought about Jack so often, comparing her English Jack with Jacques. The Englishman always won.

They had the same name but they were miles apart in every way.

She was suddenly fiercely glad that she had decided to help him. Louise knew it was dangerous. If the Germans discovered that she was harbouring an enemy she would be shown no mercy, but at this moment she didn't care.

Somehow she would make Jack well again, and then... she would find some way of getting him back to his comrades.

6

'I was looking for Jack Barlow, sir,' Joe Briggs said. He saluted the captain. 'I've been given a week's leave and I'm going to Boulogne. I wanted to know if there was anything he needed. We're mates, you see.'

'I am sorry to tell you that Barlow is missing in action,' Captain Martin said heavily. 'I have reason to think he might have been killed or taken captive by the Germans.'

'Why is that, sir? I thought he was driving you, sir?' Joe looked at him accusingly. Trust Mad Martin to get back alive. He'd warned Jack to take care!

'Yes, he was, and I shall miss him. He was a damned good man, Barlow,' Captain Martin said. 'We split up and he didn't make it back to the rendezvous. I heard the sound of fighting and an explosion, and I tried to discover what had been going on. One of the locals told me that some ammunition trucks had been blown up near a German depot. I think Jack may have been involved somehow.'

'You don't know for certain he's dead?'

'No, I don't know for certain,' Captain Martin admitted. 'But Barlow was resourceful. If he could have got there somehow he would have made it to the rendezvous on time.' He frowned. 'I shall be writing to his family in the next few days. Would you like me to give them a message?'

'Jack left some letters. He asked if someone would send them for him. I'll do that in Boulogne – and I'll write a few words to Jack's sister. Jack was the best mate I had.'

'Yes, good man,' Captain Martin said. 'I am sorry to lose him.'

'I should think you bloody well are, sir!'

Joe turned and walked away. He was seething with anger. Why should that bastard have made it back when Jack didn't? This damned war was taking all the best and it made him sick to his guts. One day he would try to speak to Rose Barlow about her brother. Jack was a good mate and he wouldn't forget him.

* * *

Luke looked at his painting. It was one of the best he'd finished and he was pleased with the result. Most of his work portrayed his fellow RFOC officers, some were of men in their planes, some showed the planes in the air, and others were of the men talking and laughing. He was gathering quite a collection. However, the picture he had been working on recently was of Rose Barlow.

He had used his sketch of her, but he'd drawn her as he would like to see her, in beautiful clothes, standing in the drawing room at Trenwith. She looked proud, her head raised, every inch the mistress of her magnificent home.

Luke laughed as he put the picture at the back of the others. It was a flight of fancy because Rose would have hated living at Trenwith, even if it were possible.

He had merely been indulging himself. It was a picture he would never show to anyone else, but he hadn't been able to resist bringing her to life as she was in his dreams.

* * *

Rose saw Rod waiting for her when she came off duty. He was wearing the uniform of the RFOC and looked impressive. Tall, good looking and a gentleman. She felt a thrill of excitement when he lifted his hand to wave at her. He was different from most of the men she met socially and she was pleased that he had come looking for her. He had promised he would as soon as he got back from duty, but she hadn't been sure he meant it. She had thought he might just have been flirting with her.

'Hello,' she said, giving him a warm smile. 'Have you been waiting long?'

'Only a few minutes. I called the hospital this morning and asked what time you came off shift.'

'You never!' Rose looked at him in awe. 'No one told me. It's a wonder they didn't call me over the coals for that!'

'Call you over the coals?' Rod looked puzzled. 'That's an English expression I don't know.'

'It means tell me off,' Rose said. 'We're not encouraged to mix our private life with work. They don't exactly encourage followers either.'

Rod laughed. He offered her his arm. 'I told them I was your brother. I thought it might be best.'

'Oh, I see,' Rose laughed as she took his arm. 'You're a proper caution, Rod Carne!'

'I hope that means you like me?'

'Yes, it does,' Rose said and laughed softly. She'd never bothered with a steady partner, but it looked as though she might have one now. 'If I'd known you were coming I'd have taken something better to work to change into for you.'

'You always look lovely to me,' Rod said. 'I expect you're hungry. Shall we go and have something to eat? I thought we might go to the theatre when you have a night off. I've got seven days' leave.'

'That's lovely,' Rose said and squeezed his arm. 'Sister told me this evening that I had been given a week off, so we can see more of each other than we would have done otherwise.'

'Looks as if it's my lucky night,' Rod said. 'Where shall we eat?'

'Can we buy some hot pies and go for a walk? I'm not dressed to go anywhere and I'd rather just spend my time with you.'

'You're so easy to please,' Rod said. 'Pies it is for tonight, but tomorrow you should put your glad rags on because we're going out somewhere special.'

'I shall look forward to it.' She felt a thrill of pleasure. She hadn't thought much about what it might feel like to be in love, but she was enjoying being sought out by Rod. 'Come on, I'll show you where they sell the very best pies...'

* * *

Jack moaned and opened his eyes. He stared round the room. It was clean and neat but unfamiliar. He had no idea where he was or how he had come here. A cold feeling went over him as he realised that he did not know who he was. He couldn't even think of his own name! He sat bolt upright in bed and then wished he hadn't as he felt the pain in his right thigh. He slid his hand down the bed and touched the thick bandage. What had happened to him?

The door opened and a woman entered. She was wearing a dress that looked as if all the colour had been washed out of it and thick black shoes with heavy soles. However, her hair was a pretty blonde colour, her eyes greenish blue. She looked attractive but tired, as if life had made her weary.

'You're awake then,' she said. 'You've slept for two days. I began to think I ought to get the doctor, but the village has been full of Germans. They were searching for the men who attacked their convoy.'

'Germans?' Jack stared at her for a moment. His memory was hazy but now he was remembering that there was a war. 'Where am I? Is this France? I can't remember how I got here...'

'You walked, or rather limped,' she replied. 'I found you when I went to feed the stock that morning. There was an attack on a German convoy the previous day. I thought you must have been involved. You must have come through the lines for some reason – this is German occupied land for the moment. We keep hoping you will break through and push them back – the British.'

Jack nodded his head. 'I'm British – but you're French. You speak wonderful English but you have an accent...'

'You don't remember me, do you?'

'For the moment I don't remember anything much,' Jack told her. 'I'm sorry. Have we met before?'

'In Boulogne when you first came over. You attended a dance and we walked for ages.'

'I'm sorry. I can't remember it at all, but then I don't remember my own name.'

'You're called Jack. We only exchanged first names. I am Louise Saint-Claire. I live here alone since – since the Germans shot my husband. I have very little help on the farm. I've been looking after you since I found you, but I have to care for the animals too.'

'Things must have been hard for you,' Jack said,

thinking that she had just explained why she looked so tired. 'I must be a burden you could do without. I am sorry. I should leave.'

'No!' Louise frowned. 'I did not mean to make you feel that you were a burden. Only to explain why I cannot be with you all the time. I have made some soup. It has bacon and vegetables, also lentils – and the bread is fresh. Will you eat some? I have given you a little water and brandy as you lay sleeping, but you need food.'

'You are very kind,' Jack said. 'For the moment I can only thank you, but I shall help you as soon as I am able.'

'That will not be for a while yet,' Louise said and smiled. Jack caught his breath. When she smiled it was as if a light had switched on inside her. She was lovely, but the hard work had taken its toll of her. He felt a wave of some strong feeling, a need to protect her. 'All I hope for at the moment is that you will get well again. I could not call the doctor for your leg, but I think it is healing. The moss seemed to help it, but I don't know why. I just know it helps. As soon as the village is quiet again I will ask the doctor to come. The wound should probably be stitched.'

'You mustn't take risks for me...' Jack gritted his

teeth. 'If you sterilise a needle and bring me some thread I can probably do it myself.'

'You would infect the wound again. The doctor can be trusted, but we must think of a story to disguise your identity. Some people might betray you to the Germans.'

'I don't think I know much French,' Jack said. 'If I open my mouth I shall betray myself.'

'Then we must say you were born dumb,' Louise replied and wrinkled her brow in thought. 'I was not born here. I shall say you are my brother Georges and that you are a little slow...' She tapped the side of her head. 'It will explain why you are not with the army. I have burned your clothes, but I kept a photograph. It is signed on the back and I think it comes from someone called Rose.'

'Rose...' Jack frowned as he tried to remember if he knew anyone called Rose. 'Was there anything else in my pockets?'

'A silver cigarette case and some French coins. Most of your clothes were ripped away in the blast. It is a wonder that you were not killed. I thought you would have papers, name tags... Something.' She shrugged her shoulders. 'It was as if you had left your identity behind.'

'Why would that be do you think?' Jack looked

thoughtful. 'Was I on a secret mission – or did I just lose everything?'

'I am sorry. I cannot tell you, but I think you may not have been alone. There was a car left in my yard on the day of the explosion. I believe it was English. It had been covered with sacks and the haystack would have hidden it from a casual observer. It was driven away in the night – and then you came in the morning.'

Jack saw a picture of an English officer standing by a car. He was saying something, but the words eluded Jack. He felt that the memories were all there, hidden behind a curtain in his mind. They would come back to him in time, but for the moment everything seemed jumbled, like the pieces of a broken jigsaw puzzle.

'I wonder what brought me here...'

'You should not try to remember,' Louise told him. 'For the moment you are safe. When you are better we shall see if your memory returns – and we may try to get you back where you belong.'

'If only we knew where that was...' Jack lay back and closed his eyes for a moment. The effort to think and talk was almost too much. 'Did you say something about some food?'

'Yes, of course. You must eat. It will make you strong again.' Louise went out, leaving Jack alone.

His thigh was throbbing with pain and he felt sore in several places. For the moment he needed to concentrate on getting his physical health back. It was frustrating not knowing who he was or where he had come from, but oddly he was happy to be here. Louise seemed familiar to him, though he could not recall their first meeting. There was something about her that made him feel comfortable.

There would be time enough to think of the future when he was on his feet again.

* * *

Rose dressed with care for her day with Rod Carne. He had told her he was taking her somewhere nice for lunch and then to the theatre in the evening. She wanted to look her best for him, and she was pleased that she had bought herself a smart new coat that winter. Rod hadn't told her about his family, but she was sure he had come from a good background. He had lovely manners and there was something about him that made her think of Luke Trenwith. It wasn't in looks, because Rod was broader, taller and had a darker complexion. She thought it was because he treated her with respect and seemed concerned to please her.

'There's a letter come for you, Rose. It looks as if it is from your brother,' her landlady said as she prepared to leave the house.

'Oh, thank you,' Rose said, surprised as she saw the handwriting. Jack didn't often write to her. He must have something important to say to her. She hesitated and then heard the car's horn in the street. Rod had arrived a few minutes early. She slipped the letter into her coat pocket and went out to meet him. Jack's letters were too precious to be rushed. She would read it when she had more time.

'You look beautiful,' Rod said and opened the passenger seat for her. 'I thought we would drive out to Richmond and have a meal at a nice hotel there near the river. We'll have tea somewhere on the way back and then make a night of it at the theatre – how does that sound?'

'It sounds wonderful.' Rose smiled up at him. Her heart was beating very fast and she felt a little strange. Rod was such a gentleman and she thought she might be falling in love with him.

He glanced at her as she settled herself in the front passenger seat. 'I didn't know how lucky I was the night I met you,' Rod said huskily. 'I might as well tell you now, Rose. I'm in love with you. One day I am going to ask you to marry me. I just thought I should give you plenty of warning.'

Rose felt as if she were floating on air. She'd never had anyone pay her compliments like this and it made her feel wonderful. She hadn't really understood why Miss Sarah was reckless enough to defy her parents for the sake of Troy Pelham, but she thought she knew now. If this was what it was like to be in love, she couldn't be happier.

* * *

Luke was surprised when they told him he was getting home leave. It was usually a matter of a three-day pass and then report back. He couldn't quite believe his good fortune, because he hadn't been wounded and it was normally only the men with 'Blighty' wounds who were lucky enough to get shipped home.

'I don't understand, sir,' he said to his CO. 'Why have I been given this leave? We're short of pilots as it is. I don't see how you can spare me.'

'If it were up to me I should give all of you home leave,' Henshaw told him with a grin. 'Apparently, this is compassionate leave. I understand there may be some trouble at home, Trenwith. Have you heard anything from your family lately?'

'As a matter of fact I haven't had a letter for some weeks,' Luke said and frowned. 'My mother sent something at Christmas but my father hasn't written for a while.'

'Well, perhaps it went astray en route.' Henshaw looked awkward. 'I don't know exactly what is wrong, Trenwith. I received word that you were being given a three-week leave and that you should present yourself for transport home immediately.'

'Thank you, sir,' Luke said. 'Is there anything I can do for you while I am there?'

'Just have a good rest and come back ready to fly,' Henshaw said. 'You've been flying more hours than most of us, because of those special missions. I understand they want to see you about that too, but no doubt you will be briefed when you get back to Blighty.'

'Yes, sir!' Jack saluted and turned on his heel. Home leave was quite unexpected. He felt anxious, because he thought it must be serious if he was being given compassionate leave. The absence of a letter from his father for the past several weeks now seemed ominous and he wished the squadron leader had been more forthcoming, but these things were often hushed up. He was just going to have to wait and see how things lay when he got home.

* * *

'I asked you to call, because I heard the news,' Lady Trenwith said. She had sent for Jack's mother and she was sitting in her private parlour, her under butler's wife standing respectfully in front of her. 'I can only say I am truly sorry, Mrs Barlow. What exactly did the letter from Jack's Commanding Officer say?'

'Missing in action, my lady.'

'So there may be hope still?'

'Barlow says we shouldn't give up on him, ma'am. He says Jack will get himself out of trouble if there's a way.'

'I respect you for your dignity in this matter,' Lady Trenwith said. 'You have our sympathy and if there is anything we may do...'

'There's nothing to be done for the moment,' Mrs Barlow said. 'I've written to Rose and asked her if she can come home for a few days. I know she's busy at work, but they may give her time off for this. I should like to have her home for a bit.'

'She would be a comfort to you, Mrs Barlow.'

'Yes, ma'am. I heard that his lordship had a little turn, ma'am. May I ask if he is recovering nicely?'

'My husband had a mild seizure in the doctor's opinion,' Lady Trenwith said. 'The events of this past year have been distressing one way and another. However, he does not want it generally known. We believe our son is coming home on leave. Confidentially, he is being given an honour. Something about bravery above and beyond the call of duty.'

'That's good news,' Mrs Barlow said. 'You'll be glad to have him home for a bit. Miss Marianne came down to see her father, I understand.'

'My daughter was always her father's favourite.' Lady Trenwith frowned. 'I lay the blame for his illness at Sarah's door. She has been the cause of much distress to this family.'

'I am sorry to hear that, ma'am,' Mrs Barlow said. Rose would have it that the truth was very different, but it wasn't her place to say so. 'I dare say she will be sorry to hear about her father.'

'I have not told her, and I have forbidden Marianne to inform her. I have not yet decided to forgive her for her disgraceful behaviour.'

'She may have behaved badly, ma'am, but she never seemed a bad girl to me. She might be a comfort to you.'

'No, I do not think so. I may forgive her one day, but that day is not yet.'

Lady Trenwith inclined her head and Mrs Barlow

got to her feet. She was thoughtful as she left the house. She wouldn't want to live in this great barn of a place. Before the war it had been alive, because there was a family and servants living there. Now Lord and Lady Trenwith were usually alone with the minimum of servants to look after them. If they had any sense they would move into the Dower House, which was more manageable and had been empty for years. With a lick of paint and a bit of scrubbing it would make a much nicer home.

She wondered what Mr Luke would think of things when he got home. Shaking her head, she put the thought from her mind. Rose should get her letter about Jack in the morning. She hoped her daughter could get time off, because she knew that Rose would be proper upset.

* * *

Rose remembered her letter and took it from her pocket when she went to bed that night. She was still glowing from her wonderful day out. Rod had treated her as if she were a princess! She'd never been as spoiled in her life.

She took the small black box he'd given her during

their meal from her pocket. It contained a gold locket in the shape of a heart on a delicate chain. Rose was stunned when she saw it.

'You shouldn't have given me this,' she'd exclaimed. 'It's real gold. It must have cost a lot of money.'

'As long as you like it, that's all that matters.'

'I love it,' Rose had told him, her eyes bright with excitement. 'It is beautiful. I shall always treasure it and wear it all the time, even under my uniform at work – but I'm not sure I should take it. My mother would say it wasn't right.'

'I bought it because I love you, and because I want you to have something to remember me by when I'm away. I can't marry you just yet, Rose. I would have given you a ring but you need time to know me. In a few months, if you want – we'll get married.'

'Oh, Rod...' Rose had felt close to tears. They had spent so little time together. She didn't know him well in one way, but in others she felt as if she had known him all her life. He made her laugh and he made her happy. She felt very lucky and privileged to have met him. 'I would marry you now if I could, but it would mean me giving up my job, because they don't like us to marry and they could sack me. But if you ask me in a few months I might say yes. The war can't last much longer, can it?'

'Damn the war,' he'd said. 'When we are married I am going to take you home to my folks, Rose. They run a store back home and I know they will love you.'

'That sounds wonderful,' Rose replied. She had believed she wanted to train as a nurse, but she knew deep down inside that if Rod asked her she would marry him. Her mother wouldn't like her going away to another country but she would understand when she met Rod.

Bringing her mind back to the present with difficulty, Rose slit open Jack's letter. It was quite bulky, and as she looked at one folded sheet of paper she saw that Jack had written something in capital letters.

The last will and testament of Jack Barlow.

A shiver went through Rose and she laid the will aside as she read Jack's letter. She understood at once why he had sent her the will. It seemed that he had something important coming up and he wanted to be sure that his savings came to her.

If anything happens to me the money is for you, Rose. The will has been witnessed proper by a couple of me mates. Besides, Ma and Pa won't

contest it. They know you have always been
special to me. I want you to have the money as
something to fall back on if you need it.

'Oh, Jack...' Rose felt the sting of tears as she folded the letter and put it with the unread will into her drawer. 'You daft thing! As if I care about the money. It's you I want.'

She felt cold all over and some of the glow faded. She'd had a wonderful time with Rod, but Jack's letter had suddenly brought the reality of war back to her. She felt uneasy, restless, and it was a while before she managed to fall asleep. She prayed that her brother was safe, but reading his letter and seeing that will had given her a sick feeling inside. It was almost as if Jack were tempting fate by sending it to her.

* * *

'It is good to see you home, sir,' Barlow greeted Luke as he opened the door to him. 'We are all very glad to hear your news.'

'You mean that gong they gave me?' Luke grinned. 'It was a complete surprise and all nonsense. I've done no more than any of the others. Have you heard from

Jack recently? How is he doing out there? I've heard they are definitely going to be using my drawing of him for a new series of posters...' He saw the sharp look of pain on the under butler's face. 'What is the matter? Jack is all right? Oh, Lord, you haven't had one of those bloody letters?'

'Missing in action,' Barlow told him, a croak in his voice, though he controlled himself with dignity. 'That's all they told us, sir. Not a word about what happened or how...'

'They probably can't give you more details just yet,' Luke said. He would have liked to offer words of sympathy but understood that Barlow could not take anything of that nature just yet. 'I will try and find out something, if it is possible. You shouldn't give up just yet. Jack showed a lot of initiative at the training camp. He may turn up one day.'

'That's what I've been telling his mother,' Barlow said and straightened his shoulders. 'She has written to our Rose, but we haven't heard from her yet.'

'It may be the post,' Luke told him. 'It isn't always reliable these days. Or perhaps she can't get time off from work.'

'Yes, sir. I dare say you are right. Sir James and her ladyship will be pleased to see you home, sir.'

'I'd better not keep him waiting. If Rose doesn't turn up today I could nip up to London and fetch her for you. I am sure we could arrange compassionate leave for her.'

'That would be kind of you, sir. I'm sure she will come to see her mother when she knows.'

'Yes, I am sure she will.'

Luke went up the stairs. He felt dreadful over putting his foot in it with Barlow. The man had struggled to hold on to his dignity. It was a damned shame if Jack had bought it out there, not least because it would devastate his sister.

Luke pushed his thoughts of Rose to one side. His own father had been ill despite his efforts to deny it. Luke was a little angry that his mother had not written to tell him; she should have done so even if his father did not wish to make a fuss.

He walked swiftly to the end of the landing and then knocked before entering Sir James's private apartments. His father was sitting in a high-backed wing chair next to the fire. He had a rug over his knees and, as he glanced up from his book, Luke saw the ravages of his illness in his face.

'Father...' He started forward impulsively and then checked as Sir James frowned. 'I am sorry for the delay. That stupid gong they gave me kept me hanging on for hours longer than I expected.'

'It was an honour,' Sir James said, and his hand clenched at the rug. 'Don't be fooled by appearances, Luke. That stupid quack of mine insists that I rest and my man will keep covering me up, as if I were a baby.' He threw the rug off and stood up, holding out his hand. 'I am glad to see you home, my boy. Did you hear about Barlow's son? He is cut up about it, of course.'

'I spoke to Barlow just now. I promised I would go up to London and fetch Rose if she doesn't come today. Mrs Barlow wrote to her but hasn't heard anything back.'

'Well, I dare say the letter was probably lost in the post,' Sir James said heavily. 'Your mother will be glad to see you, but you mustn't think you have to spend all your leave with us. If you wish to visit anyone else you must do as you see fit.' He cleared his throat. 'Sarah may like to see you if you can spare the time.'

'Mother was very angry with her. Has she forgiven her yet?'

'I am not certain. Marianne seldom visits us these days. She prefers to visit her own friends and spends as much time as possible in London. Your mother may relent towards Sarah in time.'

Luke nodded and frowned. Personally, he felt that Sarah was the one who would need to be forgiving towards her family.

'I may go down and see Sarah if I have the time. I should like to stay here with you for a few days – if I may?'

'Of course.' Sir James looked vaguely uncomfortable. 'You must know that we are always glad to have you home, Luke.'

Luke nodded. Was he imagining it or had the illness softened his father? 'Did I tell you that the War Office have decided to use some of my paintings for their propaganda posters?'

'I think someone may have mentioned it,' Sir James said. 'It is a relaxing interest for you, Luke. I imagine you enjoy painting when you have time off from your duties.'

Luke smiled inwardly. His father might have slowed down, but he hadn't changed much.

* * *

'Rose still hasn't been in touch,' Mrs Barlow said when Luke called on her the next morning. 'To tell you the truth, I am a bit worried about her, sir. She and Jack were so close. I can't believe she wouldn't find some way of getting in touch even if she couldn't come down immediately.'

'Would you like me to pop up to town and see what is happening?' Luke asked. 'I do not wish to seem interfering...'

'I'd never think that,' Mrs Barlow said at once. 'It would be a kindness, Mr Luke. Barlow keeps a brave face and I try to do the same, but I could do with a visit from our Rose.'

'Yes, of course you could,' Luke said. He felt a stirring of excitement at the thought of seeing her himself. 'I'll catch the next train this afternoon and find out whether she got your letter or not – and if it is at all possible, I'll bring her back.'

'It's good of you to give up your time for us, sir. You must have so many things you want to do yourself.'

'I want to buy a present for Sarah, so I can do that in town,' Luke said. 'It wasn't possible to send her a wedding present from France and I hope to take it down to her myself.'

'She will like that, sir.' Mrs Barlow gave him a look of approval. 'Rose went down to visit her, you know. She says it is a beautiful house and that everyone thinks the world of Miss Sarah – Mrs Pelham she is now, of course.'

'She will always be Miss Sarah to you,' Luke told

her. 'I am glad Rose has kept in contact with her. I know they were friends.'

'Well, I'm not sure about friends, sir. Lady Trenwith might not think that fitting.'

'Do you know, I don't believe that my mother's opinion is very important as far as this goes,' Luke replied. 'Rose helped Sarah at a difficult time for her and I know she will always be grateful.' He held his hand out. 'You know that I wish your family only the best, Mrs Barlow. I've told Barlow that I will try to find out what happened to Jack, and I shall. I can't promise anything, but I shall do my best.'

'No one can do more.'

Luke gripped her hand firmly. He smiled, picked up his cap and took his leave. If he caught the afternoon train he would arrive too late in the evening to see Rose, but he would call at her lodgings first thing in the morning.

Rose glanced at Rod sideways as he drove her back to her lodgings. It was nearly half-past seven and they had been together all night. They had stayed at an inn in the same room, but they hadn't become lovers. She knew that Rod had wanted it to happen, but he hadn't pushed her. They had just lain side by side on the bed and held each other. They had talked for most of the night, getting to know all the things about each other it usually takes a lifetime to learn.

'If you want it to happen it will,' Rod whispered in her ear as he held and stroked her. 'But I shan't force it, Rose. I love you and respect you. I wanted us to be together like this, but the rest of it can wait until you're ready.'

'It isn't that I don't love you,' Rose told him, and the tears were very close. 'Ma would be so shamed if anything happened and I wasn't wed – and we can't wed yet. I would have to get permission, because they would throw me out if I didn't... Especially if... you know.'

'Just let me kiss you and hold you,' Rod said, his face buried against her hair. 'You smell so good, Rose, and I want you badly, but I won't ask for more than you want to give.'

Rose hadn't given in. She had been tempted, but she remembered her mother's warnings, and she hardly knew Rod. Sometimes she felt as if he were a part of her, but something held her back. Perhaps it was her upbringing. She was a respectable girl and it wasn't just because she felt she might let her mother down; she would let herself down too – and lose the job she had chosen for herself.

Rod hadn't reproached her, but she felt a bit guilty. She knew that most of her friends had slept with their boyfriends. They told her it was something they wouldn't have done before the war.

'You never know if they will come back,' one of the girls had told her. 'If my Tim gets killed at least I'll know what it was like...'

'I'm sorry, Rod,' Rose said as they turned into her street. 'I was just nervous. Perhaps next time I get leave...'

'No, don't apologise,' Rod said and smiled at her. 'I respect you for who you are, Rose. If I wanted someone just for that I could find plenty of girls to oblige me. I love you and I'm prepared to wait until you're ready.'

'Thank you...' Rose leaned across to kiss him on the lips. The kiss was long and passionate and she was shaking when she drew away. 'Perhaps...' She had been going to say that maybe they would do it tonight when she saw a man standing outside her lodgings and felt a cold shiver. 'That's Mr Luke... Something is wrong...'

Rose opened the door and got out of the car, not waiting for Rod to open the door as he usually did.

She had almost forgotten him in her anxiety as she approached Luke Trenwith. His expression was so serious that she felt sick.

'Is it Jack?' she asked breathlessly.

'Didn't you get your mother's letter?' Luke asked harshly. 'Where have you been all night? Your landlady said you hadn't been home since yesterday morning...' His manner was so accusing that Rose caught her breath. 'Your parents are worried to death.'

'I haven't had a letter from my mother. I had one from Jack. He was going somewhere special... Has he been...?' Rose faltered, the words sticking in her throat.

'Missing in action,' Luke said. His tone and manner were still harsh. His eyes were so cold that Rose recoiled. Why was he looking at her that way? 'Your father is taking it as well as could be expected, but your mother is desperate to see you. Can you get leave? If not, I could speak to someone...'

'I still have one day of leave,' Rose said. 'If I let Sister know the circumstances she might allow me another day...'

'Go in and pack a few things,' Luke said. 'Give me the details and I'll see what I can arrange for you. You are entitled to a few days for compassionate leave. I shall come back in an hour and we'll go down on the train.'

Rose hesitated, then lifted her head proudly. His coldness could mean only one thing. He was condemning her for staying out all night. He had jumped to the wrong conclusion. He thought she was a whore!

'Thank you for coming,' she said coldly. 'It was good of you to let me know, but I can manage. I would rather speak to Sister personally...'

'What is it, Rose?' Rod asked, coming to stand behind her. 'Something wrong, darling?'

'My brother was reported missing in action and my mother needs me. I have to get to the hospital and speak to Sister – ask for a couple more days' leave.'

'I'll take you,' Rod offered at once. 'And then I'll drive you down there, Rose.'

'Thank you. If we go now I can speak to Sister and still catch the afternoon train.' She touched his arm. 'I know you would take me and I'm grateful, but I don't think this is the time to take you home, Rod. My mother will be too upset. I think you will have returned to your unit by the time I get back to London, but I'll write to you. I promise I'll write regularly.'

Rod seemed angry for a moment, shooting a look of dislike at Luke, then said, 'If it is what you want, darling. I love you, Rose. Don't you forget it!' He pulled her to him and kissed her on the lips. Rose responded and then pushed him away with a little shake of the head. He took her hand. 'Let's go. The sooner you have permission the sooner you can be on your way...'

Rose got back into the car. She turned her head to look at Luke as she was driven away. He was still staring after them. She couldn't help wondering what had made him so angry. He had no right to condemn her. She'd done nothing wrong – and even if she had, it was none of his business.

* * *

Luke felt the ache in his chest as he watched the car turn the corner and disappear out of sight. He was such a damned fool! He should have known that Rose would have a lover. She was too pretty to have remained untouched all these months. It was ridiculous to feel so betrayed.

He tried to tell himself that it didn't matter. The man with her was a fellow officer by the looks of it and he had acted as if Rose were his personal property. He had damned well better treat her properly! If he hurt her... Luke shook his head. It wasn't his business. Rose wasn't his sister. He couldn't interfere in her life. She would resent it and she had a perfect right to do as she pleased.

She had shown him that she had no intention of listening to him. She had worked for his family once, and had she had an unsuitable follower then his mother would have reprimanded her – but Luke hadn't been acting as an employer or even a concerned friend. He had been jealous.

It was ridiculous. He knew that he had been thinking of her too often in the past weeks. Rose was not for him – and now she had shown him that his thoughts were impertinent. She wasn't interested. Even if he had decided that he would risk his family's censure and ask her to marry him, she would not have been impressed. Why should she be?

Rose had the world at her feet. She was beautiful, good at her job and warm. She would never be short of admirers. He didn't know the officer she was with, even though he was RFOC – but from the look of him he came from a good family. He had sounded Canadian. They probably didn't have the wretched class system over there that had dogged Luke's footsteps all his life.

It was his own fault. If he had said be damned to it all and followed his inclination he might have spoken to Rose months ago, before she met this fellow.

He took a cigarette from his case and tapped the end to firm it up before lighting it. Since he had nothing much else to do he might as well go and find a decent present for Sarah, and then he would go down and visit her. He would just have to forget all about Rose.

* * *

'Rose...' Mrs Barlow cried when her daughter entered the kitchen. 'Thank God! When you didn't answer my letter I started to wonder if something had happened to you too.'

'You know I would have come or sent you a telegram if I'd got your letter,' Rose told her. She went and hugged her mother. 'I'm sorry, Ma. It was bad enough for you with Jack going missing without having to worry about me. I spoke to Sister and she was very good about it. I've got three days with you before I go back.'

'Couldn't they spare you for more than three days?'

'I've just had nearly a week off...' Rose saw the surprise in her mother's eyes, because she always came home when she could. 'I didn't come because I met someone. We met some weeks ago. I thought when he went back on duty he would forget me, but he didn't.

He was waiting for me when I came off duty the other day and I've been spending time with him.'

Mrs Barlow looked at her daughter's face. 'Is it serious? This is the first time you've ever mentioned a follower.'

'Rod Carne is a Canadian in the RFOC,' Rose told her, a faint blush in her cheeks. 'He is very nice, Ma. He treats me with respect and – he says he loves me. I think I may be in love with him, but I shall know for sure as time goes on. I've got an address to send to and he has promised to write to me.'

'Well...' Mrs Barlow raised an eyebrow. 'Why didn't you bring him down?'

'Because it isn't the right time,' Rose said. 'We're all too upset over Jack. Luke Trenwith said he was missing in action – what exactly does that mean? What happened to Jack?'

'We don't know anything more,' Mrs Barlow confessed. 'Jack's Commanding Officer wrote to tell us that he was missing in action. He said Jack was a brave soldier but didn't give any more details.'

'That's a bit odd, isn't it? One of the girls at the hospital had a letter from her fiancé's CO and she said he told them exactly how Terry died.'

'Maybe they don't know exactly. He didn't say Jack was dead, just missing...'

'When did it happen?'

'Just after Christmas from what I can make out.'

'But that's weeks ago,' Rose said. 'Surely they could have told you sooner?'

'I suppose they were waiting in case he turned up.'

'I think we ought to try and find out a bit more.'

'Mr Luke said he would do that for us.' Mrs Barlow frowned. 'I thought he might have come back with you?'

'I think he had something else to do,' Rose prevaricated. 'Besides, I preferred to come on my own.'

'He was very kind and thoughtful,' Mrs Barlow said. 'As soon as he knew I was worried about you he offered to go up and fetch you, and he'd only just got here.' Her eyes narrowed. 'You didn't do anything to upset him I hope? He would stand more chance of finding out what has happened to Jack than any of us.'

'No, of course I didn't upset him,' Rose said, feeling a bit uncomfortable. Luke Trenwith had seemed angry because she had been out all night with Rod, but she couldn't see why he should. 'If he said he would do it for you, Ma, I am certain he will. Luke isn't the sort to break his word.'

'It's Mr Luke to you and don't you forget it,' Mrs Barlow said. 'He said he would do his best and we'll just have to wait and see.'

Rose nodded silent agreement. However, she wasn't going to leave it there if she could help it. Luke might try to find something out for them, but she was perfectly capable of writing a letter to the War Office, and she would, because she wasn't prepared to give up on Jack just yet.

'He doesn't feel dead to me,' she said, making her mother look at her sharply. 'You know how close we always were, Ma. I think I should feel it if he were dead. I think he is in some sort of trouble, but I don't believe he is dead.'

'Well, you were closer to Jack than anyone,' her mother admitted. 'But if he has been missing for some weeks, why hasn't he been in touch? He must know that we would be told he was missing. It isn't like him not to send a card.'

'He would if he could,' Rose agreed. 'He may not be able to, Ma. He might be injured or a prisoner of war – but I don't think he is dead.'

Her mother smiled at her. 'I'm glad you came if only for a few days, Rose. I was beginning to give up hope, but I shan't after what you've told me.'

Rose was silent. Was she wrong to have hope? It would come all the worse to her mother if Jack was confirmed dead, but she couldn't help her feelings.

Jack wasn't himself, but he was alive somewhere. She was sure of it.

* * *

Jack waited until there was silence downstairs and then threw back the bedcovers. Louise was insisting that he stay in bed for a few more days, but his thigh wound was hardly painful at all now, and his other cuts and bruises had cleared up long since. He had been practising his walking while Louise was busy in the yard, but he hadn't left the bedroom. He was determined to do so for the first time that morning. He still hadn't remembered who he was or why he had been wherever he'd been, but he wasn't ill. He felt guilty about all the extra work he had made for Louise, because sometimes she looked so tired that he was concerned for her.

It wasn't right that she should have to do so much work. Running a farm was hard enough for a man let alone a woman. He didn't doubt that Louise was strong; she had become strong through necessity, but she could do without carrying trays and jugs of water to his room. She had been forced to empty slop buckets for him too, because the only toilet was outside, and that was something he'd found embarrassing. If he could get downstairs he could at least relieve her of that job and in time he hoped he could do much more.

Alone with his thoughts for much of the day, Jack had tried hard to remember something about his former life, but so far nothing had come back to him. He felt that he must have a family somewhere – at least someone who meant a great deal to him. Was he married? He wasn't sure. He didn't feel married, especially when he looked at Louise and felt a burning need to be close to her. Being an invalid didn't do much for his male ego, but he knew that once he was feeling well again and independent, he would want to know Louise better.

She had sat with him some evenings, mending or reading aloud, and she had begun to teach him French. Jack was surprised at how quickly he had managed to pick up simple phrases. He thought that perhaps he had known some of them before Louise began her lessons.

'You may need to know some French if we are to get you home,' she had told him at the beginning. 'I think there is a way of getting you through the German lines, but if you were stopped you should be able to answer in French.'

'The trouble is I don't know where home is,' Jack

told her. 'I know I must be a danger to you every day I stay here.'

'If the Germans come I shall tell them you are my brother Georges. I shall say that you are not right in the head and you must hobble and pretend to be foolish.'

'You would do better to give me up,' Jack said. 'If they discovered you were lying you might be punished severely.'

'I know they would take me off somewhere and they might shoot me – or worse,' Louise admitted. 'They have taken children from the village. They took Jacques, my husband, even though he would not be able to work for them, because of his leg. He waved a gun at them and they shot him. I do not know if he is alive or dead.'

'I am sorry.'

'I am sorry too. Jacques was not a good man but he did not deserve what they did. His leg gave him much pain and he was not wanted in the French army.'

'That must have been a bitter thing for him?'

'Yes, it was. He changed after the accident. I feel sorry for what happened but I have no grief. In time I should have left him, I think.'

Jack looked at her. 'I wish I could remember what

happened in Boulogne. I feel I ought to but I can't. I'm sorry.'

'We talked, we walked and we kissed, no more.' Louise looked odd. 'Afterwards I wished it had been more. Jacques was angry when I came home. He had not wanted me to go to my mother, even though he knew she was dying. He beat me and...' She shook her head as he started up. 'No, no, stay where you are in case you open your wound. It does not matter what he did. I think I could not have stayed with him had the Germans not taken him. I have thought that I should sell the stock and move to Paris. It is what I should like.'

'It might be better for you than living here alone.' Jack's eyes went over her, wondering how any man could treat her the way her husband had. The man must be a brute! 'As soon as I am able I shall help you with your chores.'

'Until you leave,' Louise agreed. 'I have told no one you are here, but I am sure your presence here will not remain a secret for long. I shall tell only one person who you really are, because I trust her. She may know whom to contact to help you leave here.'

'Be careful,' Jack warned. 'You can't be certain of anyone in times like these.'

'Madame Bonnier hates the Germans for taking

her son,' Louise told him. 'She would not betray you. I think most of the village people feel the same, but she is the only one I am close to.'

Jack was thoughtful as he hobbled along the landing and down the stairs. He had felt fine lying in bed but he was feeling a bit wobbly now. He grimaced, as he had to hold on to the wooden banister to steady himself. He wouldn't be helping Louise to clean out the cowshed just yet! Nor was he ready to leave.

He wasn't sure that he wanted to leave. Here with Louise it didn't matter so much that he couldn't recall his former life. If he returned to England other people might be able to tell him who he was, but here he was Jack. The war seemed distant, though they could hear the rumble of guns in the distance. He would have to return one day, but perhaps he need not go just yet...

* * *

Louise finished milking the cows. She skimmed the cream and put it aside for churning into butter, and then wheeled the churn out to the gate where it would be collected later. The spare milk was sold in the village with milk from other farms in the area, and she would receive her share of the proceeds. Sometimes she was given a few coins; at others she would ask for cheese or other foodstuffs instead. It was an easy way of exchanging goods and suited their way of life, which had always been quiet. She carried the jug of milk for her own use back to the house, but as she opened the kitchen door she almost dropped it as she saw Jack.

'What are you doing?' she asked, putting the jug on the scrubbed pine tabletop. 'You should be in bed.'

'I'm tired of lying there like an invalid,' Jack said. 'I saw the dishes needed washing so I heated the water on the range and did them.'

Louise could not hide her surprise. Jacques would never have done such a thing, even when they were first married.

'It wasn't necessary. I usually do them when I come back from milking.'

'I can't do much else for you yet,' Jack said. 'But I'm going to do whatever I can in the house until I can go outside.'

'Thank you.' The sting of tears behind her eyes surprised her. She was touched by his thoughtfulness. 'I still think you need to rest, but it was a kind thought.'

'I shall rest,' Jack said and grinned. Louise's heart jerked and then raced as she felt a tingle of desire shoot through her. Her eyes dwelled on his mouth for a moment as she recalled their kisses in Boulogne. He was handsome, generous and kind, and she would hate it when he had to leave. 'But I am not ready to move on yet, Louise. If I give myself time I may remember who I am and where I live.'

She knew it was his duty to try and get back, either to his unit or to England. The war was still raging on the Somme and he could be in trouble for deserting if he did not make that effort, but she did not want him to leave. She realised that she was falling in love with him. He was so different from her husband.

'You can stay here for as long as you wish,' she said, surprising herself, because she had been anxious for him to go at the start. 'We can tell people you are my brother. There is no need to go until you are truly well again.'

'If you are sure?' Jack looked at her face. 'I know what a risk you took bringing me here, Louise.'

Louise shrugged and smiled. 'You have repaid me by washing the dishes,' she said. 'It is a chore I have never liked.'

'I would like to do much more for you.'

There was such sincerity, such meaning in his voice that Louise's throat went dry. She looked at him, remembering their night together in Boulogne and the way she had felt then. She had wished that she'd taken

Jack back to her mother's house... to her bed. Now he was here in her home and the way he looked at her told her that he wanted to make love to her. She wanted it too. So much that she felt her stomach clench and experienced heat coursing through her. Jack wasn't strong enough to make love yet, but within a short time he would be. This time she would not let the chance slip through her fingers.

'I want you to stay,' Louise told him huskily. 'If I could I would keep you with me forever...'

'Louise...' Jack groaned low in his throat. He moved towards her and she went eagerly to meet him. He drew her close, bending his head until their lips met. His touch burned her and she moaned with pleasure as he kissed her deeply, her mouth opening to allow the searching of his tongue.

'You taste of honey,' Jack murmured. 'I want you so much, Louise. I've been thinking about you ever since I woke up and saw you.'

Louise laughed and shook her head. 'I look a mess. I have the stink of the cows on me and my hair needs washing...'

'You are beautiful to me,' Jack said. 'I think I must have felt this way in Boulogne. I can't remember it, but I feel as if we belong together – as if this was meant to be.'

'Yes, that is how I feel,' Louise said softly. She touched the side of his face. 'After we parted I wished that we had been together properly. I wanted to be with you and never come back here.'

He let her go reluctantly. 'I want you but my body isn't ready yet, Louise. I have to get stronger...'

'You should still be in bed,' she said and smiled. 'Foolish man to rise too soon...'

'I want things to be right for us,' Jack said. 'I'm going to get up for longer each day and I'll start to do more chores – but for the moment I do need to rest. I'm not going back upstairs. I'll lie down on the daybed in the parlour...'

7

'How many did we lose today?' Luke asked as his squadron leader walked into the room. 'I saw Barker go down and I think Johnson was hit too, but I saw his parachute open.'

'There were three in all today. Porter took a full hit. He didn't get out. Sorry, Trenwith. I know he was a friend of yours.'

Luke took a cigarette from his case and offered the case to Henshaw, who took one with hands that trembled slightly. They were all living on borrowed time; some of the young pilots hardly lasted the month these days. Luke lit both cigarettes with his silver lighter and drew deeply on his own. 'Would you mind if I wrote to his family? I've known Phil a while and I know his father too.'

'Of course, but spare them the details if you can, old chap. Goodness knows, it is a job I could do without.'

'It must be difficult having to write to the family of every man we lose,' Luke said thoughtfully. 'I need to find details about how an army private died if I can. His parents live on the estate and I promised I would do what I could for them. They were simply told he was missing in action.'

'His CO may not have had more details to give, but I should imagine you could speak to him yourself if you take the chance next time you have leave. See what he has to say.' Henshaw hesitated, then, 'Lillian was asking about you again. Why don't you come with us this evening?'

'Yes, I think I will,' Luke said. He had decided that there was no point in thinking about Rose or what might have been. His visit to Sarah had taken away some of the raw pain he'd felt when he'd seen Rose with that fellow Carne. Sarah was happy despite everything she had suffered. He had told her that he was proud of her for what she had done.

'I've done nothing to be proud of, but I am not ashamed of what I did either,' Sarah told him. 'I loved

Troy from the first time we met. At first he only saw Marianne but after she jilted him he became aware of me. We fell in love, Luke. If Father had allowed us to marry I shouldn't have shamed the family by falling for a child out of wedlock – but in a way I am glad it happened the way it did. Troy would probably never have believed I loved him if we were already married; he would think I was just doing my duty.'

'You love him very much, don't you?'

'He is my world,' Sarah told him. 'I don't see the scars, Luke. I just see the man I love. Besides, Troy is getting better all the time.'

Luke wished that life could be as simple for him as it was for Sarah. She had known what she wanted and gone for it. He had let himself be swayed by duty and the proper order of things, and he'd lost the woman he loved. He didn't know if he'd ever stood a chance with her and now he never would.

It was over. She had found herself a lover. Luke had to put her right out of his mind and get on with his life. When the war was over he would find that suitable girl his father expected him to marry and do his duty – but that didn't stop him having a mistress. Lillian liked him and she was pretty enough. He would go home with her that evening, and this time he would sleep with her. While he was stationed in France he would look after her and give her money.

It was an arrangement that many men of his class accepted. He knew that his father had kept a mistress for years and Lady Trenwith had never seemed to mind. Luke had wanted something more, but he knew his dreams had been foolish. If he survived this bloody war, he would forget them, forget Rose and marry as his father wished, because it no longer mattered what he did.

* * *

Rose was nervous as she made her way to Matron's office that afternoon. It wasn't often that Matron sent for the girls herself. Sister usually disciplined those who needed it, and praised them when they deserved it. Rose had felt that she was doing her job well and she had been wondering what she'd done wrong ever since Sister told her to report to Matron's office when she went off duty.

She tapped at the door and was asked to enter. She wiped her hands nervously on her skirt, her heart beating wildly as she tried to think what she had done that deserved a reprimand. Swallowing hard, she went in as she was bid and advanced towards the desk. Matron was busy writing, but she looked up as Rose stood in front of her.

'Ah yes, Barlow,' she said, her eyes going over Rose with an intent expression that made her clench her hands together. 'Sister Harris has been telling me about you. I have had some good reports of you, Barlow. I have been told that you would like to train as a nurse – is that correct?'

'Yes, Matron...' Rose's breath expelled in haste, because she had been holding it in, terrified that she was going to be sacked. 'Yes, I should like that very much.'

'Well, I have decided to put your name forward. We cannot afford to lose you for the moment, but if you are accepted your training would begin in about six months from now.'

'Thank you...' Rose could hardly believe what she was hearing. 'I am so thrilled...'

'You'll find it is even more hard work than you're doing now,' Matron said dryly. 'You will be expected to do much of what you already do, plus you will be required to attend classes and pass exams. You can thank me in a couple of years if you feel the same then.'

'I am sure I shall,' Rose told her. 'It is what I really want to do. Thank you so much.'

'Well, run along then. I am putting you forward, but mine is not the last word. You will be interviewed and you may have to sit an entrance examination. You will be informed if your application is accepted.'

Rose thanked her again and left. She was pleased to have been given the chance to better herself. It was only as she was walking home that she realised she couldn't share it with the person who would have really understood how she felt. Her mother would smile and her father would say well done, but Jack would have known what this meant to her.

Rose had written to the War Office and she received a polite reply. They were sorry but they had no further details for her. Jack Barlow had been lost in action and reported missing. Her family would be informed if any details came to light.

Rose sighed as she walked home. She'd had one letter from Rod and then nothing else. She could only pray that he was well and would come back safely. She wore his locket beneath her uniform and she touched it whenever she felt in need of comfort. Rod loved her. He had promised to marry her one day.

Nothing would ever ease the pain of not knowing what had happened to Jack, but if Rod came back safely at least she would have a future.

* * *

Jack found the black lead polish in a cupboard under the sink. The old-fashioned range Louise used hadn't been cleaned in a while, but that wasn't surprising given all the work she had to do. He fetched a cushion and knelt on it, starting work on the task he had set himself. He found the work hard after lying about these past weeks, but he wouldn't let himself give up. He had to do something to earn his keep and help Louise. Every day he was getting that bit stronger and he had told her not to worry about washing dishes or cleaning the kitchen. This was the hardest job he had tackled so far, but he felt a keen satisfaction when he got to his feet and looked at the range.

That was better! It looked a bit more like the range in his mother's kitchen now. She had always delighted in keeping her place spick and span... How did he know that? Jack frowned as a clear picture of a large kitchen came into his mind. He could see the oak dresser set with a display of blue and white china. A kettle was boiling on the range and the room smelled of baking.

'I made your favourite treacle tart today, Jack...'

Jack could see the woman. She was well-rounded but in a pleasant, attractive way, her brown hair curled in a bun at the back of her head. She wore a dark dress and a spotless white apron, but he couldn't see her face. He reached for the memory and the picture disappeared. He frowned, annoyed at his inability to get past the screen in his mind.

Jack washed his hands at the sink. Until now the pictures in his head had made no sense. That kitchen was the first thing he had seen clearly, and the woman he was sure must be his mother. He wished he could recall her face, but the more he tried the less clear the picture became.

He had a home somewhere, parents and... he wasn't sure but he seemed to remember another woman, much younger. Was she his wife or his sister? Jack felt a wave of grief mixed with guilt. If he had a family they must be anxious about him. It was his duty to get back to his lines and find someone who could tell him who he was – and yet he was conscious of a deep reluctance to leave this place and Louise.

Jack knew in his heart it was because of Louise that he wanted to stay. She had somehow found her way inside him. She made his lessons in French enjoyable, and the way that she laughed when he said something stupid made him feel good. He eagerly anticipated her return from the yard when she had been feeding the animals, and he missed her if she went down to the village to shop. His pulse raced when she came near and he caught the fresh smell of soap on her skin.

They hadn't made love yet, but he knew it was only a matter of time before it happened.

The young woman who hovered at the back of his mind sometimes could not be his wife, Jack decided. He knew instinctively that he wasn't the kind to mess about. He couldn't feel the way he did about Louise if he had a wife somewhere.

He had made up the fire and put the kettle on when Louise came in carrying a jug of milk. She gave a little cry of pleasure when she saw the range and then ran to throw her arms around him.

'You are so good to me!' she said when Jack hugged her back. 'You must have worked so hard to get the range this clean. I hated it the way it was but I did not have the energy left to clean it after my other chores.'

'I shall be able to help with the outside work now,' Jack told her. 'If I can clean the range, I can carry water for the stock and muck out the sheds.'

'Only if you are sure...' Louise looked doubtful. 'Your thigh...'

Jack kissed her, cutting off her protest. She arched into him, clinging as the kiss deepened. They were both breathless as they parted, staring at each other in mutual need.

'It aches a bit but it has healed,' Jack told her. 'I'm much better, Louise, and it will do me good to work.

Besides, I don't like to see you work so hard. You should be able to spend more time in the house. The yard work is a man's job.'

'Yes, I know, but Jacques left it to me most of the time after his accident and...'

Jack put a finger to her lips. 'Your husband isn't here, Louise. I can work now and I shall.'

'But... you should go back...' Jack bent his head and kissed her. She looked up at him, eyes opening wide. 'I want you to stay. You know I want you to stay but...'

'I have lost my memory,' Jack reminded her. 'I don't know where I belong or where my home is. They would be forced to give me leave until I recovered. I'm not neglecting my duty by staying here. If it comes back, I shall have to leave, but until then...'

'Oh, Jack!' Louise pressed herself against him. 'I hope it never comes back. I want you to stay with me for always!'

Jack pulled her close, his mouth taking possession of hers once more, his tongue exploring the sweetness of her. The kiss went on a long time, drawing them both in, making them forget about everything but their mutual need.

'Shall we go upstairs?' Jack asked huskily. 'I want to

make love to you, Louise. I do love you... want you so much.'

'Oh yes, Jack, yes,' Louise said. 'I've never felt this way about anyone before. I married Jacques because he asked but I never loved him. You are so different... so gentle and strong...'

'A gentle giant, that's what they call me.' Jack grinned at her. Pictures of a house and a large garden were in his mind. He didn't think it was his home but he had worked there somewhere. He knew that the memories were beginning to break through. It was probably only a matter of time before he could place them in the proper order, but for the moment he did not want to remember. He wanted to be here with Louise, to enjoy the feeling between them. 'I want to take care of you, my dearest one. I don't know what the future holds, but I know that I shall always want you...'

Louise smiled up at him, her eyes glowing. 'Shall we go up?' she asked, taking his hand and beginning to lead him from the kitchen. 'We can eat later...'

* * *

Louise left Jack sleeping. She went down to the kitchen to start preparing their meal. She could hear the cows calling and felt guilty because they needed to be milked. She had neglected them, sleeping after the passionate love-making between her and Jack. Her body trembled as she remembered each touch, the tenderness he had shown her as he kissed and fondled her breasts. She had responded, becoming a flame of desire, giving herself to him as she had never given herself to Jacques.

Even when he entered her, Jack had taken care to wait for her. Her climax had shocked her because it had been so fierce... so overwhelming. Even at the beginning of her marriage she had never experienced such pleasure in the act of loving. Her eyes stung with tears, because she would never have believed that she could feel like this – feel such exquisite joy. She had clung to him afterwards, tears trickling down her cheeks. Jack had been anxious until she explained that it was because she was happy – happier than she had ever been in her life.

She couldn't let him leave her. Louise knew that she would do her best to make Jack stay with her for as long as possible, because if he left it would break her heart.

* * *

Luke stopped the car he had borrowed from one of the other officers in the lane outside Lillian's house. He got out and went round to pick up the box from the boot. It was quite heavy, filled with foodstuffs and small luxuries like chocolate, dried fruit and a fresh chicken. He had asked Lillian what she most wanted him to bring her, and she had told him that she needed food for her store cupboard, but he was sure she would appreciate the chicken, because she liked to cook.

He went down the small passageway at the side of the house and let himself into the kitchen. He had been visiting Lillian for some weeks now. She was sweet and pretty and he enjoyed making love with her. She had told him that she loved him and begged him not to stop coming. She swore that she cared for him and that it was not for the money he gave her. Luke didn't mind if she did want money. He could afford her, and he quite liked holding the child sometimes.

Luke put the box on the scrubbed pine table. He was about to start unpacking when he saw the leather, flying jacket slung over the back of a chair. Even as he hesitated, he heard laughter coming from upstairs – Lillian and a man. He had no need to wonder who the jacket belonged to, because he knew it was Mike Henshaw's. Mike had encouraged Luke to visit Lillian and he was still seeing her himself.

Luke knew that he couldn't expect exclusive rights with her, but he'd thought she wouldn't see anyone else for a while. He felt sick suddenly and rushed out to vomit in the yard.

Wiping his mouth with the back of his hand, Luke walked back to the car. Lillian hadn't been short of money, because he'd given her a wad of notes two days earlier. He made a wry face as he cranked the car and then jumped in when the engine came to life. Lillian was welcome to the food and the money he'd given her, but he wouldn't be visiting again.

He could taste the bitterness in his mouth as he drove back to base camp. He had no rights over Lillian but she had sworn that he was special to her. The first chance she got she went to bed with Henshaw! Luke was aware of his anger. It seemed to him at that moment that all women were faithless.

He wasn't in love with Lillian, but he liked her. He had expected that she would turn down other offers while she was with him. Somehow it felt worse because she had gone up with Henshaw. It made the whole thing seem sordid somehow.

He thought back to the morning he'd seen Rose arriving home in company with the man she had so obviously spent the night with. Luke had been so angry. He had wanted to kill his rival. Of course he had done no such thing, because a gentleman didn't give way to emotion, especially one as unworthy as jealousy. Luke wasn't jealous now, just disgusted. He didn't feel like killing anyone. At that moment he was empty. His life seemed meaningless. He was forced to do a job he didn't particularly like and he couldn't see much hope for the future. It felt as if this pointless war would just go on forever.

* * *

Jack was whistling as he shovelled straw and dung from the cowshed. He'd come on in leaps and bounds these past few weeks. Hard manual labour suited him. He found the work came naturally to him and he enjoyed grooming the one horse they had left. He was sorry that Louise had sold the other horses. They would probably need another if they were going to work the land.

Much of the smallholding was down to grass. The cows and pigs had been penned up for the winter, but it was nearly summer now and Jack had put the cows out for the first time that morning.

'Jacques used to move the cows out much earlier,' Louise had told him as they sat together in the kitchen eating the food she'd cooked. She was a good cook, especially now that she had more time. 'I kept them in because I couldn't cope with fetching them up for milking.'

'I'll do it for you now,' Jack told her. 'I can milk them if you like. I'm sure I've done it before.'

'Do you think you were a farmer before you joined the army?'

Jack took a few seconds to answer her. 'I think I worked with horses. I felt right when I was grooming Prince even the first time, as if it were second nature. I seem to remember carriage horses. I may have worked on a big estate somewhere.'

'Your memory is coming back, isn't it?'

'Bits and pieces,' Jack agreed and grimaced. 'I can see pictures of places and people in my mind. The people aren't clear as yet, but I can see a large house. I think I worked in the stables there.'

'I don't want you to remember too soon,' Louise told him. 'I shall miss you when you go. At first I accepted that you should go, but now I want you to stay.' Her eyes held a wistful look that caught at Jack's heart.

'I want to stay. If I have to go I shall come back when I can. Even if it isn't until the war is over, I shall come back for you. I promise.'

Louise looked sad. Jack took her in his arms and kissed her, feeling the way she leaned into him, wanting more. He smiled as he recalled their loving the previous night. Louise was warm and passionate. She responded eagerly to his touch and she had cried the first time they made love. Jack had asked her why she was weeping.

'Because nothing has ever been so good for me.'

Jack kissed her tenderly. 'It has never been this good for me either,' he said. 'I feel it inside and I know I have never felt like this before.' It was strange how he knew certain things but couldn't remember his home or his full name.

Jack knew that things were too perfect. It wasn't likely that this halcyon period would continue for long. Louise was a different woman from the one who had helped him limp into the house that first night. No longer tired all the time, she took more trouble with her appearance. Her skin had a new glow and she was always smiling. He thought she was beautiful. Sometimes Jack wondered if he had died and gone to heaven. Surely this perfect happiness could not continue?

He hadn't forgotten the war completely. The sound of guns in the distance was a constant reminder if nothing else, but it seemed a long way off, as if they were somehow apart from reality.

Jack hadn't been to the village yet. Louise said

people knew he was staying with her. She'd told everyone that he was her brother Georges Marly; everyone except Madman Bonnier, who knew the truth. She was the only person to visit Louise; the only one he had met face to face.

Jack wasn't sure the older woman approved, but she hadn't voiced an objection in his hearing. Since she was Louise's friend he spoke to her politely whenever she arrived and then made himself scarce for the duration of the visit.

Having finished all his work for the morning, Jack stood for a moment looking out at the land they needed to use for growing their own food. It would have to be ploughed before much longer or they wouldn't get a crop.

Louise said that they usually grew root crops, but Jack had been thinking that they might put part of it to better use. They could have a section of it for fruit and other things that would be more useful than too many potatoes, which ended up being fed to the stock over winter. He was thoughtful as he walked up to the house. He was planning for long term, for the years to come – but was that wise?

Jack knew that if he did not return to his unit soon he could be arrested and tried as a deserter when he did return. It didn't matter that he had forgotten who he was; he knew that he was a British soldier and his duty was to get back somehow and let others sort out what to do with him. By staying here now that he was fit to travel he was neglecting his duty – and in time of war that was punishable by death.

He ought to go, but he wasn't ready to leave Louise just yet.

* * *

'He is good to you?' Madame Bonnier asked. She had called to exchange eggs and butter for meat, because she'd had a pig killed and butchered. She knew that Louise had a surfeit of eggs and might be short of meat, and it was better than seeing food wasted. 'You look better – very well.'

'I feel wonderful,' Louise told her. 'Jack is so generous, so thoughtful. I've never known anyone like him. I've never been so happy.'

Madame Bonnier raised her brows. 'He was lucky you took him in. He works now to repay you – yes?'

'Yes, but he likes the work,' Louise said. 'He is so strong and he does chores that took me all day in a couple of hours.'

'But he must leave soon, surely? He should return to his unit.'

'I suppose so,' Louise agreed. She shivered, suddenly feeling a chill of fear. 'I don't want him to go too soon. He hasn't recovered his memory. He doesn't know who he is or where he belongs.'

'But he knows he is British and a soldier. He should go back to them and let someone identify him. You do know that he could be in trouble one day if he doesn't go back?'

'You think they would call him a deserter?' Louise looked anxious. Jack could pay a heavy price for her selfishness. 'I suppose you are right, but I shall miss him so much.'

'Supposing Jacques comes back one day?'

'I couldn't live with Jacques now!' Louise was horrified. The very idea appalled her.

'He still owns the farm and the house,' Madame Bonnier reminded her. 'If he claims it after the war you would have to leave.'

Louise shrugged. 'Jack says he will come back for me if he has to leave. We could go away somewhere – perhaps to Paris.'

'It is your choice,' Madame Bonnier said with an expressive shrug. 'I was merely warning you of the consequences. I should go now, there is much to do these days...'

'You have heard no news of Pierre?'

Madame Bonnier looked hesitant, almost reluctant. 'Someone said they thought he was a captive, but there is nothing definite yet.'

'I hope it is true,' Louise said. 'If he is alive there is always a chance he will come back to you.'

'If he escaped he would join the freedom fighters,' Madame Bonnier said. 'Pierre is no longer a child.'

'I pray for him,' Louise told her as they parted. 'And for you...'

The two women embraced and Madame Bonnier left. She saw Jack walking up to the house and waited for him. 'You should go before it is too late,' she told him. 'People talk. It is only a matter of time before the Germans hear you are here.'

'I am Georges Marly and I am a little simple,' Jack told her. 'Why should the Germans bother with me?'

'If you don't go you will be expected to join them – the freedom fighters. They know you are not stupid. I am warning you for Louise's sake. Believe me, you should go.'

'Thank you, Madame Bonnier,' Jack replied. 'I shall think about what you've said.'

'Don't leave it too late,' she warned, and she walked away, leaving Jack to stare after her.

He knew she was right. He ought to have gone as

soon as he could manage to walk, but the longer he stayed here with Louise, the less he wanted to leave.

* * *

Rose looked at her letter for the sixth time that morning. It was from Rod to tell her that he was coming to London on leave and would have seven days. He wanted her to ask if she could have a week off so that they could go away together.

> *We could have a few days at the sea some-where*, Rod had written. *I've been thinking about this every day since we parted. It was such a rush that I never got to say all the things I wanted to say to you, my darling. You know I love you, but letters can't show you how much I love you. If you wanted, we could buy a special licence and get married…*

Rose folded the letter and slipped it into her apron pocket. She could ask for the time off, but she knew that getting married was risky. Rod would be home soon and she didn't have time to ask for permission. If she married without it, she might be dismissed from the service.

Rose sighed. She wanted to be a nurse so badly, and yet she understood what Rod was asking her. He knew she wasn't comfortable about going to bed with him without marriage, and he was giving her the chance to be his wife.

Rose made up her mind. She was going to ask Sister for a week's leave. If she got it she would marry Rod. If she didn't she would go for the training that Matron had offered her, though of course that wasn't certain yet. Rose was still waiting for the results of the interview she'd had with the board of the teaching hospital. It was possible that she wouldn't even get the chance, because Matron's recommendation didn't mean that she would be taken as a student nurse. They might decide she was more useful where she was, doing soulless, backbreaking work that left her hands red and chapped in the winter.

She sighed because she knew her mother was right when she said she'd had it easy working as a parlour maid. Her work at Trenwith had been easier and she'd had fun with the other servants, but she wouldn't give up what she was doing to go back there for anything. She didn't get much chance to do things for the patients, but when she could she attended to all the little jobs that the nurses didn't have time for and that gave her satisfaction.

No, Rose wouldn't exchange what she was doing for the easier life she'd had before, even if they paid her a fortune!

* * *

'Lillian has been asking for you again,' Henshaw said when Luke walked in that morning. 'She says you haven't been to see her for a couple of weeks.'

'I've been busy working,' Luke said. He didn't look at the squadron leader as he lied. He hadn't worked on a painting for weeks. He was angry, restless and sick of the war that showed no sign of ending as far as he could see.

'You've got a three-day pass this week,' Henshaw said. 'Why don't you use it to take her away somewhere?'

'If you're so interested in her welfare, why don't you take her yourself?' Luke said. 'I'm going to see Captain Martin. He is the CO of the missing private I told you about. It is all arranged.'

Henshaw's gaze narrowed. 'Lillian and I are friends. It means nothing. It's you she wants.'

'I'm not a bloody fool,' Luke said, his voice icy. 'I shall not be visiting her again so drop it, will you?' He scowled and walked away as the order to scramble came through. He was annoyed with Henshaw's persistence, but he had arranged the meeting with Jack's CO some time back and he couldn't have changed it had he wanted to...

* * *

'I'm sorry, I can't tell you very much more than I told Barlow's parents,' Captain Martin said. They were sitting together in the parlour of the hotel where they had arranged to have lunch. It was small and discreet, rather dark with its old-fashioned heavy furniture and tiny leaded windows. 'We were on a special mission that took us very close to the front line. We split up to do some scouting, and we were supposed to meet at an arranged spot. I told Barlow I wouldn't wait if he was late, and he had orders to do the same. I got back first and I waited for nearly half an hour, and then I left. He didn't show.'

'So he truly is missing. He wasn't blown up or shot to your knowledge?' Luke frowned. The hotel smelled of spices and there were tantalising aromas coming from the kitchen, but he was back in the stables at Trenwith talking to a tall, handsome groom he had known all his life. He felt a pang of grief at the thought of Barlow being captured or killed. 'You don't have any idea of what happened?'

'I heard an explosion earlier in the afternoon. We were looking for a German ammunition dump – keep that to yourself, Trenwith. When we split up, I went one way, Barlow the other. When the explosion happened I made my way towards it. I couldn't get close. The Germans were everywhere. Someone had blown up one or more trucks, probably used for ammunition I should say by the size of the explosion. I have no idea if Jack was involved. I made notes and took some pictures and then kept out of the way until dark. However, had Barlow been able to make it, I am sure he would have been there on time.'

'Barlow is or was a good man,' Luke said and frowned. 'You made no attempt to look for him at the scene of the explosion? You saw no sign of him?'

'I saw the Germans collecting some bodies,' Martin said. 'I have no way of knowing if Barlow was one of them. If he saw the attack taking place he should have stayed well clear. We weren't there to try blowing the place up, just to get information so that a task force could do the job properly.'

'Yes, I understand,' Luke said. He knew the purpose of these special missions better than most, but he didn't reveal that information. 'It wasn't your fault if Barlow got caught up in something. He should have got out as soon as he saw the dump.' He frowned. 'Do you know if Barlow had any friends – someone in the ranks he trusted?'

'There was someone,' Martin told him. 'I believe Barlow gave him a letter for his sister. I am not sure what happened to it, because he got killed a week or so later. There may have been others Barlow was friendly with, but no one I know of...'

'It looks as if I've hit a brick wall,' Luke said. His grey eyes were thoughtful. 'There have been no reports of him turning up anywhere injured? I am sure he would have got back somehow if he could.'

'I imagine he is dead,' Captain Martin said. 'Barlow knows the rules. He would have made every effort to get back if he could, poor devil. I'm sorry I can't tell you something different, something to give his family hope, but he's one of many who have just disappeared.'

'Yes, I know,' Luke agreed. 'Sometimes we see our men floating down to earth, but they don't always get back and that leaves us wondering. At least we know what happens to the poor devils that go down in flames.'

'This bloody war,' Martin said. 'I don't know who

has it worse – the Tommy in the trenches or you flyboys.'

'I know where I would rather be,' Luke said. He finished his drink and looked up as a waiter approached discreetly. 'I think that's us – our table is ready.'

'Good show,' Captain Martin said. 'They do decent food here, which is why I suggested it, though it doesn't look much. I used to come before the war. It was even better then, of course. Shall you come back when all this rubbish is over?'

'I doubt it,' Luke replied. 'I can't wait to get home and forget about the whole thing...'

* * *

'Jack!' Louise cried as she opened the kitchen door and saw him scrubbing his hands at the sink. 'Get upstairs and stay there. Go up to the attic if you have to and take the ladder with you...'

'What's wrong?' Jack asked, seeing her panic. Her face was white and she looked terrified.

'Germans,' Louise said. 'I saw them as I was putting washing out on the line. There's only one car but I think there are two of them...'

'I can't leave you alone to face them,' Jack protested. 'You know what we arranged I should do if they came. I am your brother Georges and I'm dumb and a bit simple.'

'But they might shoot you anyway,' Louise said. 'It's my fault. I should have sent you away weeks ago. I wanted to keep you with me and now the Germans are here. They have never come to the farm before. I didn't think they knew where to find us.'

'Someone must have told them I was here,' Jack said. 'If I hide they will take it out on you. I can't let that happen, Louise. I'll play my part and see what happens. I would rather they shot me than you.' He didn't mention what else they might do to a pretty woman living alone at an isolated farm.

'Jack...' Louise stared at him, her eyes wide with distress. 'I love you. I can't bear to lose you...'

'Keep calm and stick to the story,' Jack said. 'I'm going out to them now and I shall act as if I'm a mite short of a shilling. I'll take my chances. If anything happens – remember that you were the best thing in my life.'

Louise rushed at him, throwing her arms about him in desperation, but Jack put her aside gently. He opened the door and began to walk down to the yard. Louise had been right about there being just two of them. The officer was perhaps forty or so, his driver much younger. They both wore guns in holsters on their hips. Jack wished that he had a gun. He would have shot them both without compunction, but as it was he had nothing. He had to hope that his acting ability would get him through.

He was walking with a pronounced limp. It was easy enough, because he had learned to limp when his leg still burned with the pain. He gathered the saliva in his mouth, willing himself to play the part convincingly. Someone with learning disabilities may not know the difference between friend and enemy.

The Germans had seen him now. The officer went straight for his holster, taking out his pistol. Jack painted what he hoped was a stupid grin on his face. He started making odd noises. God help him! He had no idea if this would work, but he had to try.

'Halt!' the German cried in French. 'Stay where you are or I shoot.'

Jack hesitated, wondering what to do. He couldn't answer them. Would someone with learning disabilities understand what they were saying?

'Please... do not shoot him! He is my brother. He doesn't know what you are saying...' Jack heard Louise's voice behind him. She had followed him out. He smiled foolishly as she came to stand by his side, letting the saliva he had built up in his mouth trickle down his chin. 'He is strong and he helps me on the farm. But his mind is that of a small child.'

The officer stared at her. He had dark blonde hair and a small moustache, his eyes a piercing blue. 'You are Madame Saint Claire?'

'Yes...' Louise smiled nervously at the officer. 'I was here all alone so my brother came from his own village to help me. His name is Georges Marly. He is quite harmless.'

Jack made bubbling sounds and grinned at them. The officer hesitated, still holding his pistol ready.

'I was told there was a stranger staying here.'

'No one knows him,' Louise said. 'I do not let him go to the village. They would make fun of him and that makes him cry.'

'He seems fine,' the officer said and approached. He looked hard at Jack. 'What is your name?'

Jack made more bubbling sounds. He stared vacantly, praying that his acting was paying off.

'He can't speak,' Louise said. She turned to Jack and slapped him across the face as hard as she could. 'The officer wants to know who you are, you great fool!'

Jack surprised himself by giving a sob. He rubbed at his eyes and then wrapped his arms about himself, making moaning sounds and rocking back and forth as if in distress.

'I'm sorry, Georges,' Louise said. 'Please don't cry. Just nod your head if your name is Georges.'

Jack nodded for all he was worth, managing to blubber and rock at the same time. Saliva ran over his chin as he gabbled nonsense at them.

'He is clearly harmless,' the officer said and put his pistol away. 'I am sorry to have disturbed you, Madame Saint Claire. We have to investigate these claims. He could have been a British pilot you were hiding.'

'I wouldn't dare,' Louise exclaimed. 'Why should I risk my life for a stranger? It would be foolish. I have my brother to help me. I need no one else.'

'And your husband, Madame?'

'He is dead,' Louise said without hesitation.

'It must be lonely for you in such a place with only your brother for company.'

'Sometimes,' Louise agreed and smiled at him. She shrugged her shoulders. 'I struggle to survive. Times are hard. It is all I can do to feed us both.'

'Yes, times are difficult. We shall not make it harder for you by taking away your brother. He is no use to us, and if he is of service to you...' He clicked his heels, inclining his head to her. 'Adieu, Madame Saint Claire.'

'Adieu and thank you,' Louise said. She turned to Jack and slapped his face again. 'Get back to the house and watch the pots. I shall be back soon.'

Jack shuffled off, sniffing and moaning, his shoulders shaking. Louise stood where she was as the Germans got into their car and drove away. When they had gone, she walked back to the house. Jack was making coffee.

'I am sorry... so sorry,' she said and went to him. She put her arms around his waist and leaned her head against his chest. 'I shouldn't have hit you so hard.'

'You did the right thing,' Jack said and rubbed at his cheek ruefully. 'That slap really stung. It convinced them that I was your brother anyway.' He grinned. 'It was a good thing you came. It isn't easy when you're not supposed to speak.'

'At least they have gone,' Louise said and shivered. 'It was terrifying. I have never been so close to a German. I was afraid he would shoot you.'

'They've gone for the time being,' Jack said and looked thoughtful. 'They may come back, or others may come in their place. Who told them I was here – and why?'

'I don't know. Someone who bears a grudge against me perhaps.'

'You have not fallen out with your neighbours?'

'No...' Louise shrugged. 'Who knows why people do these things?' She looked at him fearfully. 'Perhaps you should leave?'

'Not yet,' Jack said. 'I may have to one day, but I told you I shall come back. I am not leaving for a while. I can't remember my name. I can't be expected to return until I know who I am.'

'Then I hope you never do,' Louise admitted. 'I want you to stay with me for always.'

Jack looked serious as he drew her close. The incident with the Germans had shown him that they were living on borrowed time. He had to make up his mind what to do, and it wasn't easy...

8

_____

Rose had been working hard all morning. She was feeling tired and her back ached. She would be glad when the end of the day came and she would be free for a whole week. Rod had sent her a card to say that he would be waiting for her when she came off shift that evening. She could hardly wait!

She still hadn't heard about her nursing training. Several months had passed since that morning in Matron's office and Rose had almost given up hope of ever being accepted or even getting the letter of acceptance she had been promised. It came as a surprise when Matron sent for her at the end of her morning shift.

She walked swiftly to Matron's office, her heart pounding. Was she going to be offered the chance to take up nursing at last? Outside the door, she took a deep breath and then knocked. Invited to enter, she went in and stood nervously in front of Matron's desk. A moment or two passed before the older woman looked up.

'Ah, Barlow,' she said. 'I have some news for you. Your next interview has been set for next Thursday.'

Rose felt dismayed. 'Next Thursday? I'm sorry, I can't manage that day. I have leave for a whole week and I am going away with...'

'This is your opportunity,' Matron said, seeming annoyed with her answer. Her gaze became distinctly frosty, her mouth setting into a thin line. 'If you turn it down you may not get another chance.'

Rose bit her lip. 'I've promised someone I will go to the sea...'

'Well, if your private life is more important...' Matron frowned at her across the desk. 'I am not going to cancel this appointment, Barlow. You should think very carefully about what you want in the future.' She handed Rose a letter. 'Take this and think about it. There is a telephone number. If you decide to cancel you must do it yourself. I have done my best for you. I am disappointed. Very disappointed. I thought you were taking this seriously.'

'I am,' Rose said, her throat tight. She felt close to

tears but she kept her head high. 'I made a promise, and I believe in keeping my promises. I shall try to change this appointment.'

'Very well. You must do as you think right. Get back to your break, Barlow.' Matron gave her a look of disapproval.

'Thank you,' Rose said with dignity. 'I am grateful for all you've done, even if it doesn't seem that way.'

She left the room, walking back to the ward. She didn't feel like eating now, because she was too upset. Why couldn't Matron have understood how she felt? Rose had promised Rod that she would go to the sea with him, and he had made a booking for them. She couldn't just change her mind at the last minute! Besides, he might be angry and she didn't want him to think she didn't care about him.

Perhaps if she talked to Rod they could come back a day or so early. Rose decided that she wouldn't cancel the appointment just yet. She would talk to Rod that evening and hear what he had to say.

* * *

Luke was sitting with a drink of whisky in his hand when Henshaw walked into the mess room that evening. He finished his drink and got up to leave, but Henshaw caught his arm.

'What is the matter with you? You never come out with the rest of us and you've been looking at me as if I were something the dog left on the step for weeks. Pull yourself together, Trenwith. We are a team. If this continues it could affect our efficiency in the air.'

'In the air we work as a team, and I shall continue to do that to the best of my ability. You have my word on that,' Luke said. 'I do as I please in my private time.'

'You are behaving like a fool! If this is over Lillian...'

'No!' Luke held up his hand to silence him. 'Leave her out of it, Henshaw. She is a pretty enough girl, but that's it as far as I am concerned. I don't want to share her – and I don't want her to myself. It was a mistake and I'm no longer interested.'

'Then why do you walk out as soon as I arrive?' Henshaw's eyes narrowed, his expression one of angry frustration.

'You are my squadron leader. I pay attention when you brief us – as for the rest...' Luke shrugged his shoulders. 'The sooner this damned war is over and I can go home the better!'

'Don't you think we all feel the same?' Henshaw glared at him. 'I am becoming seriously worried about you, Trenwith. Your attitude, the way you drink alone. If you let this feud or whatever it is affect your work you could get us all killed!'

'If my work isn't good enough for you, have me transferred.' Luke gave him an icy look. 'The remedy is in your hands.'

'Damn you! If you weren't considered our ACE pilot, I would! Watch yourself, Trenwith. I've had enough of you and your insolence. You seem to think you are better than the rest of us. Forget it! We are all expendable.'

'Thanks, I'll remember that,' Luke said and took a cigarette from his case. He didn't offer the case to Henshaw. 'If it is permitted I would rather like to get some work done...'

'Your damned paintings, I suppose?' Henshaw sneered. 'Did you know that everyone laughs at you? Shutting yourself away with a box of paints! We are all on the knife-edge. Any one of us could die any day – and we enjoy ourselves when we can. You are a fool for not doing the same.'

Luke shrugged and walked away. He was used to his work being mocked, but it was like water off a duck's back when it came from someone like Henshaw. It had hurt that his father did not appreciate his talent, but one day he would show the paintings he'd done during his time in the RFOC – and the sketches he'd made of life at the front. He was building quite a collection, and he thought some of them might be rather good.

After leaving Captain Martin he'd got someone to take him up to the trenches and he'd talked to a few of the men. He'd seen for himself what life was like at the sharp end. Henshaw talked about being on a knife-edge. He should try life in the trenches for a few days.

Luke had wanted to see things for himself and not just for the sake of his paintings. He had a letter to write to Barlow and Mrs Barlow. He had been putting it off for a while, but he would do it this evening. They should know the truth, as much as he could tell them, and he wanted them to appreciate how brave their son had been.

* * *

Rose hugged Rod when she greeted him. She was so pleased to see him that her disappointment over the appointment for her nursing training just vanished into thin air. She had missed him more than she'd truly realised and it gave her a thrill when he kissed her. He was really good looking – a gentleman with his nice manners and way of making you feel you were special.

'I was afraid something would happen and you wouldn't come,' Rod said, and the expression on his face gave Rose a thrill. 'I love you so much, Rose. I've been looking forward to this leave more than you can know.'

'Oh, Rod,' she said and squeezed his arm. She couldn't tell him that she wanted to come home from their trip early now. She would wait until they'd had a couple of days together. 'I love you too. I've never felt this way about anyone else before...'

'Will you marry me, Rose?' Rod asked. 'I've got a special licence and we could pop into the Registry Office – and then tell your mother and father before we go to the sea. What do you say?'

'Could we tell my parents first?' Rose asked. 'Ma wouldn't like it if we just turned up married. We might get married in the church at home, if you've got a special license.'

'I've got that in my pocket.' Rod looked doubtful, anxious. 'You won't change your mind if your parents object?'

'I don't think they will,' Rose told him and smiled. 'Ma said I should have brought you home before – so now I'm going to. We'll get married in a Registry Office if the vicar won't let us have the church, but I think he might.'

'If it is what you want.' Rod looked at her lovingly. 'You know I would do anything for you, Rose. I love you so much.' He stroked her cheek with his fingers and then kissed her on the lips. 'You're special, Rose Barlow.'

'I love you,' Rose giggled. 'I feel excited. Ma is going to be so surprised!'

* * *

'Surprised?' Mrs Barlow looked at the young man her daughter had brought home to them. He was good looking and his manners were those of a gentleman. She knew exactly why Rose had fallen for him. 'No, I'm not really surprised. Rose has never bothered with followers, Rod – or should I call you Flight Lieutenant Carne?'

'I should like it if you would call me Rod,' he replied and grinned at her confidently. 'I was terrified of meeting you, Mrs Barlow. I was sure you would think we ought to wait for a while.'

'Rose told me she had an admirer some while ago so I've been expecting this sooner or later. My daughter is a sensible girl. She wouldn't have mentioned you if you weren't important to her. I know you only have a week before you go back. We'll have a quiet wedding here and then you can go off for a few days on your own.'

'Do you think the vicar will marry us at such short notice?' Rose looked anxious. 'I suppose I should have said something before, but I wasn't sure it would happen...'

'You told me Rod was coming home on leave in your last letter. I spoke to the vicar and he said he would do his very best for you – if you asked.' Mrs Barlow smiled at the surprise in her daughter's face. 'I know you, Rose Barlow. I thought it was best to be pre-pared so I got a few things together for you and had a word just in case.' She laughed as she looked at their faces. 'I know what it is like to be young! Why don't you walk down to the village and talk to the vicar now? I am certain he will do his best for you.'

'Ma!' Rose flew to hug her mother. 'You're the best! The very best. I love you.'

'Get off with you. I'll send word up to your father and ask him if the kitchen can rustle up some more food. We'll ask a few of our friends to a bit of a do af-terwards. We can have it outside if the weather keeps fine for us, and if not – well, we'll manage somehow.'

Rose looked at Rod, her face glowing. She held out

her hand to him. 'Come on, let's go down to the church at once and hear what the vicar has to say.'

* * *

Rose heard Reverend Thornton's words with a sinking heart.

Thursday was the only time he could fit them in during the week, and he was doing it only because Rose and her mother had been regular church goers all their lives.

'I hope it fits in well with your plans?' he asked, beaming at them. 'Your mother told me this might happen and I kept the time free for you. You've always been a good, decent girl, Rose Barlow, and this is your reward.'

'That is fine,' Rod said. He glanced at Rose. 'Isn't it, darling?'

'Oh... yes,' Rose agreed, because she couldn't do otherwise. 'But it means we'll only get two days at the sea.'

'That is fine with me,' Rod told her. 'I have never been to this part of the country before. We can explore the countryside hereabouts until our wedding. All I want is to spend time with you, Rose.'

Rose smiled and took his hand. She loved him and

she couldn't take that smile from his eyes by asking him to postpone their wedding until his next leave. She would have to telephone the hospital board and let them know that she wouldn't be keeping her appointment. If they were reasonable people they would give her another, and if they didn't – well, she would be married to Rod and that was more important.

She put her disappointment from her mind and smiled brightly. She was getting married to the man she loved and that was wonderful! She hoped she would get another chance to train as a nurse, but for the moment she wasn't going to think about anything else but her wedding.

* * *

'It was my wedding dress,' Mrs Barlow said. 'It won't take much altering to fit you. If you think it is all right?'

Rose looked at herself in the ivory silk and lace gown, turning to see her reflection in the long mirror. 'It is perfect,' she said. 'A few tucks at the waist and a couple of inches to let down at the hem and it will fit me a treat.'

'I'm glad I saved it,' her mother said and nodded in a pleased way. 'Some brides wear their dress for best afterwards, but mine was too good so I saved it for you.

I wasn't sure you would want it, but there's no time to have a new one made.'

'I would rather have this,' Rose assured her. 'I like it because it was yours – and I can wear the veil with some fresh roses. Pa says Sir James has told him we can have flowers from the gardens at Trenwith for the wedding.'

'Lady Trenwith sent a note to say we should take all we need for the church,' Mrs Barlow agreed. 'She seems to have mellowed a bit since Miss Sarah came to see her...'

'Yes, I had a letter from Sarah,' Rose said. 'She visited her mother recently. It was time the quarrel was finished. It should never have happened.'

'No, it shouldn't,' Mrs Barlow said.

'It was good of you to do this for me at such short notice, Ma. I ought to have told you long ago that I thought I might marry Rod.'

'You did tell me,' her mother said with a smile of affection. 'Your letters said it all, Rose. You mentioned Rod quite a bit. I know my girl and I knew this was coming. Your father is giving you some money and I've got some bits of linen put by, though you won't need them yet. We shall keep any presents here for you until you're ready to set up home.'

'That won't be until after the war...'

'Will they let you stay on in the VADs?'

'I haven't told them I'm getting married yet, Ma.'

'Oh Rose! I am sure you should have.' Mrs Barlow looked dismayed. 'To marry without permission is a sacking offence.'

'I will tell Sister soon. Besides, it doesn't matter if they don't know just yet. I'll have to tell them if... anything happens...'

'You mean if there's a child. It doesn't often happen that quickly. I think you should tell them anyway, Rose. You know I don't approve of lying.'

'I haven't lied to anyone.'

'No, but you haven't told them the truth either. If you apologise and ask to be allowed to stay on for as long as you can, I am sure they will understand. It is the best way, love.'

'Yes, perhaps I shall tell them,' Rose said. She had made a different excuse when she rang the hospital board. A very cold voice had told her that she would be put back on the list, but might have to wait months for another appointment. 'Don't be cross with me, Ma.'

'I'm not cross,' Mrs Barlow said and gave her a knowing look. 'You're not quite yourself, Rose. You are sure about this wedding? You're not just doing it to please Rod?'

'Yes of course I'm sure,' Rose told her quickly. She

sighed. 'I suppose I wish that Jack could be here for the wedding.'

'We all wish that,' Mrs Barlow agreed. 'Your father had a letter from Mr Luke. He says that Jack was on a special mission behind the German lines and that is how he went missing. No one knows for sure that he is dead. He says that Jack was an exceptionally brave and resourceful soldier.'

'It was nice of him to write,' Rose said. She felt the prick of tears behind her eyes. 'I had a letter from one of his friends telling me what a good bloke he was – but we all knew Jack was brave anyway.'

'Yes, but it was nice of Mr Luke to take the trouble to find out what he could, Rose.'

'Yes, I suppose so...' Rose sighed. She wondered what Luke Trenwith would think if he knew she was marrying Rod. Of course it wouldn't matter to him – why should it?

* * *

Rose was surprised at how many people had turned up for her wedding. She came out of church on Rod's arm to be greeted by a small crowd of local people throwing rose petals at them. One little girl came forward with a straw doll, which she presented with a giggle and a curtsey.

Rose felt her cheeks turn pink. Rod raised his brows, and she leaned closer to whisper in his ear. 'It is for fertility – to help us conceive our first child. It's a local custom.'

'Quaint,' Rod replied and grinned. 'Somehow I don't think we need that, Rose love.'

'No...' Rose's cheeks went a deeper pink. She laughed as they ran from the churchyard and were showered by yet more flower petals. The sun was shining and it was a beautiful day; a day she would remember all her life. Her bouquet of lavender and roses smelled gorgeous, imprinting the twin scents in her mind forever.

Lady Trenwith had surprised them all by offering the servants' hall for the reception. She had also provided much of the food for the meal and she'd sent Rose a set of best-quality linen sheets for her wedding gift. Sir James had sent a gift of silver candlesticks with a note wishing them well.

A greetings telegram had arrived from Sarah that morning. She had sent love and the news that a gift from the whole Pelham family was on the way, though it wasn't possible for her to attend the wedding.

Rose was pleased and excited, because she hadn't

expected anything from the Trenwith family, though she'd known that Sarah would send her a gift because they were friends. Some of her mother's friends had sent small gifts, which would be stored away until she and Rod could make a home together.

They hadn't talked about that yet, but there was plenty of time because they still had three days before Rod had to leave...

* * *

Rose turned in her husband's arms, offering herself for his kiss. It was morning and she had slept deeply after Rod's passionate love-making of the previous night. He had been tender and sweet to her, and she knew now that she had made the right decision. She would still like to be a nurse if she could, but she loved Rod. She had felt right and happy in his arms.

'Good morning, Mrs Carne,' Rod said and planted a teasing kiss on her nose. 'I thought you were never going to wake up.'

Rose laughed, looking up at him with love in her eyes. 'It's your fault for keeping me awake half the night.'

'Only half the night?' Rod arched his brow and

gave her a teasing look. 'I shall have to do better tonight!'

He pulled her to him. Rose tingled as their flesh touched and she felt the pull of desire once more. She was conscious of her nakedness, still a little shy even after the way Rod had loved her the previous night, because until her marriage she had never been aware of her body. Accustomed to living with other servants, she'd pulled her nightdress on first and taken her clothes off underneath it, as all the girls did. Even when she had her own room she undressed quickly and had never looked at herself in a mirror without her clothes. Ma would think it indecent!

Rod had told her she had a beautiful body. He had caressed her and kissed her, teaching her the meaning of passion. Rose had learned quickly, discovering that she enjoyed touching and being touched. Rod's hand was stroking the arch of her back now, making her gasp as she pressed herself closer. His mouth sought her breasts, licking delicately at the nipples. Rose moaned softly in her throat, moving instinctively towards him as his hands trailed down over her quivering body, finding the warm centre of her femininity. His fingers moved sensuously, bringing her to a state of moist arousal so that she was ready for him when he entered her.

'It is so lovely,' Rose told him in a whisper as she lay in his arms, satiated and content. 'I didn't know it could be nice like this...'

'You are lovely,' Rod told her. 'I want it to be this way for us always. Promise you will always love me, Rose. You won't find another lover while I'm away?' He looked into her eyes, his hand still stroking her thigh.

'Of course I shan't,' Rose said and sat up, looking indignant. 'I'm not that sort of a girl!'

'No, of course you're not,' Rod said and laughed, pulling her down to him once more. 'But you're so beautiful, so warm and loving. I'm afraid someone will steal you from me. I wish I could stay here with you forever, that I could care for you and love you the way I want...'

'Of course they won't steal me,' Rose said and kissed him, pressing herself to him as she felt a cold shiver down her spine. 'I only want you, Rod, for always.'

'I love you,' he said and held her tight. 'Remember that, Rose – whatever happens.'

Rose held on to him tightly. She thought that he was reminding her of the war. They only had two more days before they both had to report back to work, and after that...

Rose wouldn't let herself think any further. She

had made her choice and it had probably cost her the chance to train as a nurse. She could even be thrown out of the VADs for breaking the rules, but she didn't care. All she wanted now was for this horrible war to be over and Rod to come back to her. She wanted Jack to come home too, but as the weeks passed and there was no news of him, she was beginning to fear that he was dead.

* * *

Jack glanced at the kitchen clock. Louise had gone to the village earlier that morning to take some spare eggs and butter. She hoped to exchange them for flour and salt. It was a normal event, because she bartered their produce in the village shop most weeks, but she was usually home before this time. He had finished his chores ages ago and the time seemed to drag as he watched the hands on the old-fashioned mantle clock.

He had an uneasy feeling that something was wrong. Louise should have been back before this time. His spine prickled as he heard a car engine and then saw the German vehicle draw into the yard. He stood behind the curtains in the front parlour and watched. The officer who had paid them a visit once before was driving, and Louise was in the passenger seat. There was no sign of the young man who had driven the officer on a previous visit.

What on earth did Louise think she was doing accepting a lift from a German? Jack frowned as he saw the officer open the door for her. Louise hesitated and then got out. She reached inside for her basket, but before she could move away, the officer had grabbed her about the waist from behind. He wrestled her to the front of the car, forcing her forward over the bonnet. Louise screamed as he started to lift her dress. She was struggling, but the officer had her pinned against the car. He was clearly intent on raping her.

Anger surged through Jack. He didn't hesitate or stop to think. Picking up the steel fire iron, he charged out of the house and ran full pelt at the German. His fury was such that he yelled like an avenging demon and the officer turned with a startled expression on his face. He had clearly imagined himself safe from him and for a moment the officer was stunned. Jack had got to him before he could unfasten the holster at his waist.

Jack struck him across the face so hard that the blood sprayed out. He staggered forward, wounded but still reaching for his pistol, one eye spurting blood. Jack hit him again and again, the last blow so fierce that it split his skull, and a mess of pulp and blood oozed out, before he fell face down in the dry earth.

'Jack...' Louise stared down at the German's body as it twitched a few times before lying still. 'You've killed him.'

'The filthy bastard deserved it,' Jack said. He could feel the sticky blood on his hands and face where it had spurted from that last blow. 'He was trying to rape you. I had to stop him.'

'Yes, I know.' Louise caught back a sob. 'I know you had no choice but to kill him – but what do we do now? If anyone comes here...'

'When did you get into his car?'

'On my way home. He drew up beside me and practically forced me to get in.' She let the sob go. 'I shouldn't have done, but I thought it would make him angry if I didn't...'

'Did anyone see you get in the car?'

'No, I don't think so... I am sure there wasn't anyone around. It's pretty isolated on that road most of the time. I am sure that's why he waited for me there, so that no one would see...' She gave a little sob. 'He thought I would be willing, but when I said no...'

'If no one saw you with him we might get away with it,' Jack said. 'I'm going to get him back in the car.

I'll take it somewhere and leave him. I'll drive some distance down the main road...'

'What if someone sees you?'

'I'll put his cap and jacket on,' Jack said and hauled the German into a sitting position. He removed the articles and pulled the jacket over his blood-stained shirt. There was a small pool of blood where the officer had lain in the dirt. 'Clear this up and then go back to the house and lock yourself in until I come.'

'Jack... You could be killed...' Louise cried. 'If they see you with him like that they will shoot you.'

'As long as it happens away from here,' he said grimly. 'I don't want them coming here for you, Louise. What he did would be nothing compared to what they would do if they knew he was killed here.'

Louise nodded and stood back, her face white. 'I'm sorry. I love you.'

'I'll be back,' Jack said. 'With luck he didn't tell anyone where he was going or what he intended.' He hauled the officer over his shoulder and put the body into the passenger seat, then cranked the car. The engine flared to life and Jack jumped into the driving seat. He looked at Louise as he released the brake. 'Get rid of this blood in the dung heap. Make sure you cover it – and then go into the house until I get back. Stay there and hide if you have to.'

'Yes, of course.'

Jack drove off. He didn't look back. He was taking a huge risk because if the Germans stopped him, they would shoot him without hesitation. He could feel a lump of sickness in his stomach, but he wouldn't let himself think about what he'd done yet. Shooting at the enemy from the trenches was one thing; he'd shot a few face to face and bayoneted a couple in No Man's Land when in the heat of battle, but he'd never killed like that before. He had been filled with anger and hatred and he'd committed murder; there was no other word for the violence of his action. He had meant to kill the German, and he had.

He felt like spewing up his guts, but held it in. His job wasn't finished yet. He knew the memory would haunt him, but he didn't regret it. He would do it again if Louise were in danger.

Jack knew in that moment that he wasn't going to leave her. It no longer mattered whether he regained his memory or not. He could be shot as a deserter but he didn't give a damn. Louise was all that mattered. He would sit out the war at the farm and protect her as best he could from whatever came their way. Only death could part them now.

* * *

Louise cleared up the blood and then raked over the earth so that the tyre marks disappeared, before sprinkling a little hay. No one could tell from looking what had happened here a short while earlier. She felt queasy, the bile lying uneasily in her stomach, because the horror of what had happened was sharp in her mind. It was her fault for bringing the German officer here! She had not wanted to get into his car, but he had been so insistent. She suspected that if she hadn't let him bring her home he would have raped her there on the road.

Jack wouldn't have been there to save her then. Louise was torn between wishing it had happened that way and relief that it hadn't. It wouldn't have been the first time she'd been raped: the first time it had been one of her mother's lovers, and Jacques had raped her after she returned from Boulogne. Her stomach turned suddenly and she vomited, the sour taste making her hurry to the pump to wash her mouth with clean water.

She was glad that Jack had saved her, but terrified that she would lose him because of it. He had taken the German's body away in broad daylight. He could be seen by anyone, and he might be shot.

Louise thought of the alternatives. They might have buried the body somewhere – but if they did that the disturbance to the earth might have been noticed if the Germans came looking. And the car would still have had to be driven away.

Jack had acted swiftly and she knew that it was the best he could manage. She flayed herself for her stupidity in letting that German talk her into giving her a lift. The tears were trickling down her cheeks as she walked back to the house. She would bake something, because if she sat down and did nothing she would go mad.

'Jack...' she whispered, wiping her hand across her face and tasting the salt tears on her tongue. 'Jack, I am so sorry. Please come back to me... please...'

* * *

Jack drove at a normal pace. He didn't want to draw attention to himself, because the road was far from empty. He saw a farmer with a horse and wagon, and two men standing at the side of the road talking, before he'd hardly left the farm. He passed men cutting hedges and saw labourers at work in a field, but so far no Germans. How long would his luck hold? This road often had convoys moving up and down. If he ran into one of them he would be in trouble.

Jack held the feeling of sickness back and kept driving. He wanted to get as far as he could from the farm, because the trail could lead back to them if he panicked and abandoned the car too soon. He passed the village and then realised he must be getting close to the German lines because the sound of the guns was becoming much louder.

Suddenly, he heard the noise of an engine and looked up. A plane seemed to be dogging them and he realised almost instantly that it was British. It was going to attack! Jack made his decision instantly. Instead of trying to escape it, he drew to a halt at the side of the road and jumped out, hitting the ground and rolling down into a ditch at the side. He heard the sound of firing and knew that his instincts had been right.

The explosion was loud and instant. The German car had been a sitting duck and the tank was still fairly full of petrol. Jack crawled to the top of the ditch and looked over. The car was blazing. He glanced up at the sky and saw the plane do a victory roll.

'Thank you, mate,' Jack said and grinned. He crawled out of the ditch, grabbed the cap that had fallen as he took his dive and tossed it on the fire. Then he threw the jacket into the inferno and after some hesitation, his shirt.

He ran back to the ditch as the plane circled. The

pilot had seen him and was coming back for another go. Jack cursed, because he wanted to get out of here as quickly as possible. It wouldn't be very long before the Germans came to investigate, and he didn't want to be around when that happened. He began to crawl along the ditch, which was filled with brambles in places and water in others. It was the best place to hide until he could return to the road, and then he was in for a long walk home.

* * *

Louise had the meal prepared but she hadn't started to cook it yet. She glanced at the clock. Jack had been gone three hours. How much longer was he going to be? Her stomach tightened with fear, because she knew how much of a risk he was taking. They should have hidden the car and the body, taken their chance when it was dark...

She looked out of the window and then gave a cry of relief as she saw Jack coming towards the house. He had no shirt and he looked as if he was covered with mud from head to toe.

Louise ran out of the house. 'Jack...' she cried. 'I thought something must have happened...'

'I had to hide from a British plane, and then the

Germans,' Jack told her. He grinned as he saw her expression. 'There's no need to worry. They will never know what happened here today. A British plane came over and saw us on the road. I heard him and sensed that he was about to shoot us up. I jumped out and rolled into a ditch just before he scored a direct hit. The car's tank exploded, but the pilot saw me and came back looking for me. I had to stay in the ditch, because I knew the Germans would come looking. I crawled through the mud for some distance before I dared to get out and walk. I stink like hell. I think there was pig slurry in that ditch. I need a bath.'

'Oh, Jack...' Louise gave a sob that was half laughter and half pain. 'I'm so sorry. I thought they might stop you on the road. I've been terrified that they would kill you in retribution. It was all my fault...'

'No, Louise, it wasn't your fault,' Jack said and reached for her. He stopped as he remembered that he was filthy. 'I can't touch you like this. I have to get out of these clothes and wash the mud away. Don't ever blame yourself, my darling. That pig had it coming for what he tried to do to you.'

'I've been raped before,' Louise said on a sob. 'Jacques hurt me many times and once it was rape. I married him because my mother's lover forced himself on me – and he was five times worse than Jacques...'

Jack reached out to touch her face with his finger-
tips. 'Your husband won't hurt you again, Louise. If he
comes looking for you I'll do the same to him as I did
that German. I love you more than my life, more than
my honour. I would do anything for you. I'm never
going to leave you. I promise you...'

'Oh Jack...' Louise flung herself into his arms re-
gardless of the stinking mud that had smeared all over
his body. She was sobbing, clinging to him as he kissed
her. 'I don't want you to leave me. I love you.'

'We'll stay here for a while,' Jack told her as he
looked down at her face. 'We'll get some money together and then we'll leave.'

'We'll go to Paris,' Louise said, her face glowing.
'It's what I've always wanted to do.'

'I shall need papers...'

'I'll speak to Madame Bonnier,' Louise said. 'She
knows people who help to get others through the
German lines...' She saw Jack's face and stopped.
'What?'

'I thought she might be the one who told them I
was here.'

'She wouldn't! No, Jack, you are wrong. She hates
them. She will help us, I know she will.'

'If you're sure,' he said reluctantly. 'We shall go as
soon as we can, Louise. Just in case someone saw me

in that car...' He looked serious. 'We may have got away with it for the moment, but I shall never feel safe here. I'm not afraid for myself, but I keep thinking what might have happened if I hadn't been around when he...'

Louise shuddered and pressed herself closer. 'Don't talk about it,' she said, looking up at him, her face caught with passion. 'I love you, Jack. What happened – you did it for me. I know what you did and I shall never forget the risks you took.'

'I would do it again,' Jack said, looking grim. 'He deserved what he got and I'm not sorry I killed him.'

9

Rose felt the familiar ache in her stomach and knew that her courses were about to start. She had wondered if she would fall for Rod's child during the few days they had spent together. She hadn't, but it wasn't for lack of trying! She smiled as she remembered the time they'd spent together. Rod had been so loving and generous to her, and she'd felt truly loved. She was so lucky to have found someone who sincerely loved her and treated her right.

'I'll come back as soon as I can get leave,' he'd promised her when she saw him on the train. 'Never forget that I love you, Rose. Everything is going to be wonderful. I promise.'

The train let off steam and the guard started slamming doors, blowing his whistle to let the driver know it was time to leave.

Rose had felt close to tears. She'd wanted to cling to him and beg him not to leave her, but all she'd done was smile and tell him to be good.

'Don't you go chasing after them French girls,' she told him with a roguish smile. 'I'll be after you with the chopping knife if you so much as look at them.'

Rod laughed. 'You know I wouldn't,' he said. 'You're the girl for me, Rose. You always will be.'

Rose stood back as he boarded the train, waving until it disappeared out of sight. She'd stood for a while after the train had gone, feeling bereft and then, suddenly realising the time, she'd rushed out to catch a tram to take her to the hospital.

'You're five minutes late, Barlow.'

Sister greeted her with a frown as she entered the ward.

'Sorry, Sister,' Rose apologised. 'I'll stay late to make up for it.'

She had hurried to get ready for her work. Her mother's warning that she ought to tell her superior that she had married while she was on leave had been nagging at her ever since that morning. Rose knew that if she were carrying a child she would have to tell them, because otherwise they would think she was a fallen woman and she would lose her job instantly. However, now she knew that there was no child this time, Rose didn't see the need to confess.

The hospital was always busy. The wounded men continued to be shipped home, and there was no good news in the papers, nothing to make anyone think that the conflict would be over soon. Sometimes a victory helped to cheer folk up, but then there was more bad news somewhere and another influx of wounded came along. Among the Government's disclosure of huge loans to fund the war, stories of heroism and the hanging of the Brides in the Bath murderer in the summer, the year continued. In a few more months it would be Christmas again.

They had all thought the war would be over by the end of 1914. This was September 1915 and it looked less and less likely to end, though the British and French had recently made a break through some of the German lines.

Rose found the papers almost too depressing to read these days. There was always something disturbing in the news. All she wanted was for this to be over so that Rod could come back and claim her. She knew he wanted to take her back to Canada when the war finally ended. She wasn't sure how her family would feel about that, but she would face that when she came to it. Sometimes, when her back ached and her ankles swelled, she wished she could just pack up and go home.

* * *

'Sarah!' Luke called as he saw his sister in the gardens of Pelham. 'How are you? They've given me a spot of home leave again and I wanted to see my nephew.'

'Luke!' Sarah walked to him, hands outstretched. A small spaniel dog loped at her heels, its tongue hanging out. 'What a lovely surprise. I wrote to you yesterday, but it must have missed you because you were coming here. It was just gossip, to tell you that George is thriving and I think he is teething.'

'He will be grown up before you know it,' Luke said and leaned forward to kiss her cheek. 'Are you happy, Sarah? I often think of you and all that you went through before you married.'

'Yes, I am,' she told him and smiled up at him. 'Very happy. Troy is a lot stronger now. Of course there are some things he finds too difficult, but he can ride and... do most things he wants. He is content with life and so am I. We have our son and we share so much!'

'You are lucky to have found the perfect partner,' Luke said. 'I saw Marianne before I came down. She seems discontented and her temper does not improve. I felt sorry for Barney.'

'Poor Barney,' Sarah said. 'He loves her so much. I think she does care for him, but not as he loves her. It is sad really, don't you think so?' Sarah's eyes were intent on his face. 'Have you found anyone special yet?'

'Me?' Luke shrugged. 'I shall marry when all this is over, do my duty and provide the family with an heir – you know the sort of thing.'

'You shouldn't marry unless you fall in love,' Sarah told him seriously. 'I'm very fond of you, Luke. I should like you to be happy, as I am. Marianne married on the rebound and look what happened to her. Please don't throw your life away just because you think it is your duty.'

'Yes, well, it was different for Marianne. She threw her chances away. I haven't found anyone I particularly like yet.'

Sarah hesitated, then, 'I used to think you liked Rose Barlow. I suppose that was silly of me, but I really like her. We're friends. I don't see her often, but she writes to me. Did you know she had married a Canadian? He is an RFOC officer like you.'

A tiny nerve flicked at the corner of Luke's eye. 'Mother mentioned it in one of her letters. She seemed to think Rose had done well for herself.'

'I think he must come from a good family,' Sarah told him. 'Rose says he wants her to go to Canada after the war. She hasn't told her mother yet, because she doesn't want to upset her. It is sad that her brother has gone missing, isn't it?'

'Yes, I was sorry about that,' Luke agreed. 'I tried to find out more, but there wasn't much to discover. I think he is a bit of a hero, but that isn't much consolation for his family.'

'No, of course not. They want him back.' Sarah linked her arm through his. 'Come up to the house and see Father and Troy – and your nephew. You will be surprised how he has grown.'

'You call Lord Pelham Father,' Luke said with a little frown. 'I know you visited Mother this summer. Have you forgiven her and Father for the way they behaved to you?'

'Yes, I have forgiven them,' Sarah said. 'Things were still a little strained with Mother. I do not think she will ever entirely forgive me, but Father seems different.'

'You did know he was ill?'

'Yes, Marianne told me. He seemed fine when we were there?'

'He is almost his old self, but it was a warning, Sarah. He needs to take care, but of course he won't listen to the doctor. He says it is all nonsense.'

'Mother would miss him if anything happened...'

'Yes. I hope he will hang on for a few years yet. I feel guilty at leaving all the estate business to him. I ought to be there helping, but what can I do? I had thought the war might only last a few months but it drags on and on...'

'You are doing what you have to do,' Sarah assured him and hugged his arm. 'It's lovely to have you here for a visit, Luke – but your duty is to the country while the war continues.'

'It shows little sign of ending,' Luke said gloomily. 'I never wanted any of it, but I've done rather well it seems. They gave me another gong... Ridiculous thing!'

'Oh Luke! No one told me. We are so proud of you.'

'I don't feel as if I've done anything particularly heroic,' Luke said. 'I fly over the German lines and do a bit of business every now and then – bagged a German staff car once but one of the beggars got away. We're all doing our bit, but some of the chaps aren't so lucky.'

'It must be awful when you lose a friend?'

'Yes. Squadron Leader Henshaw was shot down a couple of days before I was sent on leave. He managed to get back to our side and got out alive – but the poor devil has terrible burns. It might have been better if he'd died quickly.'

'Luke!'

Luke stared at her, horrified at his mistake. 'Sorry, Sarah. I had forgotten that Troy was burned. I never think of him that way – but he was lucky. He had you. I don't think Henshaw has anyone much...'

'Then he is to be pitied,' Sarah said. 'Oh, don't let's talk about it any more. Come and see your nephew...'

* * *

Luke was thoughtful as he stood waiting for his train the next day. Visiting Sarah had made him feel better about things. He had been pretty cut up about Henshaw, because they had parted on bad terms that last day. Perhaps it was because he didn't care much what happened to himself that he'd been having the devil's own luck these past months. He had notched up one of the highest numbers of hits on enemy kites.

Most of the chaps had accepted that he was a bit of a loner. They had stopped asking him to go drinking with them, which was okay with Luke. He'd been angry, a little bitter, and that had led to a quarrel with Henshaw. Luke regretted it now. He should never have let himself be annoyed by what happened at Lillian's house that day. He hadn't been able to bring himself to visit Henshaw before he left on his home visit. But he would visit Lillian and see if she was all right for money when he got back.

Luke had been offered promotion to Squadron Leader, but he'd turned it down. He was better at following orders than giving them, though he had disobeyed and gone off on his own in the past. Henshaw had threatened that he would ground Luke if he did it again, but he hadn't listened. He felt guilty, because he knew that if he had been sitting on Henshaw's wing that last day he might have prevented what happened. Henshaw hadn't seen the bandits coming and he'd taken a hit from the rear. If Luke had been there he might have warned his leader.

He thrust the thought from his mind. What had happened had happened. There was nothing he could do to change things, however much he might wish them different.

* * *

'Barlow,' Sister called to Rose just as she was preparing to leave at the end of her shift that day. 'Matron asked me to tell you she would like you to go to her office before you leave.'

Sister seemed a bit odd, and Rose felt a spasm in her stomach. She wondered what she'd done wrong as she hurried off to comply with the summons. As far as she knew, she hadn't made any mistakes and she hadn't been late for weeks. Perhaps another appointment had come through, though she'd been told that she would be sent a letter this time.

She stood outside the office and knocked, her pulse racing as she waited for the invitation to enter. When she went in Matron was busy writing, but she looked up almost at once.

'Oh... Barlow,' she said. 'Thank you for coming. I have something to tell you. Would you please sit down?'

Rose had never been invited to sit before. Her stomach lurched and she felt sick, because she knew something awful was coming. They must have found out she was married... but then she wouldn't have been invited to sit!

'Is something wrong, Matron?'

'Yes, I am rather afraid it is. You did not tell us you had married, Rose. I think I know why. You wished to continue to serve and thought you would be dismissed...'

'Yes...' Rose swallowed hard. Why was Matron looking at her that way? It was unnerving and it frightened her. 'I know I should have said – my mother told me it was the right thing to do, but I thought I could work for a bit longer.'

'Had you told me I should have reprimanded you, but I should not have dismissed you,' Matron told her in a gentle voice that made Rose start to tremble. 'I appreciate girls like you, Rose – and we need you.' She stood up and came round the desk. 'I am very sorry but there is no way I can make this easier for you. I have been informed that Flying Officer Rodney Carne was killed in action three days ago. He gave your name to be informed as the next of kin...'

Rose trembled; she gave a sob of despair. 'No! He can't be dead! He's missing in action, that's it – isn't it?' Rose saw the sympathy in the older woman's eyes and her hand flew to her face. 'He's dead... How?'

'His aeroplane was shot down. It crashed in flames. He did not get out. I am informed it was swift. I am so very sorry, Rose... so very sorry...'

'No! No, he can't be...' Rose flung herself at the other woman, screaming and beating at her with her fists. 'He isn't dead. You're lying to me to punish me...'

Matron caught her wrists, then she pulled Rose to

her. She was very strong and she controlled Rose, holding her in her arms as she wept. 'I am sorry. I wish I could change things for you, my dear. This is a terrible, wicked war and I hate having to give news like this to my girls.'

Rose sobbed against her shoulder, but the fight had gone out of her. Matron stroked her hair, crooning words of sympathy. 'I know it hurts, Rose. You must go home to your family...'

Rose drew away, looking at her stubbornly. 'Are you dismissing me?'

'No, I am giving you three weeks' compassionate leave. I know you broke the rules but I have no wish to make things worse for you. Go home to your family and come back to us when you feel better.'

'I shall never feel better,' Rose said, and her face was cold, proud as she raised her head. 'Thank you for not dismissing me, Matron. I shall try to make it up to you, but I don't want time off. I would rather work...'

'You will not be able to do your work properly,' Matron said, and suddenly she was the commanding person who ruled her staff with a rod of iron. 'You will go home to your family, Barlow. You will return in three weeks and I wish to hear no more of this – and that is an order.'

'Yes, Matron.'

Rose was glad that Matron had become her old self. Pity was soul destroying. She could handle an order better. 'I am sorry to have caused you so much trouble.'

She turned and walked from the office, her back straight. Inside, she was breaking into little pieces but no one would have known from the look on her face as she walked from the hospital, passing people without seeing them. She felt cold and empty, numb from distress and disbelief.

* * *

Rose made a telephone call to Pelham House. She asked to speak to Mrs Troy Pelham and after a few minutes Sarah answered.

'Rose – is that you?'

'Could I come to stay for a few days? Matron told me to go home, but I can't face them for the moment...' Rose's voice caught on a sob. 'Is it all right to come?'

'You know you are always welcome,' Sarah said at once. 'What is wrong? You sound upset, Rose?'

'Rod's plane went down in flames. He didn't get out.'

'Oh, Rose!' Sarah cried. 'I am so sorry. Of course you must come here, for as long as you wish.'

'I need a few days before I tell Ma. You understand how I feel, Sarah.'

'Yes, I do, though I was lucky,' Sarah said. 'Troy came back to me. I suppose there is no chance that Rod did get out?'

'None. His plane exploded as it hit the ground and he was still inside...' Rose couldn't hold back the sob of despair. 'I keep thinking of him on fire... burning...'

'You mustn't,' Sarah told her firmly. 'It would have been quick, Rose. He was probably dead before the plane hit the ground. Otherwise he would have bailed out.'

'I would like to believe that...'

'You have to, Rose. You mustn't torture yourself. Come to me as quickly as you can and we'll talk. I shall be waiting for you at the station.'

'Yes, I shall come. I'm catching the next train.'

Rose hung up. She was close to tears but comforted by her friend's words. It would be easier to be with Sarah than her family, at least until the raw pain had begun to ease. She loved her mother and her father but they were still grieving for Jack. Rose couldn't take the burden of her grief to her mother. In a few days she would feel stronger. She needed to cry her heart out, but then she would put this behind her and move on.

* * *

Louise showed the letter to Jack. It had just come and was from her lawyer. In answer to her request to sell the house in Boulogne, he had written a long explanation of why it was impossible just now.

'Do you trust him?' Jack asked as he returned the letter after reading it.

'Yes, I think so. I asked him to let the house. I didn't realise that I wouldn't be able to sell until the tenant was ready to leave.'

'The law is a funny thing,' Jack said. 'If you can sell the farm stock we will have something to tide us over until we can find work.'

'I have some money, but I wanted my own café.'

'I know, but if you gain experience from working in a café first it may help when you open your own.' He saw the doubts in Louise's face. 'Would you rather stay here for a while longer?'

'I'm not sure. I would sell the land but it belongs to Jacques. Without proof of his death I can't expect anyone to buy – though I've had an offer for the cows and we can sell the pigs easily. I might give the ducks to Madeline Bonnier. She has been a good friend and she likes duck eggs.'

'Think about it a little longer,' Jack suggested. 'I haven't got my papers yet.'

'Madame Bonnier said there is someone you must meet. They call him Henri, though I doubt it is his name. He wants to talk to you before he gets your papers for you.'

'I suppose that is fair enough. I have no money to give him. I don't know what the cigarette case is worth. It may not be enough.'

'I have some money...'

'You will need what you have. Perhaps he will allow me to pay some other way.'

Louise shrugged her shoulders. She did not know the leader of these men who called themselves freedom fighters. She would pay if she had to, but Jack was right. They needed what little they had for the journey and to support them until they found work. They would be strangers in Paris and they might not find work at once. It would be best to wait a little longer until they got more money together.

* * *

'This place is so peaceful,' Rose said, glancing at Sarah as they walked in the gardens. They were both wearing coats and scarves because it was cold, the grass still crusted with a fine dusting of frost. The trees and bushes looked as if they'd had icing sugar sprinkled over them, and Rose's nose was red. The weather had turned quickly and this cold snap had taken everyone by surprise.

'I'm very lucky to live here,' Sarah agreed. 'Trenwith is a lovely house but it is too big and the gardens are very formal. At least, they used to be. I noticed that some of them are becoming overgrown when I visited.'

'Lady Trenwith has a problem finding men to keep the gardens tidy,' Rose said. 'The last of the younger ones went when the government had a big recruitment drive. There are only a few older ones and the men who were needed on the land, but they don't get time to tend the gardens. Ma says she has noticed a lot of changes – a drop in standards.'

'I told Father he should close Trenwith and live in the dower house or in London for the duration of the war, but neither he nor Mother would hear of it. I know they have closed some of the rooms and covered things with dustsheets, but it is so expensive to heat the place. I'm sure they must feel the emptiness since Marianne and I left home.' Sarah looked thoughtful. 'I don't think things will ever be the same as they were before the war – do you?' Rose shook her head.

'Lady Trenwith will cling to the old ways for as long as she can. She told Ma that she thought the servants would return to their places after the war.'

'I know she clings to the belief but I think she will be disappointed,' Sarah said and shook her head. 'Luke says he doesn't want it to be the same as it was. He wants to make changes, bring Trenwith into the modern age. He may get his way if...' She broke off on a sigh, looking anxious.

'You mean if he comes home at the end?' Rose nodded as Sarah remained silent. 'No one knows for sure the way things are out there. Have you seen him recently?'

'He visited for a couple of days on his last leave. I don't think he is very happy. He joined up because he believed it was his duty, but he doesn't much like what he does.'

'I thought he was a war artist?'

'He did those posters of Jack, but he hasn't said much about his art recently. They tell us he is an air ACE. He has shot down more German pilots than most of the others in his squadron and been decorated for it, but he hates talking about it.'

'Mr Luke wasn't meant for killing,' Rose said and

smiled sadly. 'He always seemed a real gentleman to me. A lot of gentlemen aren't a bit nice, if you don't mind my saying so.'

'I agree with you,' Sarah said and laughed. 'Some of Sir James's friends aren't a bit nice – but Lord Pelham's friends are nicer.'

'You see the worst side of them when you're in service.'

'Yes, I suppose you must,' Sarah agreed. 'Rod was a gentleman, wasn't he?'

'He had lovely manners and he always treated me as if I were a princess.' Rose's smile was a bit wobbly but she could talk about Rod now without crying. 'I was lucky to meet him, Sarah. At least I know what love is all about. What we had didn't last long – nowhere near long enough. I thought we had forever.'

'Yes, we all think that,' Sarah said and squeezed her waist. 'It isn't fair that you should lose Rod so soon. I wish I could do something to help you.'

'You have helped. Just being here with you in this lovely place has made me feel able to face up to what happened. I can go home now.' She looked round at the gardens, which were beautiful even though the summer glory of the flowerbeds was over.

'Your mother will want to comfort you. She must be so worried about your brother.'

'I think of him all the time. I believe my father has begun to accept that Jack won't come home, but I still feel that he is alive. It's foolish I know, but I am sure I would know if he were dead.'

'Yes, I understand what you mean,' Sarah said. 'I worry about Luke. So many pilots are being shot down over there. I can't help wondering...' She broke off and shook her head. 'No, I shouldn't tempt fate. He has been lucky so far.'

'He will be all right. It's the new ones with hardly any training that go down quickly, so they say. Luke has been there from the beginning.'

'Yes, I know.'

Neither of them mentioned that Rod Carne had been an experienced pilot.

'Shall we go and have tea?' Sarah asked. 'I am sure Troy and Father are waiting for us...'

They began walking up to the house, arms about each other's waists, Sarah's little dog trailing at their heels.

* * *

'I heard you were asking about Henshaw?' Squadron Leader Mackintosh arched his brows at Luke. He had just walked into the mess room, where Luke was sitting with a glass of whisky in his hand staring at nothing in particular.

'Yes, sir,' Luke said and stood up. 'I heard he had been taken home to England.'

'That was the plan but unfortunately he died on the way over. I have been asked to contact you. You knew him as well as anyone, Trenwith. Would you write to his family?'

'I didn't know him that well.'

'The Big Brass seem to think differently. I can't claim to have known him at all. See to it, will you?'

'Yes, if you insist.' Luke was reluctant. He hadn't had that kind of relationship with his late squadron leader.

'I do – and you will be flying rear guard tomorrow. I know your reputation and I don't want any diving off on your own, Trenwith. You've got enough notches on your guns, give some of the others a chance. I need my experienced pilots to keep watch over the young idiots they keep sending us.'

'They are keen, sir – and most of them have only had a few hours' training.'

'You are the most experienced man on the team. In my opinion you should have been leading it, but since you refused the chance you will please do as I ask.'

Luke inclined his head. He had despised Henshaw

at times for his drinking, but the man had been human; this one was cold and clinical. Luke didn't like him, but he would obey orders, though if he saw the chance for an attack going begging he couldn't ignore it.

He frowned as he left the room without finishing his drink. He had to write a letter that he would find hellishly difficult. Before he could do it, he would have to visit Lillian. He had been putting it off, but she was the one who really knew Henshaw. Luke needed to talk to her before he could face that letter...

* * *

'He says that he will come here tonight. You must meet him by the haystack,' Madame Bonnier said to Jack. 'I do not know what he wants from you but I think there is something.'

'Thank you,' Jack said. 'Have you asked him if he has news of your son, Madame?'

'The hostages were taken to the Chateau Lorraine,' she said, and her face was grey with grief. 'No one can get in or out. The security is so tight. If my son is alive...' She shook her head. 'Who knows? It may be better for him if he died quickly. He could not have stood the torture.'

'He was a child,' Jack said to comfort her. 'There were others the Germans would suspect more.'

'Perhaps...' A flash of pain showed in her eyes. 'I wish they had taken me, but I have my other children to think of. Their father went to fight and I have not heard from him in months. If he does not come back I must be there for the young ones.'

'You must think of the children who rely on you,' Jack said. 'Thank you for what you have done for us. It was a risk talking to these men, because the Germans could be watching any of us.'

'You have been good for Louise. Be careful when you speak to Henri – if that is his name, which I doubt. I am not sure you can trust him.'

'Thank you for the warning,' Jack said. 'Louise wants to leave and I cannot travel without papers. I have no choice but to meet him this evening.'

'Just be careful,' Madame Bonnier said. 'For Louise's sake.'

Jack nodded, watching as she left the house. He had wondered if Madame Bonnier had told the Germans that he was here in the hope of learning something of her son, but she seemed genuine enough. He knew that some people would use information to buy themselves favours. If it wasn't Madame Bonnier it must have been someone else...

'Will you go? To meet Henri...' Louise's voice broke into his thoughts.

'Yes, I must,' Jack told her. 'I think we have to trust him. I need those papers. Besides, if he meant to lure me into a trap he would have forced me to go to him. By coming here he shows trust...'

'What do you think he wants from you?'

'I have no idea,' Jack said. 'Somehow I don't think it is money.'

'No...' Louise shivered. 'Be careful, Jack. I'm frightened.'

'You mustn't be. As soon as I get those papers we can leave here – go to Paris.'

Jack put his arms about her. He held her tight, stroking her hair, but his expression was serious. He hadn't got the papers yet and he was wondering what he needed to do to earn them. If it were just a question of money Henri would not have asked him to a meeting.

* * *

Jack knew that he had no choice but to agree. Henri had him by a delicate part of his anatomy and a refusal would bring certain retribution.

'Why me?' he asked, his eyes hooded, his gaze

steely. 'I don't understand why you need me on this mission.'

'We need more men. We've lost too many in the past few months.'

Jack frowned. 'Supposing I said I wasn't interested? I'm not sure I should be of use to you.'

'You pulled one of our people free of the truck that blew up that day we attacked the ammunition dump. He would have died but for you – and I saw you driving a German staff car. I heard that a car burned out on the road and a German officer was thought to have died in the fire. I am less certain how he died. You have hidden talents, Georges. You can help us – or perhaps you would rather the Germans knew that you are not quite what you appear?'

Jack registered the threat. 'And if I do help you?'

'We'll provide you with what you need.'

'So when does this raid take place?'

'Tomorrow. We leave at dawn to be there in time. When the British attack the chateau, we raid a building at the rear. The Germans have prisoners there. One of them is important to the British. We take him out with us.'

'How shall we know him?'

'He's British like you. They need him back in London. He has important information. His code name is

Red Fox but he speaks hardly any French, though they say his German is good.'

'He is a spy for the British – and that is why you need me.' Jack nodded his understanding. 'I see. All right. I'm with you, but it's just this once – agreed?'

'We need men to help us. You have a duty to help us – unless you prefer to go home?'

'I have no idea where that is,' Jack told him. 'I'll help you tomorrow and then we'll see...'

* * *

'I don't see why you have to go with them,' Louise objected when Jack told her. 'You're not one of them. You're not even French.'

'I was seen driving that German car, and apparently I dragged one of their number clear of the explosion when that truck went up. I don't remember it but Henri thinks I would be a useful addition to their group.'

'But we were going to leave here – find work in Paris.'

'We will,' Jack promised. 'I have to do some favours for Henri first, that's all. As soon as I've earned my papers we'll leave. I promise you. I can't just walk away from this, Louise.'

Louise looked doubtful. Jack took her in his arms and kissed her. She clung to him, returning his kiss and then drew back.

'Supposing something happens? You could be killed...'

'I shan't be leading the attack, believe me. They want me because one of the prisoners is British. Once we've located him my job is done.'

'Promise me you will come back!'

'I promise,' Jack said and looked thoughtful. 'There will be other prisoners released. Perhaps Pierre Bonnier...'

'Jacques could be there...' Louise's face was white. 'What if he comes here?' She pulled at Jack's coat, her eyes reflecting her fear. 'What shall we do if he is still alive?'

'He won't hurt you,' Jack promised. 'No one is going to hurt you ever again. If he tried I would kill him.'

'Jack...' Louise looked at him in distress. 'I wish you weren't going...'

'I have to go, Louise, but I'll be back.' He kissed her once more, cutting off her protests. 'I have to leave now. Stay close to the house. If the Germans come to the farm, go inside and lock the doors. Don't open them until I get back.'

Jack left the house knowing that Louise was upset and angry because he'd broken his promise not to leave her. She hated the idea of him risking his life to help rescue some prisoners from the chateau, but Jack was excited despite his initial reluctance.

He had put all thought of returning to England from his mind, because he couldn't desert Louise, but this was different. He had to earn those papers somehow and it was a way of finding himself again. Since the day he'd killed that German he'd been haunted by an odd fear that crept into his mind despite his determination to thrust it out. Jack wasn't sure what kind of a man he really was, but he had a feeling that he was about to find out.

* * *

Luke fastened his leather helmet strap under his chin and pulled on his goggles, heading for his plane. Their briefing had been clear. They were going to attack behind enemy lines. The Chateau Lorraine had been identified as an enemy stronghold. It was from here that they were pushing the drive for a new advance. The British were going to back up an attack by ground forces, which would be led by local men, but included men from other groups that had come together for this special operation. The details had come through secret channels, which were also used to get British soldiers and airmen that had been downed through enemy lines.

'Remember, Trenwith,' Mackintosh said, holding Luke's arm as he was about to climb up into his plane. 'I want you bringing up the rear today. No heroics. You are a shepherd looking after your flock.'

'Understood,' Luke said and climbed into the cockpit. He went through the routine checks and then gave the thumbs up to his ground crew. His mind was not truly on the job as he followed the squadron as it took formation. He could not stop thinking about the way Lillian had sobbed in his arms, begging him to forgive her.

'He was the father of my child,' she told Luke as she wept against his shoulder. 'We met before the war and he promised to marry me, but then he went home and I didn't hear from him. After my child was born I had to... work to feed us. Michael promised to look after me...'

Luke felt a spurt of anger. His guilt over Henshaw's death suddenly evaporated. The way his squadron leader had behaved seemed even more despicable now that Luke knew the truth.

'He should have made provision for you and his

child. I'll give you some money for now, but I'll make sure his family know that he has a daughter.'

Luke had written the letter when he returned to quarters the previous evening. Henshaw's family might be shocked when they learned of their son's illegitimate child, but it might help to ease the pain of their loss to know that they had a grandchild. Luke had not written in anger but with honesty. Lillian deserved something for the child if not for herself.

Luke's plane was climbing into a clear blue sky. He followed the formation as they headed for their destination. Attack from the air was a new form of warfare. It could be devastating, especially when backed up with a ground assault.

Luke wondered why the chateau was important, but it hardly mattered. He had been ordered to keep his eye out for the young pilots, some of whom were on their first mission over enemy positions. It was just a matter of trying to get as many of them back home in one piece as far as he could see. He would simply ride shotgun and see this mission out for what it was worth.

* * *

It was mid-morning when the planes arrived. Jack and the others had been lying in the woods just beyond the chateau for what must have been more than an hour. The first wave of planes dropped several explosive devices, which caused fire and confusion down below. A siren wailed from within the chateau as the Germans rushed out into the courtyard and responded to the attack with guns. The next wave of planes began shooting as they dive-bombed the startled enemy. The chateau was old and built solidly of stone; from the amount of chaos and confusion, it seemed the Germans had not expected an attack, because the walls were too stout to crumble easily even with such an attack.

'Let's go!'

Henri gave the order to attack from the rear. The chateau grounds backed onto the woods and were protected by high walls, but the stonework was old and, unlike the chateau itself, in some places it had been neglected and was beginning to crumble. The Germans had not bothered to repair the weak spot, believing their patrols sufficient protection. However, with the air attack diverting attention, the guards had left their posts. Henri's group soon had their grappling irons and rope ladders in place. The men swarmed over them, Jack one of the first to land the other side.

He had forgotten his promise to Louise as Henri pointed out the building where the prisoners were housed.

The sounds of shouting, screaming and gunfire were coming mostly from the front of the chateau, smoke pouring from somewhere in that area. The building they were targeting should have been well protected according to their intelligence, but the guards had rushed to the front when the attack started.

Henri shot at the stout door but the lock held until he and Jack put their shoulders against it. The wood splintered during the second charge and they thrust it open, rushing inside, guns at the ready. The stench hit them at once. Screams of fear, moaning and cries for help came from all around them. Jack halted, looking round at men, women and children who had been herded into what was obviously meant as a storeroom. There was scarcely any light and the air was stale, apart from that coming in at the open door.

'Red Fox!' Jack called in English. 'Anyone answer to that name?' A dozen voices answered in French, but among the cries for help Jack picked up a faint English voice. He spun round looking for the source. A man was sitting on a bale of straw. He raised his arm, clearly too weak to rise. Jack went to him.

'You're Red Fox?'

'Yes. Thank God you've come. I couldn't have held out much longer.'

Jack took in the situation at a glance. The man looked as if he had endured starvation at the least and perhaps torture. He was never going to walk out of here on his own. Jack thrust his rifle at one of the other freedom fighters and turned to the prisoner.

'I'm going to carry you on my back. Do you think you can cling on to me?'

'Yes. Just get me out of this hellhole.'

Jack hoisted him on to his back and someone gave him a heave up. His arms locked around Jack's neck. Jack folded the sick man's legs around his waist and held them. The building was beginning to clear as the prisoners were hurried out into the fresh air.

'Take him straight to the wall,' Henri barked at Jack. 'We'll cover your back.'

Outside, the prisoners were staggering about in the sudden blinding light of day, confused and bewildered by the noise and smoke. Some of them couldn't see, because they had been confined in the darkness for so long, and they walked with their arms outstretched in front of them, begging for help. Jack headed for the wall. Henri's men had been busy and had managed to break through a part of the crumbling wall so that it was now possible to scramble over it. The strongest prisoners were clambering over it or up the rope ladders. As Jack reached the wall he heard the sound of voices yelling, and then the shooting started. Glancing back, he saw that three German guards had arrived. They were shooting the prisoners who were stumbling blindly, lost and confused. Henri's men started shooting back. He could hear yelling and knew the three Germans would shortly be reinforced. There was no time to lose.

'Come on,' someone urged Jack. 'He's the one we want. We have to get him away. Leave the rest to Henri.' Jack hesitated and then climbed over the wall, assisted by two of the freedom fighters. A part of him wanted to go back for the poor devils who were getting slaughtered, but that wasn't his job. He had to get Red Fox through the woods to where the truck was waiting to take him where he was going...

* * *

Louise became increasingly worried as the day went on. She had kept herself busy doing the chores that Jack usually did for her. She found it hard work, but she worked her anger off as she shovelled muck, and fed and watered the animals. This was what it had been like before Jack came. If he didn't return to the farm her life would be nothing but work. The thought made her feel like weeping, but she wouldn't. She refused to cry. She wouldn't stay here without Jack. But what was there left for her without him? She had come to rely on him, to love him...

Louise went up to the house after she had finished her chores. She wasn't going to let herself think of a future without Jack. He had promised her he wouldn't take risks. Surely he would come back to her as soon as he could? He had to because she couldn't bear it if he didn't.

Since the day Jack had killed the German for her sake she had lived in fear that retribution would fall on them. She longed for the time when they could go to Paris and make a new life.

Please come back... Please come back...

The words played in her mind over and over again as the afternoon wore on. Where was he? Surely they must have done whatever they had to do by now? Something must have happened to Jack...

Louise was restless. Jack had made her promise to stay close to the house, but she couldn't settle. The chateau was too far away for her to walk to, but she would walk to the road and see if there was any sign of anyone coming...

* * *

Luke was glad when he saw the signal to disengage and return to base. The Germans hadn't been expecting an attack so far inside their lines, and they had wreaked havoc on the ancient house. It was a shame really, Luke thought as he circled, taking up his place at the rear of the formation. It wasn't destroyed, but it was badly damaged in places. However, their mission had been successful. For once no one had been hit and they were returning with all planes intact. He smiled because everything had gone so well and he'd done his job of protecting the rear.

They had been flying for a while when he saw the German fighter planes coming at them. It had taken them a while to respond, but they had arrived in time to spoil the celebrations. Mackintosh was already engaging and so were some of the others. Luke itched to break formation and go after one of them on his own. Mindful of his leader's orders, he stayed at the rear. He saw a German plane swoop on the British plane just ahead of him and diverted to assist, his guns blazing. The plane caught fire and spiralled down, taking the unfortunate pilot with him. He raised his hand to salute the young pilot and received a frantic signal in return from one of the others. Realising too late that a formerly unseen bandit had sneaked up behind him, he swooped off to his right hoping to out fly him, but the German followed, tagging onto Luke's rear.

For some minutes they played tag as Luke used all his skill to keep out of his sights, and then the German got the drop on him and fired. Luke knew he'd taken a slight hit to the engine somewhere, but there was no fire and he didn't lose height. He pulled the plane out of a dive and then saw his squadron leader behind the German plane. Mackintosh fired and the German's plane became a fireball. Luke raised his hand in salute, then made a signal that he was heading for home. Mackintosh nodded his understanding. Luke was hit and he couldn't hang around to help win this dogfight. He had to get as far as he could before the damage forced him to land.

* * *

Jack hitched a lift part of the way home with a farmer. He had taken leave of the freedom fighters as soon as his part of the job was over. He had no intention of hanging around waiting for the Germans to send out patrols looking for the escaped prisoners.

After his lift came to an end, he was forced to walk the rest of the way. He knew it would be late in the afternoon by the time he got back to the farm. Louise was going to be anxious. He was sorry that he'd had to put her through this, but he wasn't sorry he'd done it. The slaughter of those prisoners, who had been too weak or ill to escape, had taken away any guilt he might have felt over the German officer he'd killed. The man had deserved it anyway, but the whole thing had left a nasty taste in Jack's mouth, because he had wondered if he was a natural killer. He knew now that he wasn't a murderer by nature. He had killed to save Louise and because it was the only thing he could do to keep them both safe. He would do it again if he had to, but he didn't enjoy killing or seeing people killed. He felt the burden lift, giving him a sense of freedom.

He knew he was getting near to the road where he needed to turn off for the farm when he heard the strange noise. It was a whining, stuttering sound that made him look up at the sky. The plane was flying dangerously low, only just skimming some trees. He realised it must be out of control even as the noise stopped and the machine seemed to just drop the last few feet from the sky like a stone.

Jack was running before it hit the ground with an almighty crash. Flames started to shoot from the engine immediately, but Jack was there. He saw the man inside. He was slumped forward, obviously knocked unconscious by the crash. Jack didn't stop to think. He ran to the plane, scrambled up into the cockpit and dragged the pilot free. He could feel the heat and smell the sizzle of burning, but it wasn't until he had dragged the pilot well clear of the plane that he re-alised the back of his coat was on fire. He tore it off and threw himself on the ground, rolling back and forth until he was sure nothing else was burning. The pilot was still unconscious as Jack got to his feet once more and started to pull him away from the plane, which was now blazing like an inferno.

'Let me help you! We have to get him away before it explodes...'

Jack stared at Louise as she grabbed hold of one arm. His mind rejected the fact that she was here when she was supposed to be in the house with the doors locked, but her efforts helped and they hoisted the pilot to his feet, hauling him away to the side of the field. They were still close enough to feel the blast when the explosion came. It rocked Jack and threw Louise to the ground.

'Are you all right?' Jack asked as she sat looking up at him for a moment. 'You shouldn't have done it. You might have been killed.'

'You can talk – and you promised not to be a hero,' Louise said and glared at him. 'Come on, we have to get him away from the road before the Germans come to investigate.'

'I can carry him. Give me a boost and I'll take him over my shoulder,' Jack said. 'Just push now – that's right. Now get going! I'm right behind you...'

got him away from the road before the Germans come
to investigate.'

'I can carry him. Give me a boost and I'll take him

10

'It looks as if we got him out in time,' Jack said as they
laid the pilot on the mat in the kitchen. Louise placed
a cushion under his head as Jack removed the leather
helmet and goggles. He sat back on his heels, staring
at the man's face. It was streaked with blood and black
smears but there did not seem to be any sign of burning. 'Good grief... I think...' He shook his head as
Louise brought a bowl of water. 'Let's get some of this
muck off...' Jack wrung a cloth in the water and wiped
the pilot's face. 'He cut his face as he fell forward on
impact and there's a blow to the side of his head,
which must have knocked him out...'

'He brought the plane down in a controlled
manner so that the impact was minimised,' Louise

agreed. 'It was a brave thing to do. I was watching it until I saw you run towards it. That was a stupid thing to do, Jack. You could have been killed. You've singed your hair and your hands...'

Jack glanced at his hands. He had hardly been aware of the stinging pain, but now he saw that there were burn marks on both of them, though far less than he might have expected. He pulled away as Louise tried to take his hand.

'No, leave that for later. We have to make sure he doesn't have more injuries and we need to get him upstairs.'

'We should get his clothes off and burn them in the stove,' Louise said. 'The fire will have been seen and the Germans may search for him.'

'They won't know he is missing the way that thing went up just after we got him clear,' Jack said. 'I've looked for signs of broken limbs but I can't find any. Unless there are injuries inside that we can't see, I think it is just the blow to his head.'

'We can't risk fetching the doctor yet,' Louise told him. 'He will just have to take his chances.'

Jack turned his head to look at her. 'I know him. I remember him. I remember everything. His name is Luke Trenwith and his father owned the estate where I worked in the stables. He is a good man, Louise. We have to do all we can for him.'

Louise stared at him in silence for a moment. 'Take him upstairs while I burn his things, Jack. We'll see how he is for a few hours – but if he seems worse I'll go for the doctor once it's dark...'

'Yes.' Jack pulled Luke up and hoisted him over his shoulder. 'We'll talk later, when I've got him settled.'

'Yes...' Her face was white, her eyes wide with fear. 'Does this mean you will have to leave?'

'I don't know what it means just yet,' Jack told her. 'But I shan't leave without you, Louise. I told you. I love you and for me that is everything...'

Louise nodded. She bent to gather the clothes and the leather helmet as Jack went up the stairs, pushing them into the stove and holding them down with a poker until they caught. She shut the door as the smoke billowed out, tears stinging her eyes. The leather helmet and jacket were making a horrible smell as they burned, but that wasn't the reason for her tears.

Jack loved her, but could he stay now that he knew who he was and where he belonged? Would he want to go home to his family?

* * *

Jack came down to the kitchen an hour later to find Louise pounding dough for bread. He could see that she was distressed and he went to put his arms about her, holding her close. He felt her relax against him as he stroked her hair, kissing the top of her head. He kissed her neck, feeling her tremble and arch into him.

'You always smell so good,' he told her. 'Don't distress yourself, my love. I promised I would never leave you, and I'm a man who keeps his word – as much as possible anyway.' He grinned as she looked up at him. 'I couldn't let him burn, Louise. Even though I didn't know who he was, I had to do what I could for him. I have to help him now.'

'I know that,' Louise said and smiled. 'I was shocked and frightened when I saw you go in there, and your hair...' She touched the front where it had sizzled, leaving an odd looking patch on the front and side of his head. 'You could have died with him.'

'Neither of us died,' Jack told her with a smile. 'I think he will be okay without a doctor, Louise. He has a couple of small burns on his neck but the fire had hardly started when I got there. If I hadn't seen him before he actually came down that last bit... But we got him out and I think he has been lucky. I can't find anything broken and there's no blood on his body, no damage that I can see. He'll probably be bruised all over, but if he comes round he should be fine.'

'He banged his head,' Louise said. 'He may not remember...'

'You mean he might lose his memory the way I did?' Jack frowned. 'It is a possibility, but don't count on it. When he comes round he will know me.'

'I wish he hadn't crashed...' Louise cried. 'You will have to go. He will tell you it is your duty to your family... Your sister...' She stared at him wildly. 'The girl in the picture is your sister, Rose. You told me about her that night in Boulogne. I didn't tell you because I didn't want you to leave. I'm sorry...'

'Shush...' Jack kissed her, touching her face tenderly. 'I've been remembering for a long time, Louise. It was all coming back, piece by piece. I couldn't fit it all together until I saw Luke's face, but it was only a matter of time.' He brushed the tears from her cheeks with his thumb. 'It isn't going to be easy, but I promise I won't leave you behind...'

'Promise me,' Louise said, clinging to him desperately. 'I was so lonely today, so afraid. If you died I should have nothing to live for.'

Jack drew her closer. 'We have something special,' he whispered against her ear. 'Nothing can change that, Louise.' She leaned her head against his chest, holding him.

Jack's expression was grim as he looked beyond her. While he had been able to keep the last pieces of his memory at bay he could stay with Louise and plan for their life in Paris without guilt, but now he knew that he had a grieving family. He was thinking of his mother and father and of Rose. Rose was the one who would miss him most if he could never go home. It hurt him to think of Rose grieving, because they had been so close.

* * *

'You shouldn't have come in this morning,' Sister Morris said, looking at Rose's red nose and streaming eyes. 'You've obviously got a nasty cold. You should be at home in bed.'

'We are already short-staffed,' Rose said thickly. 'I didn't want to let you down.'

'You will infect the patients,' Sister Harris said. 'I can't let you near them in that condition, but I suppose you could help out in the sluice room.'

'Yes, Sister...' Rose turned obediently.

'Don't look so downcast,' Sister Harris called after

her. 'You're one of my best volunteers, Rose Barlow. I don't know what we would do without girls like you.'

Was that supposed to make her feel better? Rose was aching all over; her throat felt as if she had swallowed cut glass, and she had a fever. She must have been mad to come in. When she joined the service she'd had such high hopes of making a career out of nursing, but her dreams were fast vanishing into the blue. She had turned down the chance of an interview and it looked as if she wouldn't get another. Sister Harris said she was useful for scrubbing bedpans and that was about it.

She approached the pile of dirty pans that needed scrubbing, her head whirling. She felt dizzy and sick, and at the moment she would have been happy to lay down and die. After all, what was there left worth living for? Rod was dead, and Jack was missing. Sometimes she thought it was the loss of her brother she felt the most. She had known Rod only a short time, but Jack was her brother.

Sinking her hands in hot water that stung her hands, Rose let the tears run down her cheeks unchecked. She felt empty and unhappy, and she couldn't see anything changing for her.

'Oh, Jack,' she whispered. 'I miss you so. I just wish I knew what had happened to you...'

She felt that she could have faced all the rest if only she could have news of her brother.

* * *

Luke stirred, his eyelids flickering as he became aware of soreness all over. His body ached like hell and he felt as if he had been run over by a traction engine. He put out a hand gingerly to touch his head, discovering a thick bandage. He was aware of other discomfort but the worst was the pain in his head.

He opened his eyes and saw a woman looking down at him. She was pretty but she seemed to be angry about something, and there were tear marks on her face.

'Hello,' he said and tried to sit up but found his head swam. He lay back and closed his eyes for a moment. Hearing the sound of a door closing, he opened his eyes again. The woman had gone. Had he really seen her, and where the hell was he?

Hell! Luke remembered his plane being hit on the return from a successful raid. He had tried to nurse it home, but towards the end he'd known that he wouldn't make it. He had begun to lose height so he'd taken it down, hoping to land, but at the last it had fallen and he... couldn't remember a damn thing after that!

Where was he? Luke glanced around the bedroom. It was neat and tidy, furnished adequately but not well. There was a washstand with a jug and basin, a large heavy chest of drawers and an ugly wardrobe. A thick white cotton counterpane covered the bed; everything was spotlessly clean. It reminded him of Lillian's bedroom, but he wasn't there. The room was French though, so he must have been found and brought here. Had he managed to get back to the British side of the lines?

He stiffened as he heard the sound of a heavy tread, and then the door opened and a man entered. Luke stared in disbelief. He was staring at a man he had never expected to see again.

'Jack?' he asked. 'Is it you – or are we both dead?'

'You're alive,' Jack told him. 'I was afraid we might have to fetch the doctor after all. You've been out cold for hours.'

'Where am I?'

'Behind the German lines,' Jack told him. 'This is a French farm. Louise Saint Claire owns it and we brought you here when your plane came down.'

Louise had come in behind him. 'You owe your life

to Jack,' she said. 'If he hadn't pulled you out you would have died when the plane exploded.'

'I wondered how I got here,' Luke said. 'I remembered the kite going down and then nothing. Thank you – thank you both. You must have taken a hell of a risk. If the Germans had seen you...'

'We've learned that they have been searching the village,' Jack said. 'That's why we dared not fetch the doctor to you. I couldn't find anything wrong with you, except that bang on the side of your head.'

'I feel as if I've been through the grinder,' Luke said. 'Do you think I could have some water please? I am very thirsty.'

Jack went over to the washstand and poured water into a glass. He brought it back, handing it to Luke, who drank a few sips and then gave it back.

'You should eat,' Louise said. 'I have soup...'

She left the room abruptly. Luke frowned as he watched her go.

'Am I imagining it or does that young woman resent my being here?'

'Louise brought me here when I'd been wounded,' Jack told him. 'I was caught in the blast from an ammunition truck and I lay in a ditch for hours. When I came round I made my way here. I was supposed to meet someone here and I sort of remembered it...

though when I woke up in Louise's bed I couldn't re-member anything. My memory didn't come back fully until we brought you here and I saw your face. Sud-denly, all the vague pictures slotted together.'

'I spoke to Captain Martin,' Luke said. 'Your family were told you were missing so I tried to find out more...' He frowned. 'Surely you could have got back through the lines? Once you were with the British they would have discovered who you were soon enough.'

'I couldn't leave. Louise is alone here. She took a huge risk saving my life. I can't just leave her.'

'I know you owe her something but...' Luke shook his head. 'Rose is very upset and so are your parents.'

'I know that now I have remembered who I am.'

'What are you going to do?'

'As soon as you are better I am going to arrange to get you back,' Jack told him. 'I know someone who will get you through.'

'If you know...' Luke's eyes narrowed. 'Have you been working with them? I don't know what they call themselves, but we call them the French resistance...'

'I was on a raid with them the day you crashed...' Jack nodded. 'You must have been coming from there. We got your man out. What was so important about him that it was necessary to risk so many lives?'

'I have no idea,' Luke said. 'I couldn't tell you if I

had – but I really don't know. I was given orders the same as everyone else.'

'The Germans shot the prisoners that weren't strong enough to make a break for it. They had been shut in a building with hardly any light, left without much food or water or medical attention. Some of them were stumbling about because they couldn't see... and they shot them down.'

'Bastards!' Luke growled. 'I used to feel guilty every time I shot a German pilot down, but they deserve it.'

'Do they?' Jack looked doubtful. 'I was up at the front line last Christmas. We exchanged gifts with the soldiers from the other side and played football. They are just like us, Luke – they follow orders. This bloody war is wrong. I can't fight for a government that allows men to lie in the mud, freezing their balls off and shitting themselves every time the order comes to go over the top.'

'You have to go back,' Luke said. 'If you refuse they could accuse you of desertion and shoot you.'

Jack shrugged. 'They will have to find me first.'

'Think of your family! If you do this you can never go back home, Jack.'

'Maybe that's the price I have to pay.'

'I should report what happened,' Luke told him. 'If you explain about the loss of memory and I vouch for the fact that you saved my life you might get a medal rather than a reprimand.'

'I'm not sure,' Jack said. 'Louise is bringing your soup. Don't say any more. I have to think about this – and I have to see someone about taking you out. You can't stay here. The Germans might hear stories and then...' He turned away.

'Think about Rose,' Luke said as he reached the door. 'She is breaking her heart for you.'

'I'll let Rose know somehow,' Jack said. He smiled at Louise as she entered, carrying a tray. 'That smells delicious, love. He will feel better once he gets some of that inside him.'

* * *

'You did well the other day,' Henri said when Jack met him at the appointed place in the woods that afternoon. 'We could have got him without you, but it would have taken longer to find him.'

'Someone would have pointed him out to you.' Jack shrugged. 'I have another favour to ask.'

'I know. You have the British airman who was shot down. You were seen, Jack. You saved his life and now you want us to get him back through the lines – no?'

'Yeah, that's about the size of it.' Jack looked grim. 'It is what you do most of the time, isn't it?'

'It is one of the things we do,' Henri agreed. He looked up as a bird fluttered overhead. He lowered his voice. 'We must be careful. There are those who would betray us to the Germans. You have proved yourself, Georges. We want you with us. We need you. Either you go back with the British pilot or you stay with us for the duration of the war.'

'And if I stay?'

'When we no longer need you, you shall have what you need. A French identity and papers that will allow you to work and live in France.' Henri shrugged expressively. 'It is your choice, my friend.'

'I can't desert Louise,' Jack said. 'I could take her with me, but I'm not sure what would happen then. I could still be shot for not returning to my post months ago. She might be left alone in a strange country with no one to help her...'

'Then it seems you do not have a choice.' Henri held out his hand. 'Come, take it. We are not so bad. Besides, I think you enjoyed our little outing the other day – do I lie?'

'No, you're right,' Jack agreed. 'It beats lying in a mud hole waiting to be shot at by a mile. If I must fight

I would rather fight with you than take orders from a green officer who has no idea what he is doing.'

'A kilometre, not a mile,' Henri told him. 'You are a Frenchman now, Georges. You must try harder to think like one or you may betray yourself. How soon can your pilot be moved?'

'Tomorrow I should think. He could do with a rest but he is in pretty good shape considering.'

'You will come with us,' Henri said. 'The sooner you are truly one of us the better for all concerned.'

'Yes. I shall be glad to see him safely on his way,' Jack said. 'He is a good man, Henri.'

'You know him? He will not betray you?'

'Not if he gives his word,' Jack said. 'He would rather die than break his word. He's one of the old school – an English gentleman.'

'He has given it?'

'Not yet – but he will...'

* * *

'It is too much,' Louise said. 'Why should you have to pay for his freedom?' She tossed her head resentfully towards the bedroom where Luke lay resting. 'Besides, they would have taken him anyway if you had refused.'

'I am not sure they would,' Jack said. 'I couldn't

take the risk. I saved his life and I owe him this much, Louise.'

'You owe him nothing! He will persuade you to go with him and leave me.'

'I've given my word to Henri. I am staying here for the rest of the war – or until they no longer need me. After that I'll have my papers and we'll be free.'

'Do you trust Henri? Supposing something happens to him? You might be killed – what good are the papers then?'

'Listen to me!' Jack took her by the shoulders. 'I have two choices. If I go back with Luke I could take you with us, but they might not let you stay – they might lock you up for the duration in case you're a spy. They might shoot me for desertion...'

'No!' Louise stared at him with desperate eyes. She clung to him. 'You can't go back.'

'If I don't go back I have to stay here and fight with Henri and the others. It is the only way I can get the papers we need.'

'It is blackmail...'

'No. It is what I want to do,' Jack said. 'When I couldn't remember who I was I thought I could go to Paris and forget about the war, but I can't – I can't be a coward, Louise. I have to fight, either with the British or the French freedom fighters. I prefer to stay here and take my chances. I am sorry if you are disappointed about going to Paris but...'

'You promised me!' Louise said and broke away from him, her eyes accusing. 'You are like all men – you never keep your promises...'

'Louise...' Jack stared after her as she rushed from the room in tears. There was no point in going after her if she didn't understand that he needed to do this for the sake of his pride and his self-belief. He loved Louise more than his life, but even for her he couldn't run away from this chance to fight in his own way.

* * *

It was hardly light when they left the house. Jack looked at Luke as he paused for a moment, wondering if he had pushed him too far in his eagerness to get him away. His face was pale, and it was clear that it was costing him to walk.

'If you can't make it I'll find Henri. Maybe they can find transport of some kind.'

'I'll be fine,' Luke said and straightened his back. 'My head hurts like hell and I felt a bit faint, but I can't stay here. Every moment I delay I could bring danger for you and Louise.'

'They may still come looking for you,' Jack said.

'Henri thinks they believe you were burned to a crisp; there wasn't much left of the wreckage by the time they got there. The search was routine, but it's better that you go sooner rather than later.'

'Yes...' Luke glanced at him in the half-light. 'You're certain you don't want to come back? I would stand by you... speak for you...'

'I have given my word to stay here,' Jack said. 'You won't give me away – will you?'

Luke hesitated, then shook his head. 'You saved my life. I couldn't betray you – but what about your family? Do I just let them think you are dead?'

'My father would think I had let him down,' Jack said, a grim line to his mouth. 'He wouldn't understand why I stayed here. It is probably best if he believes that I am dead – the same goes for my mother.'

'What about Rose?'

'Will you tell her please? Not just yet – perhaps when the war is as good as over. Rose might understand. I hope she will...'

'She got married you know...'

'Did she?' Jack smiled for a moment. 'That's good. I can think of her being happy. I leave it to you. If she is happy you may not think it right to tell her – but perhaps one day...'

'I'll see how I feel,' Luke said. He held out his

hand. 'Thank you for what you did, Jack. I know you're no coward. I owe my life to you.'

'It wasn't as heroic as it sounds. I didn't think, I just grabbed you and pulled.' Jack shook his hand. 'We should hurry. Henri says there isn't much time.'

'Thank Louise for me when you get back please.'

'Yes, I shall,' Jack said. 'We need to go now or we may miss our contact...'

* * *

Louise stared out of the window. The day was passing and she was worried because Jack had not returned. Anything could have happened! They could have run into a German patrol... or Jack could have changed his mind and decided to go through the lines with his friend.

She hadn't bothered to wish him luck. She had been so angry because of what he had promised Henri that she had refused to speak to him. She had moved to the other side of the bed when he lay down beside her, refusing to touch him. If she had let him touch her she would have wept and given in, because she loved him so much. She couldn't bear it if he were killed. If he left her, he would forget all about her...

Louise tortured herself as the hours ticked by so

slowly. She knew that this was what must be if he stayed, because Jack was too proud a man to run away to Paris with her. She had to accept it or lose him...

Glancing through the window, she saw a man walking very slowly towards the house. Jack had been hurt! Louise ran out of the house and across the yard, stopping in dismay as she saw the man clearly for the first time. It was not Jack!

'Louise...' he croaked. 'Help me... please...'

Louise froze to the spot, her heart pounding. She stared at her husband in dismay, hardly daring to move. Jacques, alive! Here and asking for help! She swallowed hard, not moving. She didn't want to touch him. She didn't want to go near him. Even as she hesitated, Jacques gave a moan and fell to the ground at her feet. She stood over him, fearing a trap, still reluctant to help him.

'Louise!' Jack's voice was anxious as he sprinted towards her. 'What is it?'

'Jacques...' she whispered. 'It's Jacques...'

'The poor devil looks exhausted,' Jack said, and dropped to his knees beside the unconscious man. 'He must have been one of the prisoners we released. Some of them were desperately ill. He has walked all the way here and by the looks of him he is half dead.'

'I wish he were dead!' Louise said. 'He asked me for help. I don't want to touch him...'

'He can't hurt you,' Jack told her. 'I'm here with you, my love. I promise he can't hurt you. We have to help him.'

'No...' Louise backed away, her face white. 'Let him die...'

'I can't do that,' Jack told her. 'It's all right, Louise. You don't have to touch him. I'll take him in and I'll do what I can for him.'

Louise stared at him for a long moment, then inclined her head. She didn't want to help Jacques. She wished he had died in the German prison.

* * *

Rose was feeling better when she came downstairs that morning. She saw the letter lying on the hall table and picked it up, turning it over to look at the writing. It was from Sarah. She opened it as she left the house and went to queue for a tram. It was cold and she shuffled her feet as the icy wind nipped at her nose.

Scanning the few lines on the single sheet of notepaper, she saw that Luke Trenwith had been reported missing in action.

His plane was reported as taking a slight hit. He signalled that he was going to try to get back to base, but he never arrived. They think he may have had to land it behind enemy lines. They say that other pilots have got back safely after being forced down and they have hopes that he may do the same. I wanted you to know, Rose, because you are my friend. I am trying to keep strong and not cry. I know how you felt about Jack now. I am sure I should feel it if Luke was dead, so I am keeping an open mind. He will come back if he can.

Now, I want to tell you some better news. My cousin Lucy is to be married to Troy's brother Andrew. We have been expecting this for a while, but Andrew thought they should wait because of the war. I think Lucy gave him an ultimatum and he decided to marry rather than lose her! That is a joke, because she would never have left him, but she did want to be married – just in case. I supported her, of course, and the wedding is next week. Please try and get leave. Lucy would love you to come and so should I. Your ever loving friend, Sarah.

Rose smiled as she put the letter away. The news

about Luke was upsetting. She had always liked him. In fact there had been a time when... before she met Rod... but there had never been any chance of anything between them. Rose hoped that Sarah was right to be optimistic about her brother, but she wasn't sure her feelings were a true indication. She had been so sure that Jack was still alive, but as the weeks passed without news, she had begun to lose her certainty.

Rose knew that both her father and mother had accepted that Jack was dead. They had grieved for him and they would always honour his memory, but they had no hope of his return.

'Jack would have been in touch if he could.' Mrs Barlow said it over and over. 'He's gone, Rose, and we have to accept it. He was a good brave lad and your father is proud of him.'

Rose felt the familiar ache inside as she thought about her brother. She would always feel as if a part of her were missing, and she suspected her mother would too. However, grieving wouldn't bring him back. It was probably time to move on.

She would ask for leave. She knew she had a week or so due and she would take as much as she could. She could stay with Sarah for the wedding and then go home for a couple of days...

* * *

'He is very ill,' Jack told Louise as he came back down to the kitchen. 'The fever is raging and he keeps calling your name. It might help him if you would go up and speak to him. You need not do any more.'

'No, I don't want to,' Louise said. She looked at him angrily. 'After what he did to me... How can you ask me to help him?'

'I know what he did was terrible,' Jack said. 'I think it may be playing on his mind. I'm not sure he will live, Louise. It might make his dying easier if you forgave him.'

'Don't look at me like that!' Louise felt ashamed. There had been a time when she'd cared for Jacques. 'All right, I'll go up to him, but don't expect me to help him.'

'I've told you, I'll do all that is necessary.'

Louise walked past him and up the stairs. Her stomach was tying itself in knots and she felt sick. She had been hoping that Jacques was dead for so long and now she was supposed to feel sorry for him!

She hesitated and then went into the bedroom. There was a sickly smell that she immediately disliked, but she couldn't think what it was. It got worse as she moved towards the bed and she knew it was coming from her husband. His face was flushed, damp with sweat, and he was restless, tossing and crying out in pain.

Louise stared at him resentfully, but then he called her name and put out a hand as if entreating her.

'Forgive me...' Jacques cried. 'Louise... sorry... so sorry... loved you...'

Louise felt the resentment melt away. Nothing could take away what he had done, but her heart was moved to pity. She went closer, taking the damp cloth Jack had been using and bending down to wipe his brow.

'It is all right, Jacques,' she told him softly. 'I have forgiven you.'

'Louise...' His eyes flickered open for a moment, though she did not think he could see her. He was gripped by fever. 'Forgive me... never meant to do...' He sat up in bed suddenly, his eyes wide with terror. 'No... Don't touch me... Don't touch me...'

Louise knew that he must have suffered in the prison. Whatever he had done he didn't deserve that fate. She touched his hand, uttering soothing words, and he lay down, closing his eyes. His words were fainter now. She couldn't hear them properly.

'I forgive you,' she said softly. 'It doesn't matter any more, Jacques. Believe me, I have forgotten it...'

She thought he seemed a little easier. Hearing a sound behind her, she turned to see Jack watching her.

'He is very ill...'

'He is dying,' Jack told her, his expression serious. 'Can't you smell the gangrene? I saw the puss oozing out of his leg. It has too great a hold. Even if we called the doctor and he took the leg it wouldn't save him. I've seen this before with men in the trenches...'

'That awful smell...' Louise applied the damp cloth to his forehead again. Pity stirred within her. 'It's all right, Jack. I can tend him now. You get on with your work. I'll sit with him for a while.'

'I don't think it will be long,' Jack said. 'I'll go down to the yard and make sure the stock is settled. Henri told me I'll be needed again in ten days. Until then I can carry on as usual. I shall be here with you most of the time.'

'Yes...' Louise bent her head over the dying man, tears trickling down her face. The bitterness had gone with her acceptance of Jacques. She knew that Jack was right. He had chosen to stay with her and that meant she must accept what he had to do. 'I understand.' She turned to look at him and smiled. 'It's all right now. Don't worry. I love you. I always shall...'

'And I love you,' Jack told her. 'More than you will ever know.'

'I do know,' Louise said. She knew in her heart what it had cost him to stay when he'd had the chance to go back. He had given up so much for her sake. She could accept what he must do for his. 'Our time will come, Jack. I can wait...'

'I'll be back soon,' he promised and went out. 'We'll have that café in Paris, Louise – and I'll have my garage. I promise you. We'll have everything you want one day.'

'I have all I need right now.'

Louise looked down at her husband as Jack closed the door softly. Jacques was getting weaker. He would not last the night.

* * *

'It was so good of you to come!' Sarah hugged Rose when she met her from the train. 'I was afraid that you would not be able to get leave. I really wanted you to be here for Lucy's wedding, and she does too. You are one of us now, Rose.'

'I think it is lovely that they are getting married at last,' Rose said. 'I've bought Lucy a present. It's a lace tablecloth. I hope she will like it.'

'I am sure she will,' Sarah said and tucked her arm

through Rose's. 'She is very excited and I am so thrilled for her.'

'Yes, she must be happy. It is the best day of her life.'

'Oh Rose,' Sarah said, looking at her sadly. 'Is this upsetting for you? I know it isn't long since Rod...'

'It is just what I needed,' Rose told her firmly. 'Things have been getting me down lately. They finally turned down my application to train as a nurse. Sister Harris said they were out of their tiny minds. She was furious because she said they didn't have the slightest idea of what they were missing. I think she was pleased though, because she went out of her way to tell me how good I was at my job – and she asked me to join the hospital choir this year.'

Sarah nodded, looking interested. 'I remember you used to sing in the choir at home. You have a lovely voice.'

'I like singing,' Rose said. 'I haven't done much since I went to London, but I said I would give it a go. We're going to sing carols on the wards this Christmas.'

'The patients will appreciate that,' Sarah said. 'Are you very disappointed about your nursing training?'

'I was,' Rose said. 'Somehow it doesn't seem to matter so much now. There are more important things

– like your brother. Have you heard anything more about him?'

'No, not yet,' Sarah said. 'I just keep thinking he will turn up. I had a letter from Father. He was very distressed, as of course he would be – but Mother hasn't said a word. Luke was always her favourite. I don't know how she will feel if...' She shook her head. 'I refuse to even think it! Luke can't be dead.'

Rose squeezed her arm but didn't say anything. She had felt the same about Jack for a long time. She still wanted to believe he was alive, but her hopes of ever seeing him again were fading fast.

'We shouldn't talk about it,' she said. 'We mustn't let anything spoil your cousin's wedding. It has to be a perfect day so that she can remember it for the rest of her life.'

'Yes.' Sarah smiled as they got into the car Lord Pelham had sent to fetch Rose from the station. 'I don't want her to have shadows hanging over her wedding day.'

'Mine was perfect,' Rose said. 'Sometimes I can hardly remember – but I know it was perfect.'

Sarah nodded, a hint of shadows in her eyes. Because of Troy's terrible injuries it had taken a long while for her to find the happiness she now enjoyed in her marriage.

'That is how it should be,' she said and smiled. 'I am determined that is the way it will be for Lucy – though I know she is worried about Luke. She was always fond of him.'

'He will come back,' Rose told her. 'Just keep hoping and praying, Sarah. I am sure he will come back.'

She wasn't quite sure if she was thinking of Luke Trenwith or Jack.

* * *

'I asked you to call, because I wanted to know if there was anything I could do for you, Mrs Barlow,' Lady Trenwith said. 'I should have liked you to come back to us, but I quite understand that you feel you don't have the time. Sir James has been thinking we might have to close the house and move to the dower house for the duration. It would make things easier as far as keeping the place in order is concerned, though I am not sure my husband realises how small the dower house is.'

'I dare say he thinks it would be more economic until things become easier, ma'am. You can always open the house when the war is over.'

'Yes, of course. We shall certainly do so,' Lady

Trenwith told her. 'But if we leave the house empty we shall still need caretakers. I wondered if you and Barlow would care for the position? It will not require so very much attention if we are not here, I think.'

'Perhaps not, ma'am,' Mrs Barlow said. 'I am sure Barlow wouldn't mind keeping an eye on things for you – but you should speak to him. I wouldn't want to leave the cottage.'

'Well, you need not,' Lady Trenwith said. Her expression did not change. 'You will have heard that my son is missing?'

'Yes, my lady.'

'I am convinced that it is all a storm in a teacup. Luke will turn up shortly, as I have told his father. I suppose you have heard nothing of your son?'

'No, ma'am. I hope Mr Luke is safe and sound somewhere.'

'Yes, well we must hope for the best. Well, I shall speak to my husband about the move. He will talk to Barlow if we decide to go ahead.'

'Yes, ma'am, thank you,' Mrs Barlow said and went out.

Lady Trenwith frowned and reached for her pen. She ought to make a list of what needed doing if they were to close up the house.

11

'I am sorry about Jacques,' Madame Bonnier said. 'You will have him buried in the churchyard?'

'Yes, I suppose so,' Louise said, though she looked doubtful.

'He deserves that at least,' Madame Bonnier told her. 'I know what he did to you, but he endured much in that prison. The Germans thought he was one of the freedom fighters. They tortured him...'

'Yes, Jack thought he had been tortured,' Louise said and crossed herself. 'I shall speak to the priest. I hear that you have Pierre back?'

'He was set free in that raid, but it was too dangerous for him to stay with me. The Germans might have come looking for him. I have sent him to Paris to live with my sister.'

'That must have been a wrench for you. I wonder that you do not all go?'

'I must keep the farm going for my husband,' Madame Bonnier told her. She looked around the kitchen with an appraising eye. 'This belongs to you now that Jacques is dead. He had no family but you. You are at liberty to sell now if you choose.'

'I know. I was aware of his will. He left everything to me,' Louise said. She sighed. 'At least we know the truth at last.'

'Will you leave for Paris now? There is nothing to stop you.'

'Jack has thrown in his lot with the freedom fighters. We stay until they say he is not needed here.'

'You have no need of Henri's services,' Madame Bonnier said. 'Jacques is dead. It would be easy for Jack to step into his shoes. They are of similar build – he wears Jacques clothes, why not assume his identity? He needs no other papers.'

'I have thought of it,' Louise admitted. 'Jack does not like the idea. He says he made a promise and he will honour it.' She shrugged and smiled. 'It no longer matters. I was afraid that Jacques would come back; he did – and I forgave him before he died. I am no longer afraid of him, only of the Germans.' Louise shuddered as she recalled the day the German officer had attacked her. Madame Bonnier knew nothing of what had happened, and she never would, for Louise knew they could tell no one. Even Henri was only guessing when he hinted to Jack at knowing about something hidden.

'They say the British have made a significant breakthrough on the German line this year...'

'But the papers say that the news is bad elsewhere,' Louise reminded her. 'There have been defeats as well as victories. I fear that it will be a long while before the war is over for us.'

'Then we shall just have to grit our teeth and bear it,' Madame Bonnier said and lifted her wine glass in salute. 'To all brave men everywhere – and that includes Georges Marly.'

Louise raised her glass. 'Damnation to the enemy,' she said. 'The one good thing in all this is that we have become good friends.'

Madame Bonnier nodded her head. 'You have a good man now, Louise. You should marry him as soon as you can.'

'I would marry him tomorrow, but people think he is my brother. We must wait until we can leave and live our lives elsewhere.'

'But will he not have to go home one day? Surely he must want to see his family – unless he has none?'

Louise looked away. She knew that Jack had stayed for her sake and sometimes she felt guilty. 'Jack will decide for himself...'

* * *

'Lucy looks beautiful,' Rose said as she stood at the bottom of the stairs and watched the bride walking down. 'And so happy...'

'She is happy,' Sarah replied and went to greet her cousin. She kissed her cheek and told her that they all thought Lucy looked wonderful.

'It is a good thing Mama had some material put by for me,' Lucy told her. 'I don't think I could have bought silk this fine now. And the veil is the one she wore at her wedding.'

'I wore a family veil at mine too,' Sarah reminded her. 'I didn't have the chance to buy anything. At least you have a trousseau, Lucy.'

'Yes, I do,' Lucy said. 'I have no idea where we are going for our honeymoon, but Andrew says he is taking me somewhere. I think it may be Scotland.'

'The cars are waiting,' Sarah said. 'You ought to go

out now, dearest. We're about to leave and you don't want to keep Andrew waiting.'

'He told me he would wait forever if need be,' Lucy said, her eyes bright with laughter. 'I was the one who refused to wait any longer.'

Sarah smiled. She followed behind her cousin, picking up her train as she went outside. Most of the staff had gathered to see her leave, happy because the sun was shining even though the weather was bitterly cold. Lucy wasn't shivering. She was too happy to feel the chill, but everyone else was hopping from one foot to the other, glad to get into the wedding cars or go back inside the house to finish getting ready for the guests.

Rose was in one of the last cars to leave. As they were turning out onto the main road she saw another car approaching from the opposite direction. She couldn't see who was inside, because she only caught a glimpse as it swept into the drive. She smiled because she imagined it was a guest arriving late. They would have to hurry if they wanted to get to the church in time to see the ceremony!

* * *

'You just missed them,' Lord Pelham's housekeeper
exclaimed as she welcomed the late arrival. 'They all
left for the church a few moments ago. If you hurry
you might just get there in time.'

'Who is getting married?' Luke inquired. 'I had no
idea there was a wedding going on or I should have
asked before I arrived. I dare say you will wish me to
the devil?'

'Oh no, Mr Luke. It's Miss Lucy getting married to
Mr Andrew. Mrs Pelham is always pleased to see you.
She will be delighted to know you're safe, sir. Your
room isn't in use. Madam asked me to keep it free just
in case.'

'That is exactly what I might have expected of
Sarah,' Luke said. 'I did try telephoning just before I
left home, but I couldn't get through so I thought I
would turn up and surprise her. However, I don't want
to appear as the spectre at the wedding and upset
everyone.'

'Perhaps you would like to rest, sir? If you want to
go up and get changed, perhaps have a bath – I'll tell
Mrs Pelham the good news when she gets back.'

'Thank you, I am a little tired. I haven't slept too
well. They kept me in hospital for a while, just to make
sure I was all right. Apparently, they thought I was a
walking miracle once they knew what had happened.'

'It is just like a miracle, sir. The answer to Madam's prayers, I dare say. And your mother's! Lady Trenwith must have been delighted?'

'Yes, perhaps.'

Luke nodded to her and went up the stairs. He needed no one to show him the way, because Sarah had told him that the room he'd used last time would always be his if he wished to visit. He went inside, leaning against the door for a moment, feeling drained. He had probably made the exhausting journey through the enemy lines too soon, but he'd known that Jack wanted him gone because of the risk to Louise. He couldn't blame him. Besides, he had wanted to leave once he understood the situation.

Jack was a damned fool! Luke couldn't see why he hadn't just brought the girl back with him if he was that worried about her. There was an element of risk involved, of course, but Luke was pretty sure he could have swung it. Jack might have ended up as a war hero who had suffered tremendously and then made it back against the odds. He had saved Luke's life and that would have gone a long way to clearing any doubts. He had chosen to stay in France, which meant that if he came back after the war he would be arrested and shot as a traitor and a deserter. At the very least he would go to prison for years.

Luke couldn't understand how Jack could be so selfish. His duty was to his country and his family, not to some girl he'd fallen for over there. He might be in love with her, but he could have arranged something for her until the war was over. Love shouldn't be allowed to get in the way of duty and honour.

Knowing what he did, Luke had avoided meeting Jack's parents when he went home to see his father. He'd paid a flying visit to Trenwith, promising he would return later. It was probably because he hadn't stayed more than an hour or two that his father had forgotten to tell him about Lucy's wedding. Luke would have bought her a present if he had known, but it would have to wait now until he got a chance to go up to town. However, he could ask her what she wanted. He was just glad to be here in his sister's home. At least she would show some emotion when she learned he was alive!

He loosened his tie and kicked off his shoes, sitting and then lying down on the bed. He was so damned tired! He would rest first and get changed afterwards. Maybe he felt low because his mother had taken his homecoming in her stride. She had said she was pleased to see him back, but that was it. He was a fool, but it would be good to feel that someone actually gave a damn what happened to him. Jack might have it right after all. Perhaps love was the only thing that really mattered.

* * *

Rose and Sarah stood together to throw rose petals and confetti as Lucy came out of the church. The sun had been bright earlier, but dark clouds were blocking it out now and everyone was getting cold. The photographer took some pictures, and then everyone piled into the cars with a sigh of relief. A warm reception would await them at Pelham, huge fires in all the big hearths throughout the beautiful, spacious rooms and a feast of lovely food that the servants had been preparing for days.

Rose was invited to join Sarah in her car this time, because the guests had mingled and were riding back with whomever they wished, rather than in formation as before.

'It was perfect,' Sarah said and laughed softly. 'I knew it would be.' She looked proudly at her husband sitting up front with the chauffeur. 'Even Troy remarked on how pretty Lucy looked and how happy his brother was.'

'Are you taking my name in vain, Sarah?' Troy asked, glancing over his shoulder lovingly.

'I was telling Rose you enjoyed the wedding.'

'It was all right, as weddings go...'

'He's just teasing you,' Rose said. She thought it was marvellous the way Troy Pelham had come on this last year. When she'd first seen him after he was badly burned on one side of his face, she'd thought he had changed too much to be the same as he'd once been – the man Sarah had fallen in love with – but she'd been wrong. Troy's face would never look as it had before the war, but he was as charming and loving to his wife as he had been when they were courting. Their mutual love and happiness was there in their faces for all to see.

'I know,' Sarah said and laughed huskily. 'Isn't it wonderful?'

Rose nodded and smiled. She couldn't help a small feeling of envy, because seeing all the happy faces at the wedding had made her more aware of her own loss, her own loneliness. She had friends but there was no one special who truly cared for her. She had her parents of course, but they hadn't been the same since Jack went missing.

That was it, of course, the feeling of missing Jack that never quite left her. It was strange that Rod's image had begun to fade from her mind soon after his death. She had tried desperately to bring him back, but she could never quite picture his face unless she looked at her wedding photographs. Jack's image was always there – as a child, a young lad and a man. She remembered the day she had seen him onto the train vividly. She had told him not to be a hero, but she might as well have kept her mouth shut.

Rose blinked away her unshed tears as she followed Sarah into the house. The large rooms seemed to be overflowing with guests and Sarah was immediately drawn into the thick of it, greeting guests, congratulating Lucy and her husband.

Rose joined the line to greet the happy couple. She shook hands with Andrew and kissed Lucy, wishing them luck and future happiness, and then she took a glass of champagne from the waiters circling and went to stand by the window. She didn't feel out of things because Sarah's family was always welcoming, but many of the faces were new to her and she did not want to intrude.

Barney Hale came up to her as she stood looking out, hardly touching her drink. He was Sarah's sister's husband and a more frequent visitor to the Pelham household than his wife Marianne.

'How are you, Mrs Carne?' he asked. 'I was very sorry to hear your sad news.'

'Thank you,' she replied and smiled, because she

liked Barney and he always went out of his way to speak to her, though his wife usually just gave her a nod in passing. 'It is nice to see Lucy so happy today.'

'I agree. She is a lovely girl.' Barney nodded thoughtfully. 'Have you heard the good news?'

'No – has something happened?'

'Luke Trenwith turned up when we had all left for the church. He is upstairs resting, but I dare say he may come down this evening. Sarah has popped up to see him...' He broke off as one of the footmen approached. 'Yes, Chivers – did you need me?'

'No, Mr Hale. I have a message for Mrs Carne.' He turned to Rose, his expression grave. 'I am sorry to intrude, Mrs Carne, but there was a message from Lady Trenwith. She said that your father was very ill and your mother wishes you to return at once.'

'My father...' Rose stared at him in shock. 'Thank you. Yes, of course... I must go home immediately...' She was too bewildered to think clearly. She turned to Barney in confusion. 'I'm not sure... Is there a train soon?'

'Go upstairs and get your things as quickly as you can,' Barney told her. 'Don't worry about anything, Rose. I'll drive you to the station. If there isn't a train I'll drive you home myself.'

'I am sure there must be a train, but thank you.

Will you explain to Sarah and the others why I had to leave?'

'Yes, of course. Don't worry about a thing. Just grab what you need. Anything you leave can be sent on. Now go!'

'Thank you,' Rose said. Her throat was tight and she blinked hard to stop herself giving way to tears. She was numb, too stunned to think properly and very grateful to Barney for being there when she needed help.

* * *

Luke hugged his sister tightly, feeling an overflow of love because of her obvious delight in seeing him. Sarah was the one person he'd ever known who had given him unconditional love, and he realised how lucky he was to have her.

'I kept praying that you would come back,' Sarah said. 'It's so wonderful, Luke. I know Mother was devastated, because she was convinced you were dead.'

'She was quite unemotional,' Luke said as he let his sister go and looked at her. 'If she missed me, it didn't show. You look as beautiful as ever, Sarah. No one told me about the wedding. I thought I would come down and surprise you. At least I did try to phone but couldn't get through so then I thought why not make it a surprise. I hope it isn't inconvenient?'

'How could it be? To have you here is all I needed to make things perfect, Luke. It is the most wonderful surprise,' Sarah said. 'We thought your plane must have crashed? What happened to you – if you don't mind talking about it?'

'I managed to get the plane a part of the way back and then I knew I wasn't going to make it, so I tried to land but couldn't quite bring it down. I was knocked unconscious on impact and I would have died, because the plane caught fire and exploded. I was lucky...'

'Did someone get you out?' Sarah stared at him in wonder.

'Yes...' Luke hesitated. He had decided that he couldn't tell anyone the truth, because Jack Barlow had made his decision and the truth might be harmful to others. 'A man pulled me clear and took me to his farm a short distance away. He and his... wife looked after me, but I wasn't too badly hurt, just bruised and unconscious for a while. They knew people who could get me through the lines and back home.'

'He must have been so brave to do that,' Sarah said, eyes bright. 'I think he deserves a medal.'

'Yes, I believe he does,' Luke said thoughtfully. 'I

think he is working with a group of men who call themselves freedom fighters. They make a general nuisance of themselves, blowing up ammunition trucks and things like that on the German side of the lines...'

'Do you know his name?'

'Georges Marly.'

'I should like to shake his hand one day,' Sarah told him. 'He saved your life, Luke, and for that I shall always be grateful.' She looked at his face and saw a slight scar on his temple. 'You were so lucky. You weren't even burned.'

'I was very lucky,' Luke agreed. 'Shouldn't you be getting back to your guests?'

'Yes, I must, though they are Lucy's guests,' Sarah said. 'But I must tell Rose you are here. She will be so happy for us. Her husband wasn't so lucky. His plane went down and he didn't get out.'

'I am so sorry,' Luke said. He was stunned. 'No one told me. That is rotten luck. Rose must have been terribly upset.'

'Yes. She was devastated when her brother was reported missing. Then she lost her husband, all in the space of a few months.'

'Yes...' Luke frowned. He had almost made up his mind not to tell anyone that it was Jack Barlow who had pulled him from the wreckage of that plane, but now he wasn't sure. He had promised to tell Rose when the time seemed right. Perhaps it would help her. He couldn't be sure. 'You go down, Sarah. I'll come down and join you in a few minutes, if that is all right?'

'Yes, of course it is,' Sarah told him. 'Lucy will be thrilled to see you. We have tried to make this a happy day despite worrying about you – and now it truly is.'

* * *

'This is so good of you,' Rose said as Barney gave her a first-class ticket, some magazines and a bar of chocolate. 'You didn't need to do all this for me.'

'It was my pleasure,' he said. 'Sarah has told me how good you were to her when she was in trouble. This is the least I could do in the circumstances. I do hope things are not as bad as you fear when you get home.'

'I think they must be serious or Lady Trenwith would not have telephoned,' Rose said. She shook the hand he offered. 'Thank you again for helping me. I was so stunned I hardly knew what to do – and I didn't want to throw a blight over Lucy's wedding...'

Barney nodded. 'Have a good journey,' he said, and he stepped away from the door as the guard blew his whistle and the train began to get up steam. 'Take care, Rose.'

'I shall – thank you.'

Rose waved and then took her seat. She had never travelled first class before and for the moment she had the carriage entirely to herself. She glanced at the magazines Barney Hale had bought for her, realising they were all the kind of thing she had looked at on the stalls but would never dream of buying, because they were the type society ladies usually read. The clothes shown on these pages would be way beyond her means, though she had seen enough of them when she worked as a maid at Trenwith.

Rose choked back a sob as she thought of those days. It wasn't much more than a year since she'd left to volunteer, but it felt like a lifetime. So much had happened that it all seemed as if it was like a story she'd heard about someone else. In a way that was true, because the Rose who had worked at Trenwith had vanished long ago. She'd been a girl then, but she was a woman now.

Rose leaned back against the comfortable seat and closed her eyes. Tears trickled down her cheeks un-heeded as she thought about her father, brother and Rod. She hoped her father wouldn't die, because she didn't know what her mother would do if he did. She had lived at Trenwith all her life, and the cottage belonged to the estate. Would she have to move?

Rose shook her head. She was being morbid! Her father was ill. That didn't mean he was dying. He might get better. She could only pray that he did – and miracles did happen. Luke Trenwith had come back and that had seemed most unlikely after his plane went down behind enemy lines. Sarah must be so happy!

Rose wiped her eyes. She realised she was hungry; she had skipped breakfast in anticipation of the wedding feast. She broke herself a piece of dark chocolate filled with white cream and put it in her mouth, letting the chocolate dissolve. Then she reached for the magazines. She might as well make the most of them since they had been given to her.

Marianne didn't know how lucky she was to have such a kind and considerate husband, but then she'd wanted Troy. She had jilted him in a fit of pique and she had been horrible to her sister when Sarah and Troy got together, though she seemed to be on reasonable terms again now.

It was strange the way things twisted and turned, Rose thought. Only a few months ago her parents had been planning what they would do after the war and now her father might be too ill to retire to the sea as he'd hoped.

* * *

'I am pleased you got back,' Marianne said as her brother came up to her. 'We all thought you might not, though Sarah was more optimistic than the rest of us. Mother must have been pleased to see you.'

'Yes, perhaps,' Luke said and kissed her cheek. 'You look very well. How are the children and Barney?'

'The children are with Nanny at home,' Marianne said and pulled a face. 'Barney wanted to bring them, but I thought it might be too much for them.'

Luke nodded. What his sister truly meant was that they were too much for her. She preferred to see her children for a few minutes when they were clean and tucked in bed at night, unlike Sarah who was often to be seen playing with her son in the gardens or her private sitting room.

'Mother said she didn't feel like coming to a wedding, and of course Father still isn't fully fit...' Luke frowned and glanced round the reception room. 'Have you seen Rose anywhere?'

'You mean Rose Barlow – I suppose her name is Carne now.' Marianne pulled a face. 'She had to go home in a hurry. I think her father is ill or something. Barney is playing the gallant. He offered to take her to the station and see her on the next train.'

'That was good of him,' Luke said. 'I am sorry to hear that family has more trouble.'

'Yes, they have been unfortunate,' Marianne said. 'Barlow will be missed. He was in line to step up to the position of butler when Matthews leaves, you know. I believe he was going to be the caretaker if Mother finally moves into the dower house – I'm not sure she will.'

Luke was silent. How could she think that was important? It was the grief Rose had suffered and must be suffering now that mattered. He wished that he had been the one to drive her to the station. He couldn't have told her about her brother at such a time, of course, but he would have done his best to comfort her in whatever way he could.

'That was very good of Barney,' he said. 'You were lucky when you married him, Marianne. He is a decent chap.'

'Barney is all right,' Marianne replied. 'He can be assertive when he puts himself out. I suppose I have been lucky in a way.' She glanced across the room to where Sarah was standing with their cousin Lucy. The two of them were laughing. Troy and Andrew were with them, all of them clearly pleased with life. She might have been a part of that if she hadn't been so stupid as to throw her chance away. The undamaged side of Troy's face was turned towards her. From this angle he still looked the most attractive man of her acquaintance. 'Oh, here he comes now. Rose must have caught her train...'

'It's good to see you, Luke,' Barney said as he reached them. He offered his hand. 'We are all delighted to have you home.'

'Thank you. I've been given a couple of months' leave,' Luke said. 'They seem to think I need it, though I'm not sure I shall know what to do with myself.'

'You must come to us for a while,' Barney said. 'For Christmas or the New Year if you wish. My father would be delighted.'

'Thank you, but Sarah invited me for Christmas and I must spend some of the time at home, but I might come for a couple of days.'

'You are always welcome,' Barney assured him. 'Marianne, if you are tired you should sit down, my love.'

'Please do not make a fuss, Barney! I am going to talk to Sarah.'

Barney looked rueful as his wife walked away. 'Marianne isn't too pleased to be having another baby just yet. She didn't want me to tell anyone, but I don't want her to overdo things.'

'Congratulations,' Luke said. 'You must be delighted.'

'Well, yes, I am pleased of course. I shall be when it is over. Marianne takes these things hard and I feel for her, but I shall be pleased to have another child, naturally.' Barney looked at him. 'You haven't made any plans for marriage yet?'

'No, not as yet,' Luke told him. 'I shall have to think about it after the war. My father is anxious that there should be an heir, but I don't feel that I want to marry while this damned war is going on. Not fair to the lady.'

It was only a part of the reason, Luke thought as they walked to join the little group around Sarah and Lucy. He hadn't met anyone he could contemplate spending his life with – except Rose Barlow. He had put that out of his mind when he discovered that she had a lover. Perhaps he had misjudged her? She had married the man... It didn't mean she'd slept around just because she had stayed out all night with the man she loved.

Luke felt something ease inside him. It had hurt him deeply to believe that Rose was that kind of girl. He had placed her on a pedestal, refusing to let himself imagine having an affair with her, because she was decent and pure. Marriage had been out of the question. It still was, of course.

He made an effort and put Rose from his mind. If she was staying at Trenwith when he returned he would speak to her. He would decide then whether or not he should tell her about Jack...

* * *

'Thank God you're home,' Mrs Barlow said. 'I was sorry to send for you because I knew it was the wedding, but I've been at my wits' end. Your father is so ill, Rose. I think he may die...' Tears began to slide down her cheeks. 'I don't want to lose him. We had plans...'

'Oh Ma,' Rose said and put her arms about her mother. She smelled of baking and herbs, familiar and dear. Drawing back, Rose looked into her mother's face. 'You can't cope with everything yourself. I'm here now. Tell me what the doctor said please.'

'It is heart trouble,' Mrs Barlow said. 'He just collapsed at work and they sent for the doctor. Her ladyship would have kept him there. She has been very good, Rose. Your father wouldn't stay and so she sent him home in her carriage.'

'That was good of her, but the least she could do, Ma. This family has worked hard for Trenwith.'

'I dare say you're right, but I thought it was kind of her.' Mrs Barlow sniffed. 'The doctor told me that your father had been lucky this time. It was a severe warning. He must rest and not worry or he could have another one and that might be fatal.'

'Where is he?'

'In bed. He asked for you, Rose. He hates being there. Especially when he's sick. He doesn't like being a trouble to me. He said you were used to nursing people and it would be easier for you.'

'Yes, of course,' Rose said and smiled. 'Do you have a bedpan? If Father shouldn't get out of bed that would make it easier all round.'

'I've got one, but I'm not sure he will use it. He keeps trying to get up, but he fell over twice and I had to get him back to bed. You talk to him, Rose. He might listen to you, because you're a nurse.'

'I'm not really,' Rose said with a smile, 'but if Pa thinks it, it will make him happy. I know how to deal with patients who try to get out of bed anyway.'

'How long can you stay?'

'I'll ask for compassionate leave,' Rose told her. 'Don't worry, Ma, I shan't desert you.' She was smiling because she felt relieved. Her father was still alive. She hadn't arrived too late, and perhaps if they could make him rest, as the doctor had ordered, he would recover. 'I'll go up to him now and see if there is anything he wants...'

Rose went quickly upstairs. She was smiling as she tapped at her father's door and then entered.

'Pa...' she said cheerfully. 'Ma sent me to see if...' She stopped abruptly, a chill going over her as she looked at the figure on the bed. He was lying in an odd way, his hand outstretched as if trying to reach something. Rose approached the bed slowly, her throat catching. She had been so full of hope after talking to her mother – but it was too late. Her father's eyes were open wide, staring in horror at something. The heart attack must have been massive this time. She touched his body. It was still warm. He hadn't been dead for long enough to go cold. 'Oh Pa...' she choked. 'Pa...'

Rose moved his arm to his side and then closed his eyelids. He didn't look quite so bad now. She bent to kiss his cheek, tears sliding down her own, falling onto his face.

'I am so sorry, Pa,' she told him. 'We love you. We all love you.' She stroked his hair away from his face. He was still a young man. He shouldn't have died like this, alone in his bed – perhaps while she was talking to her mother. 'We shan't forget you...'

Rose stood looking at him for a moment longer, then turned and went down to the kitchen. She was dreading telling her mother. Mrs Barlow had thought he would recover, and she was going to be devastated to think of him dying alone.

* * *

'Barlow died the day before yesterday,' Lady Trenwith told her son. 'Rose came home immediately, but it was too late. She found him, I believe. Mrs Barlow will be devastated.'

'Yes, of course. Barlow was only in his fifties. She must have expected they would have several more years together.' Luke frowned. 'We must do what we can for them, Mother.'

'Your father has arranged the funeral. They will remain in the cottage for as long as they wish, naturally. It would be wrong to ask them to move out.'

'I should think so!' Luke said. 'It would be disgraceful to think of it, Mother. I hope no one has suggested it to them?'

'It is usual when no one works for the estate. However, in this case I think the custom should be waived and your father agrees. Perhaps you would wish to be the one to let them know?'

'After the funeral,' Luke said. 'I shall attend, naturally. I don't know if Father intends to be there, but I certainly shall. I have good memories of Barlow – of all the family.' Especially one of waking up in a French farmhouse when he should have been dead, fried to a crisp in his burning plane.

'You must do as you see fit,' Lady Trenwith said. 'It isn't fitting that I should go, of course, but I dare say Rose and her mother will be there. There are no males left and he cannot go to his rest unescorted.'

'Sarah may come. I shall telephone her,' Luke said. 'I know she feels that Rose is like a sister to her.'

'Ridiculous,' Lady Trenwith said. 'I do not approve of your sister's friendship with Rose Barlow, though I understand there are special circumstances. I prefer not to discuss it, Luke. As I said, you must do as you see fit.'

'Yes, I shall,' Luke told her.

He turned away to contemplate the magnificent view from the parlour window. The formal gardens were looking a bit neglected in places, but beyond them was a wide sweep of grass and the lake in the distance. Trenwith had a timeless beauty that touched him deeply. Luke wondered what his mother would say if she had any idea how much they owed the Barlow family. He wished he could tell her it was Jack

Barlow who had saved his life, but that was impossible. He was not sure it would make her grateful even if she knew.

'If you will excuse me, Mother. I have a phone call to make and some letters to write.'

Luke left his mother's parlour and walked into the hall. He would ring Sarah and let her know the situation, and then he must write a letter to a certain Monsieur Georges Marly...

* * *

'Oh, Sarah,' Rose said and stifled a sob. 'Thank you for coming. I didn't want to trouble you myself. It was good of Mr Luke to telephone you himself.'

'You know I would want to be here with you,' Sarah said. 'I am so sorry, Rose. I don't know what to say. You've lost so much – and we've been so lucky.'

'I'm glad Mr Luke came back,' Rose said, and tears trickled down her cheeks as Sarah put her arms about her. She had tried to be strong for her mother, but with Sarah she could let her grief show. 'And it makes me happy to see you and Troy together. It was a shock for Ma, because she thought my father would get over it. I was glad I found him, because I was able to tidy him up a bit before she saw him...'

'What will she do now?' Sarah asked. 'Will she want to stay on here? You told me your parents had plans to retire to the sea...'

'They were waiting until the war was over, because they didn't want to leave Lady Trenwith in the lurch,' Rose said. 'I told them they should go now but you couldn't move Pa. He always took his time, but it wasn't that he was overworked here. Ma says he hadn't been the same since Jack went missing. He broke his heart over that but he kept it inside and that is what killed him – at least that is the way my mother sees it.'

'Do you think people do die of a broken heart?'

'I don't know,' Rose admitted. 'It may have been coming on for ages. Pa would never admit to being ill. Even when he had a bad cold he went to work.'

'Yes, I know – just like you,' Sarah said and smiled. 'I'll just go in and see your mother. I shall walk with you behind the coffin tomorrow, Rose. Luke told me that he would too. You won't be alone.'

'A lot of the servants have asked permission to follow too,' Rose told her. 'Pa was liked and respected. I think the church may be full.'

'That is good.' Sarah hugged her waist. 'You know that you could always come and live with me, don't you? I spoke to Lord Pelham. He said that he has several good houses on the estate and you and your mother would be welcome to live there for as long as you wished.'

'Oh, Sarah, that's so good of you. I'll talk to Ma about it, but not until after the funeral. It wouldn't be right to think about it until then.'

* * *

'Come and sit down, Rose,' Mrs Barlow said. The funeral was over and all the friends who had come for a glass of sherry and a sandwich afterwards had gone, leaving them alone in the large kitchen. 'Leave the rest of the washing up for now. I want to talk to you.'

'All right,' Rose said. She dried her hands and sat down opposite her mother. The look on Mrs Barlow's face told her it was serious. 'I did tell you that Mr Luke says it is all right to stay on here, but Sarah says we can live in a house on the Pelham estate if we want.'

'That is what I want to talk about,' Mrs Barlow said. 'You have a good job and you're happy, aren't you? I know you're still grieving for Rod – but with your life in general?'

'I suppose so,' Rose said. 'I wanted to go into nursing but I didn't get the chance. I shall stay where I am until they tell me I'm not needed – unless you want me to come home?'

'No, I'm not asking that of you,' Mrs Barlow said. 'Your father was proud of you – almost as proud as he was of Jack. He thought you were doing a good job and I agree.'

'Will you stay here alone in the cottage?' Rose looked at her doubtfully. Her mother seemed to have aged in a few days, all the life gone out of her.

'No, I shan't stay – at least only for a few months until I get myself sorted. I shan't be taking up Miss Sarah's offer either.'

'Where will you go?'

'I have an aunt who lives in Bournemouth,' Mrs Barlow said. 'She writes to me sometimes. She runs a small hotel, Rose. She always said that if ever I wanted to I could go and help her. It was her letters that gave Barlow the idea that we might have a little boarding house. Aunt Beatrice is my only relative apart from you now, Rose. She doesn't have anyone else either. It makes sense that I should go to her. You have your own life. I know Beatrice would welcome you if you wanted to stay – or even live with us, but I doubt you will. You're pretty and you're bright, Rose Barlow, and you could make something of yourself. You might marry again.'

'Perhaps,' Rose agreed. 'If I meet someone I like enough.'

'There's no hurry.' Her mother smiled at her. 'You're a good girl, Rose. I couldn't have got through this alone. Now I want you to leave me here by myself. I need time to grieve before I join my aunt, and I'll do that best alone.'

'Are you sure?' Rose asked, looking at her anxiously. 'I can take another two weeks off if I want.'

'I was glad you came when you did, but we can't help him now. He has gone. There's only you and me now – and my aunt. I don't want you wasting your time here worrying about me. I know what I want and I'll do best by myself.'

'If that is what you want...' Rose felt as if her mother were pushing her away. She understood her need to grieve alone, but it hurt. She wished that Jack were here. He would know how to comfort their mother. 'If you need me...'

'I know you'll come. You're a good girl and I love you,' Mrs Barlow said. 'I have to do this in my own way. Now there's something else I have to say. You have never touched Jack's money. I know you're leaving it in case he comes back. Your father left me three thousand and five hundred pounds. I don't know how he managed to save so much, but I want you to have half of it.'

'No, Ma. I don't need it. You might want it yourself.'

'I shall be all right with Beatrice. She will treat me fair. She has always said she will leave me her place when she goes. God forbid that will be anytime soon. I want you to have half the money. I'll keep the rest for the time being just in case...'

'Oh, Ma...' Rose felt her throat tighten. She had thought her mother had given up hope of Jack, but it seemed she was still keeping at least a tiny spark alive in her heart. 'I'll put the money aside in case I need it one day. Thank you, but you can ask if you need anything.'

'I've never needed much,' Mrs Barlow said. 'I like to do my baking and keep things nice, and I'll be doing that in Bournemouth soon. When you get a decent leave you can come and see us.'

'Yes, I shall,' Rose said. 'I think I shall go for a walk now – unless there's something I can do?'

'You've done more than your share,' her mother said. 'I'll finish up here and then I'll have a rest.'

Rose nodded. She shrugged on her coat and scarf and pulled a felt hat down over her head. It was cold out, but she needed to walk. She was hurting inside and she couldn't let her mother see. She might go up to the house and talk to Sarah.

* * *

Luke saw Rose walking towards him, her head tucked down against the wind. It was very cold out this evening. He had decided to walk down and talk to Sarah. He had mentioned the cottage to her after they left church, but he was still undecided as to whether he should tell her the truth about Jack. Was this the right time to tell her that her brother was both a hero and a deserter?

'Good evening, Rose,' Luke said as he drew closer. She looked startled and he knew she hadn't seen him until the last moment. 'I was just coming down to see if there was anything you need?'

'You have been good to us, sir,' Rose said. 'Ma wanted to be on her own for a bit so I came for a walk.'

'I hope you reassured your mother about the cottage. It is hers for the rest of her life if she wants it.'

'She was very grateful,' Rose said. 'She has her own plans. She means to live with her aunt in Bournemouth. My great-aunt has a boarding house and Ma is going to help her run it – my father had an idea of doing that and I suppose it came from reading Ma's letters from her aunt.'

Luke had fallen into step beside her. 'Did you know about this?'

'Not until a few minutes ago. It will be a good thing for her. She will like to be busy.'

'My mother spoke of her coming back to us...'

'No, I don't think she would have considered that,' Rose told him frankly. 'Ma gave up service when she married. I think she will be happy working with her aunt.'

'Yes, of course. I wasn't suggesting anything else.'

'I can stay with them when I like. I shall continue in the VADs until they tell me they don't need me any longer.'

'Have you thought about what happens then?'

Rose glanced at him. 'I don't know. I wanted to nurse but they turned down my application. I shall find something when it comes to it, I dare say.'

'You won't come back here?'

'Not now,' Rose told him. 'I would never have gone back into service, but if Ma had stayed I should have visited.'

'Then I don't suppose I shall see you very much in future,' Luke said. 'I'm going to stay with Marianne and Barney for a while, and then I shall go to Sarah's for Christmas. I intend to make the most of this leave. You won't be at Pelham?'

'No, I shall work through Christmas,' Rose told him. 'I've had a lot of time off this year and there's no point in taking more when others have families to visit. I've joined the hospital choir and we're going to be singing carols on the wards Christmas Eve and on the day itself, I expect.'

'I remember you used to sing in the choir at church,' Luke said. They were nearing the house. He knew that if he was going to tell her about Jack he must speak now. 'Jack sang as a young boy...'

'Until his voice broke,' Rose agreed. 'After that he wouldn't try. He said he croaked like a frog.' She sighed. 'Ma says Father broke his heart over Jack. He was convinced that Jack would have got in touch somehow if he were alive. I'm not sure if that's what killed him, but Ma thinks it...'

Luke looked at her. She had been so brave, supporting her mother. She had lost her husband of a few months and now her father. How could he break it to her that her brother was alive but didn't wish to return home? Jack hadn't remembered who he was for a while, but he'd known he was a British soldier. He could have come home had he wished, because someone would have known him.

'He might have been taken prisoner...' he suggested. 'Or there could be some other reason he couldn't get in touch. It doesn't mean he is dead.'

'I think he must be,' Rose said. 'Perhaps it is best that way – best we grieve for him and move on.'

'Yes, perhaps that is best,' Luke said. They had almost reached the house. 'Were you going to see Sarah?'

'Yes.' Rose looked at him. 'I am glad you got back alive, sir.'

'Please, call me Luke.' He offered his hand. 'You don't work for my family any more, Rose. Sarah thinks of you as a friend – and if we ever meet in the future I should like you to think of me that way too.'

'Thank you... Luke.' Rose smiled at him. 'I have thought of you as Luke for a while, because Sarah says your name so often. I hope we shall meet sometimes. Perhaps at Sarah's?'

'Yes, perhaps.' His hand clasped hers. He had an urgent desire to sweep her into his arms and tell her that he had loved her for a long time – long before she married. He killed the instinct instantly. This wasn't the time. There would probably never be a time, but if it came he might ask her to be his mistress. Rose wasn't an innocent girl any more but a lovely woman. He couldn't marry her, but one day he might ask her to be his lover. 'Excuse me... I have something I must do. I wish you happiness and success for the future, Rose.'

'Thank you.'

Rose went in at the side door, as she had always done when she worked here. Luke stood watching until the door closed and then walked away. He had thought that he no longer wanted her, but the old desire had come back as strong as ever. If she hadn't been grieving for her father he might have kissed her. Luke smiled as he walked away. He wished it was possible to speak of love and ask Rose to marry him, but he retained a strong sense of duty and he knew he must do what his father expected of him.

He had once thought that meant he could never have Rose, but now he wasn't sure. There was a chance that she might want a friend and protector one day.

12

Louise saw Jack coming through the window. She ran outside to greet him. It was Christmas Eve and he had been away for three days with the freedom fighters. She had been afraid that something might have happened to him.

'I missed you,' she said and flung herself into his arms. 'I thought you would be back before this and I worried.'

'I am sorry you were worried,' Jack said and pulled her to him, kissing her long and deep so that she thrilled to his touch. She arched into him, her body melding with his as the desire rose hot and strong between them. 'I hate leaving you, Louise, but it has to be done.'

'Yes, I know,' she said and smiled at him. 'I don't mind now that you are back. I have been baking, hoping that you would be here to share the Christmas feasting.'

'I managed to buy you a present,' Jack told her. 'I sold that cigarette case and bought you something pretty. Do you want it now? Or would you rather wait?'

'Keep it for later,' Louise said. 'I have something for you, but it is a surprise. We will exchange at midnight. Come and get warm by the fire and eat. Are you hungry?'

'Only for you,' Jack said and reached for her again. 'Shall we go to bed, Louise?' As he pulled her close, he saw the envelope propped up against the mantle clock. 'What is that – a Christmas card?'

'It is a letter from England.' Louise frowned. She had picked it up several times but stopped herself opening it. 'It is addressed to Monsieur Georges Marly...'

'Impossible...' Jack said. 'Unless...' He let go of Louise and went to the mantle, taking down the envelope. He hesitated for a moment and then tore it open, reading the contents swiftly. 'Damn! I should have been there...'

'Who is it from, Jack?' Louise was alerted by the look of anguish in his face. 'Is it bad news?'

'It is from Luke. It had to be. No one else would write to me using that name – no one in England knows it...' He crumpled the letter and threw it into the fire. 'He wrote because my father has died suddenly of a heart attack.'

'Oh, Jack. I am so sorry.' Louise went to him, looking anxiously at his face. 'You blame yourself, because you were not there... It is my fault.'

'No, of course it isn't,' Jack told her. He reached out and drew her close once more, kissing the top of her head. She smelled so good, like flowers, and he felt the love swell inside him. 'Never think that, Louise. I made my choice when Luke offered me the chance to go back. If anyone is to blame it is me, but I would do it again if I had to.'

'But you wish you had been there before he died?'

'Yes... and no.' He looked down at her. 'I might not have been there even if I had returned to England. I might have been arrested. I might even have been shot. Yes, I wish I had been there for him, but I don't regret what I did. You are my world, Louise. I love you and I gave the rest up for you, because it was what I wanted. My life is here in France. I can never return to England – and I do not want to.'

Louise gazed up at him. 'You are sure? You could still go back... Make some excuse...'

'No!' Jack touched his lips to hers. 'I shall never go back, Louise. I gave up my past for a future with you. You are my love and my life.' He kissed her hard with a passion that sent her senses spinning. 'Now, I think we were about to go to bed...'

* * *

Louise was sleeping. Jack left the bed and went down to the kitchen. It was early yet but he was restless. He had made his choice to stay in France and he would never change his mind. He did not regret what he had done, because his love for Louise was all that mattered.

It did not stop him grieving for his father or for his mother's pain – or for Rose. He felt for his sister the most, because he knew that she would feel so alone. Luke had told him that she was married now. Perhaps she had put her grief aside and hardly thought of him these days. Even if he knew she was grieving, he could not go back. Rose was like him. She was strong. She would make her own life.

He began to make up the fire. His life here was good. He smiled as he thought of the previous night. Louise had come to his arms so willingly. She was passionate and lovely, and she gave him all he would ever need. When the war was over, they would go to Paris and they would marry. She would have her café and he would work with engines. It was a good life and he would not allow regret to spoil what he had.

Jack filled the kettle and put it on the range to heat. He would wake Louise with coffee and croissants in bed. It was Christmas Day and the beginning of a new life. After today he would never look back again.

* * *

Rose joined the carol singers making the rounds that morning. She liked the feeling of spreading joy, because the atmosphere was wonderful. Some of the men were so severely injured they would never return to their homes, but even they had managed a smile for the carol singers. Christmas was meant to be a time of joy and peace for the world. Rose hoped that by next year the war would be over and there would be no more killing.

When the carols were done, Rose lingered to talk to the patients. She knew all of them by name, because she spent time with each of them whenever she could. She was always the last to leave at night, and usually the first on in the mornings.

'Merry Christmas, Rose,' a soldier called to her as

she stopped at the bottom of his bed. 'Give me a kiss and I'll give you a present.'

Rose hesitated, shaking her head at him. 'You know that's against the rules. Sister will have my guts for garters if she sees me.'

'Damn the old battle-axe,' he said. 'Anyway, she knows I've got a present for you, because she wrapped it for me. I couldn't do it myself.' He waved his right stump at her.

'I meant the kiss,' Rose said. Several patients had given her small gifts. She approached him, shot a quick look over her shoulder and then bent to kiss him. He turned his face so that the kiss caught him full on the mouth and grinned. 'Naughty, naughty!' Rose scolded, though she didn't mind a bit. Even if Sister saw, she would be lenient because it was Christmas.

'Take your present,' he said. 'I hope you like it.'

'I am sure I shall.' Rose picked up the small parcel lying on the bed next to him. She hesitated then tore off the paper and opened the box inside. It contained a pair of pearl earrings that clipped on the lobe and the pearl dangled from a gold link.

'You shouldn't have,' she said. 'They are lovely. I shall treasure them always.'

He looked pleased. 'Wear them for me when you go dancing.'

Rose smiled. She hadn't been dancing since her wedding. She kissed him again, on the cheek this time, and then moved on through the ward. Sister stopped her as she was about to leave.

'Ah, there you are, Rose,' she said. 'I'll pretend I didn't see that kiss as it is Christmas – but I wanted to ask if you would like to come to dinner at my house this evening? I know you are on your own...'

'My landlady is cooking this evening specially for me,' Rose said. 'It is very kind of you, but I ought to get back. I don't want to disappoint her.'

'Off you go then. I didn't want you to spend Christmas alone.' Sister smiled at her. 'I shall see you tomorrow. Like you, I am working all through Christmas.'

Rose pulled on her coat, scarf and hat, going out into the crispness of a cold Christmas night. She was feeling happier than she had for a while. The carols and the patients had somehow broken through her feelings of loneliness and regret. The patients had so much more to bear than she could even imagine; they had suffered terrible pain and many had lost limbs. Some had lost legs and arms, and yet they had managed to joke somehow. She had lost a great deal too, but she was young and she was strong – stronger than she had realised. She had been grieving hard, but she was pulling through it now. She had really enjoyed the carol singing and all the training. Sister Harris had told her that she ought to have her voice trained professionally.

'You could be a singer,' she had said when Rose did her solo. 'I'm not joking, Barlow. You should think about it when the war is over.'

Rose smiled to herself. She wasn't good enough to be on the stage. It would be daft to think about it, and yet she was thinking about it. She laughed as she ran to catch the last tram home.

* * *

'Ah, there you are, Rose,' her landlady said as she got in and took her coat off. 'Finished at last and ready for something to eat, I'll bet.' Mrs Hall beamed at her as she fussed round. 'They keep you all hours at that place. I am sure they don't know what a treasure they've got!'

'It was lovely. I didn't want to leave. Everyone enjoyed the carols so much and I had several presents. I'll show them to you later.'

'Well, there's another one waiting for you. It arrived by special delivery this morning.'

'A parcel for me?' Rose said in surprise. She took it

from her landlady and looked at the postmark. 'I've already had something from Ma – but this isn't from Bournemouth. It was posted overseas...' Her hand shook as she unwrapped the brown paper. Could it be from Jack? A card fell out and she picked it up, feeling shocked as she read the message. 'Oh, it is from Luke Trenwith. He says it is to wish me a Happy Christmas...' She opened the box and looked inside. She saw another pair of pearl earrings, but these had diamonds as the studs and the pearls were real; they must have been very expensive. 'He shouldn't have...'

'They look as if they're worth a lot of money,' Mrs Hall said and frowned. 'Isn't he part of the family you used to work for?'

'Yes. I told you he was good to us when my father died.'

'You want to be careful of him, Rose,' her landlady said. 'Men don't give presents like that for nothing...'

'I am sure he doesn't mean anything wrong,' Rose said, but there was a blush in her cheeks. She remembered the looks he'd given her a few times when she was working at the house. She'd dismissed them as meaning nothing, thinking she was imagining things, but now she couldn't help wondering what Luke meant by sending her a present like these earrings. 'I'm not interested anyway.'

'Well, if I were you I should send them back,' Mrs Hall advised. 'You mark my words. He'll expect something in return.'

'I shall probably never see him again,' Rose told her. 'That roast smells good, Mrs Hall. What are we having?'

'I managed to get a cockerel,' Mrs Hall said. 'Come and sit down, Rose. I'm ready to serve it up now...'

Rose went to the sink to wash her hands. She looked at the table, which was laden with food and the happy, smiling faces of Mrs Hall, her daughter and grandchild. She was spending Christmas with people who cared about her, and she knew that some of the patients loved her, and she cared about them. She had a lot to be thankful for, and who knew what might happen in the future?

FROM THE AUTHOR

Dear Readers. I hope you will enjoy these books as much as I enjoyed writing them. Best wishes, Rosie Clarke.

ALSO BY ROSIE CLARKE

Welcome to Harpers Emporium Series

The Shop Girls of Harpers

Love and Marriage at Harpers

Rainy Days for the Harpers Girls

Harpers Heroes

Wartime Blues for the Harpers Girls

Victory Bells For The Harpers Girls

Changing Times at Harpers

The Mulberry Lane Series

A Reunion at Mulberry Lane

Stormy Days On Mulberry Lane

A New Dawn Over Mulberry Lane

Life and Love at Mulberry Lane

Last Orders at Mulberry Lane

Blackberry Farm Series

War Clouds Over Blackberry Farm

Heartache at Blackberry Farm

Love and Duty at Blackberry Farm

The Trenwith Trilogy
Sarah's Choice
Louise's War

Standalones
Nellie's Heartbreak
A Mother's Shame
A Sister's Destiny
Dangerous Times on Dressmakers' Alley

Sixpence Stories

Introducing Sixpence Stories!

Discover page-turning
historical novels from your
favourite authors, meet new
friends and be transported
back in time.

Join our book club
Facebook group

https://bit.ly/SixpenceGroup

Sign up to our
newsletter

https://bit.ly/SixpenceNews

Boldwood

Boldwood Books is an award-winning fiction publishing company seeking out the best stories from around the world.

Find out more at www.boldwoodbooks.com

Join our reader community for brilliant books, competitions and offers!

Follow us
@BoldwoodBooks
@TheBoldBookClub

Sign up to our weekly
deals newsletter

https://bit.ly/BoldwoodBNewsletter

Milton Keynes UK
Ingram Content Group UK Ltd.
UKHW041830190524
442864UK00002B/25

9 781835 181812